DEAD MONEY

STEVE O'BRIEN

First Printing 2012

Author Services by Pedernales Publishing, LLC
www.pedernalespublishing.com

Distributed by:
New Shelves Distribution
103 Remsen Street #202
Cohoes, NY 12047
(518) 391-2300
www.newshelvesdistribution.com

ISBN 13   978-0-9881843-0-5
ISBN 10   0-988184303
LCCN 2011917728

Printed in the United States of America
10 9 8 7 6 5 4 3 2 1

www.AandNPublishing.com

Also by Steve O'Brien

Elijah's Coin
Bullet Work
Redemption Day

Critical Acclaim for *Bullet Work*

O'Brien weaves this tale of exciting characters, breath-taking horse racing action; right into our lives…He opens up the equine world to readers, with the grace of an artist sweeping his brush across a canvas.

—US Review of Books

Poetic ruminations about randomness punctuate the action in this mystery…These philosophical, foreboding passages transcend the novel's specificity—its insular, transient community of racetrack devotees who endure long hours and low pay to be near the creatures they adore—to become insightful analysis of character and motivation. O'Brien refuses the pat, satisfying wrap-up mystery readers may anticipate.

—Foreword Magazine

This is a wonderful tale, full of stories of the people behind the scenes. People are often interested in the "horse whispering" phenomena and O'Brien brings it to another level…[A] must read for the Dick Francis fans, another direction for the aficionados of the horse racing field.

—Seattle Post-Intelligencer

The manner in which O'Brien introduces each of these characters in brief focused chapters is a stroke of writing genius, a polished version of the manner in which some other novelists such as Cormac McCarthy have always used. O'Brien continues to impress with his skills as a writer and his underlying concern for humanity that is so lacking in the work of other writers of this genre.

—Grady Harp, Amazon Top Ten Reviewer

Critical Acclaim for *Elijah's Coin*

Elijah's Coin by Steve O'Brien is a very thought-provoking book of change. It will make you look at who you are, what you want and where you are going.

—Chicago Sun-Times

This story is spiritual, moving and incredibly hopeful. It is about finding your way in your life, even if you don't want to anymore. It's about finding the good in people, but more especially, it's about finding the good in you. The author has written a wonderful, wonderful story of possibilities and love and I absolutely devoured it.

—Front Street Reviews

This is a deceptively simple, feel good story that is a sheer delight to read…The quality of Steve O'Brien's writing cannot be bettered…[A]lthough written as a novel it could easily share space in the psychology or self help sections of the book store.

—Blogger News Network

Critical Acclaim for *Redemption Day*

A challenge worthy of Bond or Bourne. At pulse-pounding speed, the plot races toward a catastrophic, coordinated terror strike in the nation's capital.

—Foreword Magazine

Tantalizing novel…a definite page turner combining decades of news headlines with conspiracy theories and age old government corruption.

—U.S. Review of Books

O'Brien is one of those authors who gets an idea that seems a bit out of the ordinary and then works into the fabric of his novels so that not only does it work to propel his page-turner books, but it also teaches about something with which we are not familiar.

—Grady Harp, Amazon Top Ten Reviewer

Smoothly written, fast-paced, exciting and intellectually intriguing…feeling all the time as if I could easily be watching a movie.

—Shiela Deeth

A tense and compelling novel about terror here on our own shores…a dose of danger and terror spawned here in our own country.

—Leslie Wright

Alexandra,
This one is for you—the spirit of Aly Dancer

A hard-bitten, cynical gambler who watched Equipoise, one of the gamest horses in history, drive home in the 1930 Pimlico Futurity after he had gone to his knees at the start, said, "When you see a horse like that, you believe in God for a minute."

...David Alexander, *A Sound of Horses*

There is an old saying, often attributed to Winston Churchill, that adequately sums up man's relationship with the horse. "There is something about the outside of a horse that is good for the inside of a man." Anyone, from the smallest child to the most wizened old curmudgeon, who has ever seen a horse run—unfettered, graceful, and with the look of eagles in his eyes—knows this saying to be true.

...Frank R. Scatoni, *Finished Lines*

DEAD MONEY

Chapter 1

Hurting people was just a part of business.

Words had modest impact. Actions transformed.

Business associates remembered action, especially if accompanied by plaster casts, stitches and bloody gauze.

Vasily Korsakov sat patiently behind a scarred wooden desk. A plywood table would have been more accurate. Shelves were organized with customer files in green folders. They stood level and perfectly aligned. A brown metal folding chair sat vacant on the other side of the desk. Nothing was new. New things drew suspicion; Vasily avoided suspicion.

The smell of dry cleaning chemicals was familiar and burned his nostrils. To Vasily, it smelled like money. For Vasily, everything smelled like money. His office sat in the back of Sunshine Cleaners off Dozier Avenue. It was one of several offices Vasily occupied in East LA.

He punched a number on a cell phone, his pudgy fingers looking for an approximation of the number he intended. He put the phone to his ear and rubbed his silver short cropped hair. His eyes were sharp and alert, though framed by fifty-year-old skin which gave in to gravity around his wide nose. He tugged on the loose skin below his chin.

The silence of the vacant business was interrupted by a scream and a slap in the room behind him—then a dull thud. Sounded like a gut punch, Vasily thought.

The line engaged. "We got a deal?" Vasily asked.

"Not yet, boss. Guy's kinda cagey," the man said. Vasily's eyes rolled to the ceiling. "Hard to get a straight answer," the voice on the phone said.

"She's not worth what we've offered," Vasily grumbled, mostly to himself.

"Today might change everything, Mr. K. We might have a breakthrough today."

A door behind Vasily creaked open. In the gap of the door a face like a steam shovel peered through. It bore the twisted toothy grin of a man who was quite pleased with himself. With hands the size of a Virginia ham, the man thumbed over his shoulder indicating they were ready. Vasily nodded.

"Get the damn horse bought, Anton. Get it done fast."

Vasily clicked off the call and set the cell phone on the desk. He reached down and produced a hammer, which he banged four times on the cell phone, reducing it to shards of plastic and electronic guts. Using the front of the hammer he swept the parts into a wastebasket near his knee.

"How is he, Mickey?" Vasily asked.

"Like a little girl." Mickey laughed. "Probably wet his pants."

Vasily rose and walked into the adjoining room. Mickey followed.

"He get that job?" Vasily whispered.

"Yep."

"That's one good thing."

Franco Wolletti sat trembling. A trickle of blood ran from his left nostril down to the silver duct tape that covered his mouth. His curly black hair was mussed as if he'd missed his shower and shave today—which he had. More tape secured his arms behind the folding chair. His feet were propped on another chair and taped tightly.

"This saddens me Franco," Vasily said as he walked close to the bound man.

Franco tried to speak, but nothing made it through the tape—just pleading noises.

"How long have we done business?" Vasily asked. "Five, six years?"

Franco nodded vigorously, appearing hopeful.

"In all those years, I have trusted you. I have given you opportunity. I have taken care of you. Why do you make me do this, Franco?"

Pleading noises and garbled sounds came again. A tear ran down his face, mixing with the sweat erupting on his cheeks and forehead. Vasily walked behind the man and picked up a crowbar. As soon as Vasily was back in his sights, Franco's legs contracted, pulling the chair nearer the one on which he sat. Mickey pulled the chair back into position and stood on it, securing it in place. The grin widened as Mickey crossed his massive arms across his barrel chest.

Vasily stood near Franco calmly tapping the crowbar against his open palm. "What do I tell you? What is our deal? You lie to me, I cut out your tongue. You steal from me, I cut off your hand. You give me up, I kill you."

Franco nodded frantically, his eyes wide and fearful.

"I'm not smiling." Vasily slowed his delivery. His words were well chosen and deliberately stated. "This hurts me deeply." For Vasily the timing was more important than the outcome. The tension would build. A significant part of the pain was the tension. It was a card he knew how to play well. "You, my friend, were late."

Franco shook his head.

"You were late. I get nervous when people are late. It is not only disrespectful, it is bad business. Two days late. Where could he be?" Vasily looked to the ceiling and spoke as if lecturing a child. "Who could Franco be talking to? Is Franco safe? Is Franco gone?" The only sound was the muttering of the man and the iron slapping against Vasily's palm. "That was a bad thing to do, Franco. Very bad. It won't happen again."

Franco shook his head trying to work a deal without words.

Vasily stopped tapping the bar. "It won't happen again, friend."

Seconds passed. Eyes locked. No words, no sound. Vasily waited. It was a tactic that was well honed.

After several breaths, Vasily looked down, then back at Franco.

He dropped his arms, paused, then gripped the bar with both hands. He slashed downward and connected with Franco's kneecap. A sickening crack and dull pop erupted. Franco screamed, muffled and animal like. Huffing against the fabric of the duct tape, cheeks puffing in and out, Franco shouted and cried in pain.

Vasily slashed again, and again, and again.

When he finally dropped the crowbar, Franco's knee

was bent the wrong direction, blood seeped through his pants, and the point that connected his thigh to his shin was shattered like a porcelain vase dropped on a concrete step. Franco was slumped, head back, unconscious.

"Get him out of here," Vasily said.

Mickey chuckled. "For a second there, he actually thought you might let him go."

Vasily straightened his collar, brushed his hands on his pants, and walked out of the room.

Chapter 2

What was it about trust?

Why in God's name did we trust the things we did?

We trusted the airline pilot to safely operate an aircraft. We trusted the traffic light to alert crossing traffic as we zoomed through the intersection. We trusted the elevator not to free fall dozens of floors. We trusted TSA to keep terrorists off airplanes.

We trusted grocery clerks. We trusted bank tellers. We trusted newspaper reporters, bus drivers and talking heads on television.

We trusted our memories, our mentors, and our computers. We trusted the innocence of small children.

Why was it so hard to trust the ones we loved?

~

Dan loved her, of that he was certain. But he just couldn't reveal the million dollars. The relationship was too fragile. Their relationship was like a toddler chasing a bouncing rubber ball across the New Jersey Turnpike. He might make it to the other side, but what's the point?

A million dollars would change everything.

That's a one with six zeros behind it. Dan leaned back in his office chair.

Put it out of your mind.

He stood and carried the transcription tape into the reception area and dropped it on Mindy's desk. "Dan Morgan and Associates LLC." reflected backwards through front window. It still made him smile. He was the only attorney at Dan Morgan and Associates; had been for two years. "And Associates" was an aspiration, but one that possibly made a difference to prospective clients.

Mindy was his part time receptionist. Occasionally a law student interned with them during the summers. Someday there would be associates, but on this Saturday morning, the whole legal engine of the enterprise stood in the reception area of his three room empire.

This was his baby.

No more long hours in the library of Simpkins, Miller and Gains, no more politics shoveled by incompetent supervisors in the prosecutor's office. This was the life he wanted-—his own firm.

His Toyota was the only car in the lot, pulled up to the door. The morning sun teased the Virginia landscape. Late April, the sun was out, blue skies overhead, and someone had offered him a million dollars for his undefeated filly, Aly Dancer.

Put it out of your mind.

Dan had the first draft of a reply brief to finish and he made a mental note to order Mindy some flowers for her desk. She was reliable, steady, and a calming influence. A single mom with two elementary school kids was his calming influence. Made sense—Dan grew up with a single mom. He knew the routine. He respected it.

Speaking of Mom, he thought, I could buy her a new house. She could retire from her secretarial position at the CIA. She deserved that. I could pay off all my credit cards and the operating line for the firm, hell pay off my condo, maybe get a new one, buy a couple of yearlings. Start over again.

Put it out of your mind.

The phone on his desk rang and brought him back to the moment.

"Lennie."

"You coming today?"

"You bet. Where?"

"Tycoon's."

"See you."

Dan smiled. One of their longer telephone conversations, he thought.

Dan's three-year-old filly, Aly Dancer, was entered in the Magnolia Stakes at Gulfstream. His workload kept him away from south Florida, but he'd watch it on simulcast at Laurel Park.

Lennie Davis was a fixture there. A full time handicapper and horse aficionado, Lennie was a voice of reason in Dan's life. Though he looked like a regular at a Grateful Dead concert with his zero body fat and long gray hair held back in a ponytail, Lennie held a PhD in Mathematics from Princeton and had used his brain power to handicap horses for a living. Many people tried, few survived. Lennie was a survivor.

Dan picked up his Dictaphone and thumbed it forward. "Mindy this is Maxwell versus Janssen Floral, insert caption head, reply brief." He clicked it off and thumbed through his research and notes.

A million dollars.

He'd sold horses before, never for this price. He sold Partego as a three-year-old for seventy-five. Bought him for twenty. Sold Mythical Mime for fifty, bought her for fifteen. Of course it was easier to avoid thinking about the horses that had eaten his bank account. He was wise to unload them, but many times only after significant financial pain. He had promised himself he would buy to race and sell.

This time was different.

He'd owned horses for six years, back when he was still married to Vicki. She never understood the attraction. Vicki thought he was foolish, the business too risky. Maybe she was right.

But this time *was* different.

Aly Dancer was a star. She'd won a maiden effort at Fairfax Park last summer and followed it up with a win in the My Lassie stakes. Jake Gilmore had taken her down to Florida for the winter and she was training like a beast. He put her in a "non-winners of two" allowance at Gulfstream last month and she dusted the field by six lengths. She was the morning line favorite for today's stake and if all went well, the Kentucky Oaks was on the horizon. This time was different. Or was it? A million dollars.

Put it out of your mind.

"Plaintiff brings this action for replevin of business equipment…." He clicked it off again.

It had also been a month since he'd seen Beth. He leaned back and stared at the ceiling. Beth DeCarlo was one of Jake's grooms and she was the principal caregiver for Aly Dancer. He'd made three trips to Florida over the winter, the most recent for the allowance race.

Two days of great racing, vibrant restaurants, hitting the town, but most importantly, two nights spent with Beth. The first night they celebrated. Unbeknownst to Jake, Beth had taken the trainers' exam in Florida. As a kid growing up on the backside, becoming a trainer had been her dream. Two days before she'd received word that she'd passed.

Dan took her to MiCielo and they toasted to her new status. Having a trainer's license and being a trainer were completely different spheres. The test was about animals, regulations and ethics. The world of the trainer was about managing egomaniacal owners and cash flow. Currently Beth had neither.

Beth was patient though. She said she still had plenty to learn and connections to make. She had time on her side.

Her eyes glistened in the candlelight and she flashed the smile that melted Dan to his core. It became an evening, a precious moment he couldn't shake from his mind's eye. He never would.

Dan was initially drawn to her conqueror's spirit and thorough knowledge of horses, but deep inside there was another reason—one more physical, one more desperate.

Did he love her?

Did he even know what the word meant? Was it just an attraction? A passing fancy?

He couldn't drag his thoughts away from her—the short cropped blonde hair, the devilish gleam in her eyes, the laugh that made his knees quiver. He was like a nervous teenager around her despite being seven years her elder.

After the last trip, those two nights, everything

was altered. There was an understanding, an unspoken commitment. This was getting serious and for the first time, Dan was becoming frightened by the prospect.

He had not mentioned the offer for Aly Dancer to Beth. Only Jake knew. Dan didn't even know who the potential buyer was. He didn't want to know. As was customary, all communication came through the trainer. For Dan, the trainer/owner privilege was to be respected as much as the attorney/client variety.

Dan couldn't tell Beth—couldn't. She loved that horse and selling meant Aly Dancer would go to another barn, another trainer, another groom. There was too much anxiety in the relationship, both professional and personal. He didn't like withholding information from Beth, but this was information that would do her no good and could do significant harm--—to both of them.

She would never forgive him if he sold the filly. The transaction would become a permanent barrier in their relationship. They could try to ignore it, but at every moment of trust, it would slap him in the face. He could have Beth or have the million dollars. He couldn't have both.

Still, it was a million dollars. He could get her through it, couldn't he?

Put it out of your mind.

"Replevin of equipment arising out of a contract for delivery of…." He clicked it off again and sat staring at the photo of Aly Dancer from the My Lassie Stakes. His biggest win as a thoroughbred owner and the worst day of his life—all rolled into one.

A friend had died that day. A boy named AJ Kaine. He died as Aly Dancer stood in the winner's circle.

Dan had sworn to protect AJ. He had promised the boy.

Dan had failed.

Was it my fault? Was I too caught up in thinking about myself?

There was nothing he could have done to prevent it. That's what friends had told him. When he wanted to feel better, Dan agreed with them. The rest of the time it was simply unresolved.

He stared at the photo on the wall.

A million dollars would change everything.

Chapter 3

Two hours later Dan turned left across three lanes of traffic and wheeled onto the grounds of Laurel Park. To his left the track was deserted and the grandstand appeared dark and vacant.

Laurel's famous paddock appeared to his right. The white and green structure shaped like a circus tent stood next to the grandstand. Dan drove ahead to the valet section of the parking lot. It cost him three bucks and was hardly worth the few hundred feet closer to the entrance which his money bought, but the industry was in trouble. At least the valet guy had a job. Dan's three bucks wouldn't make a huge difference, but every little bit counted.

Dan shook his head and chuckled as he passed the bronze statue of Billy Barton. The horse stood regally peering toward the railroad tracks where the MARC trains dropped off patrons who would flood the grandstand. There was a day that happened, not today, not recently. Billy stared at less and less foot traffic each year and waited in vain for the jammed passenger trains to drop their cargo of gamblers at his gate.

It always seemed odd to Dan that someone decided to build a statue of Billy Barton. They immortalized a horse that had been ruled off North American racetracks because of the gelding's "cussedness." Although the Kentucky bred had won several races in Cuba, he was never much of a racehorse in America.

Billy had become what gamblers and tracks hated most in racehorses. His last flat races were defined by one word—"refused." Despite the efforts of his jockey, Billy would not leave the starting gate.

He'd become a nonstarter.

It was a tag that defined him as a wagering entry that screwed up mutuel pools and frustrated gamblers and racetrack officials alike. All bets on nonstarters were refunded and odds recalculated on the remainder of the field's entrants. It was as if the horse was never in the race.

Years later Billy Barton's connections launched a second career as a jumper, coming a few yards shy of becoming the first American horse to win the Aintree championship in the UK. Despite that Billy was still an odd pick to be honored with a bronze statue at a flat racecourse.

Why you, Billy Barton? Why Laurel Park?

Dan squeezed through the turnstile and stepped toward the table where a grizzled, unshaven man chomped on an unlit cigar. Dan's request for today's form and program drew a grunt and some wrinkled bills in exchange for Dan's twenty. It cost him nothing so Dan wished the man a great day, folded the form under his arm and turned into the grandstand.

With no live racing the place had the charm of a warehouse albeit with hundreds of high definition television monitors. The crowd, mostly men craned their heads at odds boards and monitors for the dozen or so tracks whose races were pumped in via satellite. Some calmly studied their forms while others stood and shouted at a stretch run where money was on the line. With a televised race going off every five minutes, there was a constant stream of betting action.

This was modern racing. In Billy Barton's day forty thousand fans would show up to experience a live match race between two horses. Today, barely a thousand would show up to wager on simulcast offerings beamed from all over the globe.

"Hey, Morgan."

Dan turned to look. The voice was gravely and distinctive. A willow-thin man in ripped blue jeans and a faded Redskins t-shirt with a large oil stain down the front limped forward.

"Goldie, how are you?" Dan didn't know if Goldie was a first name, last name or nickname. Like many of his racetrack acquaintances, they shared a history, but knew only names-—and most times they were merely nicknames.

The two shook hands. Goldie's dingy ball cap bobbled atop his uncut, unkempt salt and pepper hair.

"Your filly going to do it today?"

"I sure hope so, but take it easy. It's a tough field. She's no sure thing," Dan said.

It was hard to discern Goldie's age, except that he had to be at least two decades Dan's elder. Goldie removed his cap and leaned in.

"Could I ask a favor?"

There was only one favor asked in this venue, and it involved cash.

"Goldie," Dan said, as if scolding a hunting dog.

"No, no, Morgan. Not to bet. Just ah, wondering if you could spare a little so I can get something to eat, you know."

Dan smiled and pulled some bills from his pocket. He peeled off a twenty and extended it. Goldie's eyes never left the bankroll and he quickly reached forward. Thinking better of it, Dan yanked it back.

Goldie looked up, confused.

"Come with me," Dan said. He led Goldie across the concourse. An overweight woman in a white shirt with a rental bow tie stood sentry at the snack counter. Dan handed the woman the twenty and thumbed toward Goldie. "Give him whatever he wants. No alcohol, no cash back. If he doesn't spend it all, the rest is yours."

The woman nodded. Goldie gave him a sheepish glance from the corner of his eye.

"See you Goldie."

"Right. Good luck Morgan."

As Dan walked away he could hear Goldie snuffle and say to the bow tied woman, "Yeah, guy owes me money. Lettin' him work it off a bit at a time."

~

Dan plopped down in a seat at Lennie's table in the traditionally appointed Tycoon's club. This venue, adorned in dark maple and green, Scottish influenced carpet and drapes was a betting room for regular high rollers.

A dozen big screen TV's covered one wall and an angular bar graced the other. Two sets of betting windows meant no waiting at the mutuels for the two dozen fans who occupied overstuffed chairs tucked under tables covered with handicapping paraphernalia.

Dan found space to open his form on the table bearing stacks of computer printouts colored with Lennie's scribbled notes.

Across the table sat Milton Childers, or Magic Milt as his friends dubbed him. His chair was pulled back from the table to accommodate his massive belly, making his arms appear childlike.

Milt's section of the table included a half-eaten cheeseburger, a chili dog, and a plate of fries covered by a wave of orange cheese sauce. Milt was a regular, but gambling took a backseat to an endless quest for calorie consumption.

"She gonna win today?" Milt asked as he stuffed a handful of fries into his mouth. A dribble of cheese sauce was skillfully pushed into his mouth using his thumb.

"I hope so. Jake thinks she's doing well. Tough bunch today, though," Dan said. "What's the data say, Lennie?"

"I like her. Good spot for her. She'll improve off her first out," Lennie said as he shifted some pages looking for something. "She'll be a bet down favorite, so I'm looking to move the odds on her."

"Move the odds? How's that work?" Dan asked.

"Well, what do you think her post time odds will be?" Lennie said, pushing his glasses up onto his forehead. "Five to two, maybe two to one?"

Dan nodded. "Probably."

"So the return is somewhere between six and seven bucks for every two dollars bet to win. Now, I like her chances, but I need to make more than a three to one return to make her a solid wager. The next question is what bets with her winning will yield a larger return?"

"You mean like exactas and tri's?" Milt asked.

"That's always an option, but pick threes and the late double also give me a chance. So I have to check the other races, see if I can narrow the fields."

"Yeah, but you have to hit the other races too," Dan said. "That's no simple task."

"So let's say two favorites win and your horse wins. What's the pick three going to pay?"

"No clue." Dan said.

"It is a bit of a guess, but the pick three should pay fifty or sixty bucks. These aren't likely to be terribly over bet favorites. At that rate, I'm working at odds of twenty-five or thirty to one. Now, every time I add another horse in those other races to cover myself, the odds go down because I'm making more bets, covering more potential horses, but if I can keep the margin well above three to one, it's a bet."

Lennie shuffled more pages and scribbled a note. "Because of the added risk, I need a higher return. As I add horses in the other races, the payoff should go up because a favorite ran out. So I develop a target range for acceptable risk. The decision point is still relatively simple."

"Simple to you," Milt said, holding his chili dog and eyeing up his carnivorous attack route.

"Remember, I'm trying to beat three to one. Given the risk, I will target a six to one return to factor a risk premium. My worst case payoff—all three favorites winning has to be six to one. From that six to one return worst case, I can calculate how much I can bet and therefore, how many other horses I can include."

"But if you miss one of the other races, you're out," Dan said.

"Correct, so they need to be playable races, where I think I can hit or else I'm just gambling."

"You are just gambling," Milt said laughing.

"No. You, my friend, are gambling, I'm investing, hedging, and seeking a return. The other thing to keep in mind is the long term. I may miss a given race or have a horrible day, but over time I'm able to show a return. So I make a calculated wager like this, my chances on any specific bet could go wrong, but over time, if I'm playing overlays and structuring appropriate bets, I will come out ahead. I can't guarantee any specific bet, but I have been able to squeeze out a net positive return over the years. Better than ninety nine point nine percent of everyone who walks through the turnstile."

"You're a real Wall Street gambler," Dan said.

"It's not that much different from the stock market. With a stock you can hold it decades before you learn whether it was a good bet or not. With horses, you find out in two minutes. But seriously, if you had a good feeling about a publicly traded company, you could simply buy a share of stock. If you are convinced you are right, you can leverage up your bet on the company. You could buy options, LEAPs, or buy on margin. I guess the one advantage that the market has is you can bet on dogs."

"Huh?" Milt grunted as he chewed on his cheeseburger.

"Well you can bet that the price of a stock will go down, a put option," Lennie said. "In horse racing, you have to pick winners. I could make a fortune telling you who won't hit the board in a given race. The problem is, that information doesn't pay anything."

Chapter 4

Three thousand miles away, Vasily Korsakov stepped into the gloom of mid-morning East LA. Sunnyside Cleaners' sign was flickering to light as his staff prepared for their day. Next door was Ace Pawn Shop, another business owned by Vasily. Cash businesses were his stock in trade, but of course neither carried his name on the registration. None of his businesses did.

The street was deserted at this hour, save for the cars that occupied random spaces along the street, like broken teeth.

Half a block up the street two men approached—one black, one Hispanic. A hooded gray jacket adorned one, unzipped to reveal the dingy wife beater t-shirt festooned with multiple gold chains. The Hispanic was shorter in a Kobe Bryant jersey. Both had high tops which had never been properly tied and that distinctive fashion Vasily could never fathom—pants hanging below their underwear. The shorter one had covered his head with a red bandana. They walked like they were going sideways more than forward, arms slashing through the air like they were casting aside underbrush in a jungle.

Vasily shook out a cigarette and expertly lit it with his

gold Colibri lighter. American cigs were pussy smokes, not like the chavakas he smoked in Solntseva as a boy. But that was part of the trade-off he'd chosen. He inhaled and released the smoke which melted into the haze of the city.

The men neared, talking their trash in voices louder than they needed. Vasily watched them in the corner of his eye. They sashayed past. One of them made furtive eye contact. That was a tell. Fifteen feet past him, they toggled their heads and checked surroundings. They were coming back, he knew.

Vasily crossed his arms and leaned against the building, slipping the cigarette into the left corner of his mouth. He detested what these clowns represented. Not their race or age, but their attitude—their whole sense of being. Allergic to real work and entitled to others' income. They took from those who earned, either directly through forced robbery or indirectly through government redistribution. Like dogs trained to roll over, these guys had been trained to be parasites of the system.

He didn't feel sorry for them. He hated them.

"Hey ol' man," the taller one said.

Kobe wannabe fidgeted with a blade, twiddling it so Vasily could see.

"Yo, need some cash. Help a brother out?" They were both laughing in a menacing way.

Vasily locked eyes with Kobe. His blood pressure remained steady, his heart rate unchanged. He stared with a feral intensity. His black eyes revealed that not only was he unafraid, he was relaxed. The look conveyed not only that he had killed before, but that it wouldn't bother him to do it again, right now.

"Money or we mess you up," said the taller one.

Vasily directed his dead-eyed glare to the speaker. He inhaled smoke, reached up grasping the cigarette, and blew the smoke into the man's face. Then he replaced the cigarette in his mouth. Their bodies started hopping as if their aggressive motion would change Vasily's mind. Kobe took a low broad stance and waved the knife like he was filleting the air. He surveyed the street quickly. That was his mistake.

Vasily grabbed the knife wielder's wrist, pulled him in, and cracked him with an elbow across the nose. Kobe collapsed backward. It was a move that needed super slow motion, like a frog's tongue capturing a fly. The knife skittered to the ground. With the same ferocity, Vasily gut-punched the taller one. His body folded forward. Vasily grabbed his head with both hands and introduced the black man's face to his rising knee. A sickening crack permeated the East LA air. The man's head snapped back and he collapsed.

Vasily turned back to Kobe and launched a kick to the ribs. An animal sound was emitted as the ribs collapsed and pushed his breath into the street. He kicked him again which caused the man to roll onto his back. With two powerful stomps, the man's nose was flattened and front teeth dislodged. The force of the motion rendered the man unconscious. Lucky for you, Vasily thought as he booted him in the ear for good measure.

The taller one was scrambling to get to his feet, clearly attempting to flee. Vasily grabbed the hooded part of the shirt and yanked him to his feet. With one hand filled with Hoodie and the other grasping the belt of his low riders, Vasily hurled Hoodie face first into the craggy brick building. Blood smeared the brown bricks as he slid to the ground.

Vasily grabbed Hoodie's belt from behind and hoisted him onto his knees. Then taking two steps back, he approached his target as if it were a fifty-yard field goal in the NFL. His Italian loafer connected with the groin of the downed man sending him head first into the brick wall. Vasily looked to his right. Kobe wannabe was still splayed on the ground. He wasn't going anywhere. Vasily grabbed the back of Hoodie's pants again and hoisted him onto his knees. The first kick may have been wide of the uprights, so he executed another one.

Both men were motionless, groaning. Vasily reached up and removed the cigarette, calmly exhaling the smoke. His blood pressure had not changed, his heart rate remained steady. He replaced the cigarette and inhaled deeply.

Vasily noticed Mickey approaching in the silver Cadillac. The car stopped in the street and the passenger window dissolved into the door.

"You okay?" Mickey said.

"You're late."

"Jesus, a little gangland fight?"

Vasily bent down and picked up the knife. He examined it as if determining its make and origin. Then he knelt down next to the moaning field goal prop. Vasily tossed the blade up catching it backhanded and drove the blade into the man's thigh. A primal though muted scream erupted. The body twitched, airless and in agony. He reached back desperately for the blade, but wasn't able to reach it. He groaned and pulled his hands toward his groin. Probably where he has the most pain, Vasily pondered as if conducting a scientific study.

Vasily rose calmly, dusted the street grime from his knees, removed the cigarette, and blew smoke at the two broken bodies. With his thumb and middle finger he flicked the cig onto the ground.

Vasily stepped over the carnage and got in the Caddy. Mickey was chuckling and shaking his head.

Vasily made eye contact. "Punks."

Chapter 5

"Okay, let me see if I can put this into a context you can understand." Lennie leaned back and rubbed his chin. "What is your favorite kind of pizza?"

"DiRicci's Pizza in Silver Spring. Best damned pizza on the planet," Milt said, suddenly excited. They had delved into his passion.

"All right, I was thinking pepperoni or Hawaiian, but—"

"No way, man," said Milt. "They make the Explosion. Not like the crap this place serves." Milt swiveled his head as if a customer service rep was hanging on every word.

"You don't seem to have a problem with the pizza here as far as I can tell," Dan added.

"The Explosion has Parma ham, green olives, four kinds of cheese, bacon, ground beef—"

"Sounds like a gut bomb," said Dan.

"Stay with me," Lennie said. "Odds are like buying a pizza."

Milt gave him a quizzical stare, but at least he was paying attention.

"So how much does DiRicci's charge for a pizza?"

"With tax the Explosion is twenty-six seventy-four."

"Why am I not surprised you know to the penny," Lennie said mumbling to himself.

"That's an expensive pie," Dan threw in.

"If you want the best, you gotta pay," Milt said defiantly, scooping a claw full of French fries.

"Okay, focus for a second," Lennie said. "Let's call the pizza twenty-five bucks. You with me? Now, the pizza comes in eight slices."

"DiRicci's pies are twelve pieces, for a large anyway," Milt said.

"Do you want to learn this or not?" Lennie said to Milt.

"Learn what?"

Frustrated, Lennie said, "Learn the difference between overlays and underlays."

"I thought we were talking about pizza."

Lennie shook his head, then continued. "For twenty-five bucks you get twelve slices of pizza."

Milt nodded, fully engaged.

"So you order the pizza, give them twenty-five bucks and all is right with the world. Fair price, fair trade. Now what if you ordered the pizza, gave them twenty-five bucks, but when you open the box, there are only ten pieces of pizza?"

"Then I'd talk to Luigi."

"Whatever," Lennie said. "Just pay attention for a minute. If you only got ten pieces, then you overpaid. That's an underlay. You paid a fair amount, but didn't get all that you should have. Underlay. Got it? Now, if you paid your twenty-five bucks and opened the box and you had fourteen pieces of pizza, the full pie with twelve and two extra—"

"Well they'd have to separate the two otherwise they'd be sitting on top of the full pizza and would get all smooshie on the bottom."

Dan let out a chuckle.

"Lord save me," Lennie muttered. "Forget about the smooshiness, okay. If you paid twenty-five bucks and got fourteen pieces of pizza, that's an overlay."

Milt nodded again, but chances were he was dreaming of two free slices of pizza.

"So if you could get the fourteen piece for twenty-five bucks deal, how many pizzas would you buy?" Lennie asked.

"DiRicci's doesn't freeze well and it's best when it's right out of the oven—"

"You're hopeless," Lennie said sighing heavily, but soldiered on. "In betting, you always want an overlay. Quite simply that the payoff is fourteen pieces of pizza when the world expects twelve. To beat the fifteen to nineteen percent takeout the tracks keep on every straight bet, you have to bet overlays to come out on top. If you don't, over time, the vig just eats you alive. If you constantly bet underlays, you pay full price for ten pieces of pizza. Got it?"

Dan laughed, picking up his racing form. "That's the best explanation I've ever heard. The sixty-four thousand dollar question though, is how you find overlays."

"That's a lifetime pursuit and serious study. Horse racing is all probability theory. If each race was run a thousand times, how many times would each entry win?"

"Here we go again," Milt said, throwing his hands in the air.

"Actually it's a series of conditional probabilities," Lennie said. "The updated position of each horse at given points in the race. If A, then B. If A is true, let's say the half mile pace is as expected, then B will follow. See?"

"I have no idea what you're talking about," Dan said. "But it sounds like college algebra."

"Actually statistics. Essentially, I am factoring that information into a theoretical betting line, then searching for inefficiencies in the wagering pools. And dear friend," Lennie said, pointing at Milt. "That's why you can't bet every race on the card and hope to beat this game. You have to be selective; otherwise this place will just gobble up your money."

"So how do you find these inefficiencies?" Dan asked.

"First," Lennie said. "You have to establish a betting line for each race."

"You mean like the morning line that the track sets?"

"Right. The morning line is a Bayesian inference—"

"A bay what?"

"Forget it. It's a statistical starting point. I analyze the field, evaluate the past performances, factor in likely pace scenarios, known jockey and trainer tendencies, workouts, equipment changes, training shifts, early and late pace figs and calculate the expected odds of each horse to win. Then I watch the actual odds in the minutes leading up to post time. If one of my horse's track odds are higher than my expected odds, that's an overlay. I also look at betting pools and expected payoffs for exotics and do the same thing. Variations from my expected odds determine overlays and underlays. I only bet overlays."

"How do you know your odds line is right?" Dan asked.

Lennie cocked his head and gave him a "you kidding me" stare.

"Okay, maybe you can do it, but what about a guy like me or Milt?"

"You guys don't have to make money at this," Lennie said. "You have jobs. This is my job, this is my source of income. If your income depended upon your wagers, you'd quickly learn that you have to put in the time, study the form, create odds lines, do all the advance work. Otherwise you're just a lamb being led to the slaughter. Guys who walk in, crack open a racing form and expect to make money are just kidding themselves. Like a guy walking into a casino and expecting to make money. Occasionally they do, but over the long haul, they lose money. Lots of money. That's what keeps these places in business. But it's a good thing from my perspective."

"Why would you be happy that others are losing their shirts?" Milt asked.

"It's simple. Some believe pari-mutuel wagering creates a Nash Equilibrium, when it is really more like Zermelo's game theory."

"Try English this time," Dan said, with a chuckle.

"Because bettors create inefficiencies in the market. They over bet favorites. They take careless stabs at hopeless long shots. This is pari-mutuel betting, we're betting against each other. A big collective. Bad bettors fill the pools with dead money. Bad bets. That allows guys like me to exploit their mistakes."

"Like the greater fool theory of the stock market," Dan said.

"Very close," said Lennie. "I did my doctoral thesis on inefficiencies in the US stock market. People fall in love with a company and have no idea what the financial internals look like," Lennie said.

"Buy low, sell high," Milt interjected in a sing song manner, displaying the depths of his market knowledge.

"Those who make money in the stock market calculate the true value of the company," Lennie said. "Divide it by the number of shares outstanding and create their own betting line on the company. If the price is less than they think the company's worth, they buy. If higher they pass."

"Just like passing on a horse race," Dan said.

"Very good, grasshopper," Lennie said. "Warren Buffet had a wonderful quote. He said investing is like a baseball game with no called strikes."

"No called strikes? What's that?" Milt asked.

"Wow. Let me slow this down for you," Lennie said. "You know when the pitcher throws a pitch and the batter doesn't swing and the umpire calls a strike. Three strikes and you're out. Anyway, betting horses is a game of no called strikes. You can watch pitches go by all day long and wait for the one you want to take a swing at. As opposed to Milt here, who swings at every pitch."

"Hey, I get my share of wood on the ball."

"Sure you do. You just keep believing that." Lennie said picking up his computer sheets and pulling his glasses down onto his nose. "Your middle name could be Dead Money."

Chapter 6

Mickey steered the Cadillac to the stop light.

"Where'd you take him?" Vasily said, staring out the passenger window.

"ER. Figured that was the right thing."

Vasily nodded. After several seconds Vasily spoke. "He understand?"

"We didn't do a lot of talking," Mickey said smiling and shaking his head. "I think he's got the picture."

"Good."

The neighborhood on the eastern edge of Boyle Heights peaked in the sixties and was now on life support. Brick storefronts and dusty shop windows created a tunnel as they drove. Half the stores were vacant, some with broken windows taped up with flattened cardboard as if that would keep out the vandals.

In contrast to these eyesores, Vasily's companies did well. They always did well, that was his requirement. He owned three of them in this quarter. The rest of the neighborhood withered like rotting fruit. The liquor stores did steady business, Vasily noted. Then again they were framed with steel cages and employees who were packing heat. The remainder of the shops crept along or succumbed to economic destiny. Nothing new was ever built here. Why bother?

"Where to?"

"My place."

At a stoplight Vasily fired up another cigarette and stared at three young boys standing on the street corner. Ten, maybe twelve, he thought. One was telling a story furling his arms to give it life. The other two were engaged in rapt attention, smiling and nodding.

Here, the country's talking heads would say these boys didn't have a chance. Someone had to help them. Bullshit, Vasily thought. They ought to help themselves.

At their age Vasily was already part of the Bratva, the brotherhood as it was known. Moscow's streets were unforgiving, but Vasily had made it out. The streets of East LA were like a nursery school compared to home.

He didn't need or want a handout. That was for the weak. Vasily watched the system beat down his father. Every time the family made a step forward, some government yahoo changed the rules and pushed the Korsakovs back to their original state. Work hard, keep trying, the system said. But it was never true. They'd never have a chance to advance.

Frustration broke his father's will, just as the leadership designed. It broke the will of entire communities, entire classes of people. Vasily swore they would never break his.

His father warned him about the Bratva. They make you a criminal, he'd said. You embarrass the family. Vasily couldn't take it anymore. "You embarrass the family," he'd shouted. "You let the politicos steal from you. Treat you like a punk. You don't fight back." His father struck him. It wasn't the first time. Vasily clenched his fists, eyes stinging from the blow. He could kill him. It wouldn't be the first. Then he turned and walked out, never to return.

In the early days Vasily was a foot soldier for the Bratva. It was never random violence like here in the States. It was organized. It was a business and that's where Vasily became a businessman.

Everything he touched made money. He had a sense about how to build something, that endeared him to the leadership of the Solntsevskaya Brotherhood. At eighteen he was managing money for the leadership. He not only knew how to keep cash safe, he knew how to invest it, how to buy legitimate businesses.

It was always easier to negotiate when the seller knew the Bratva was backing Vasily, but he wasn't a street thug, they'd seen that. He could actually turn loot into steady streams of income. It changed the face of the organization and Vasily was a rising star.

By twenty-two he was wearing suits and expensive loafers. He didn't need to carry out the dirty work of the soldiers, though he'd proven he was able if called upon.

Vasily had a vision. Acquisition of small businesses in a neighborhood gave them leverage in addition to income. Soon they could take over entire neighborhoods and control the local economy. It was one thing to take by violence; it was another altogether to take because you were the only game in town. They laughed that they were just like the government. Come to power by violence, then enrich themselves through economic control.

It was a beautiful system, and Vasily was the Minister of Finance.

Sergei Mikhailev was the leader. Vasily was the wunderkind. Nobody messed with Sergei's wunderkind.

Moscow wasn't big enough for the Bratva, especially because they were flush with cash and struggling to find higher yielding investments. Europe was the logical choice.

Vasily was buying legitimate businesses throughout the continent. The challenge was building and maintaining an army of Bratva soldiers that could protect their ever expanding turf. This also led to inevitable skirmishes with established criminal enterprises in their headlights.

Brutal violence and death was the result, but the Bratva moved forward like a bulldozer, crushing smaller gangs and local toughs. The smart ones joined the Bratva, the dumb ones were collateral damage. Though the smart ones would never become associates—as they were not Russian and not part of the Solntseva inner core—the recruits knew they were on the winning team and got to keep breathing as a bonus.

That stood to change in 1986 when Sergei was arrested in Switzerland and charged with multiple crimes of thuggery. The Swiss government went to work to build the case. A vacuum of leadership for the Bratva would lead to chaos and coup attempts. That couldn't be tolerated. The prospect that Sergei might serve time was something that couldn't be permitted.

Through bribes to Swiss law enforcement personnel, Vasily and a select group of the Bratva inner circle learned the names of the principal witnesses. There were three.

Vasily took a deep drag and leaned back against the headrest. With eyes closed, his mind drifted.

~

The breeze was cool off Lake Geneva. It was always cool and overcast. Vasily had little use for the whole country. Banking laws and secrecy were the only value on this piece of dirt between Germany and Italy.

His mark was an amateur. Most naïve, law-abiding witnesses were that way. They lived as if virtue was an impenetrable shield. Vasily was the only truth that mattered and he would set Marco Pelier free.

Nosy, do-gooder bankers were unnecessary. He was not a challenging prey. Marco had gone to the prosecutors first. He'd identified Mikhailev. It wasn't the frequency of his transactions, but that they were all cash deposits. Some multi-billionaire slug could transfer millions with a keystroke. Somehow they were pristine. But a man who built his enterprise with his bare hands from the ground up? Hell, he couldn't be trusted.

Vasily wanted this guy. What he had done to Mikhailev was enough, but Marco threatened Vasily's plan. If Mikhailev was behind bars, instability would rattle the organization. Instability was bad for Vasily's plan. This obstacle had to be eliminated for his plan to stay on course.

Marco sat with his back to Vasily on the patio of the coffee shop. The Swiss were crazy for coffee. Maybe it was the gloomy weather. A half dozen other patrons were scattered at small round tables. If it were Paris, they would drink wine. If Moscow, it would be vodka. In Geneva, it was coffee.

Vasily stood on the sidewalk and watched Marco thumb his newspaper and pitter patter with the teenage server. He laughed as he handed the girl a few coins—an unnecessary tip. Everything Marco did was soon to be unnecessary. The girl blushed, covered her mouth and swept away.

Marco cracked his newspaper open which caused three pigeons to scurry away. Damn things were like pets, Vasily thought.

Without a sound Vasily was behind Marco. His left forearm went over the seated man's forehead and yanked his neck back.

Vasily knew what would happen next. It was predictable. Marco's hands went up instinctively. The triangle formed by the slender man's forearm, bicep and face appeared perfectly. So predictable. Vasily's hand reached through the triangle with a flash of light. The knife ripped across Marco's throat. Silent, except for the crunching sound as the knife severed the trachea.

Vasily shoved him with his left shoulder. Marco tumbled to the cement, scattering more birds. His hands slithered in the expanding blood as if he could do anything about it.

A five-ruble note was dropped onto the newspaper, a calling card from the Bratva. Then Vasily quickly scooted up the street. A woman screamed. Chairs shuffled on concrete. Vasily didn't turn to look. No one would follow him. No one would pursue.

Swiss were docile people and innately selfish. That's why they never fought in a war. It was culture. No heroes. No one would chase or confront him.

Vasily turned the corner and hopped into a waiting van.

Obstacle removed.

~

"You okay?" Mickey asked. "You look like you're out of it."

Vasily nodded.

"Not a young man anymore, Mr. K. You need to leave the street brawls to me."

"I wait for you, they take me to the morgue." Vasily said, staring out the window into the distance.

Vasily also killed the second witness against Sergei Mikhailev. Another trusted soldier killed the third. Without witnesses, the case couldn't go forward and though it angered European governments to no end, Mikhailov had to be released.

While sipping Dom Perignon at a sidewalk café in Paris, Vasily laid out his plan. It was very simple. No one left the Bratva, at least no one who wanted to remain standing upright. All income and effort was for the Bratva. That was the code. And the Bratva protected its soldiers. That was the return promise.

But Vasily was a special case. Sergei owed him. They made their deal.

Vasily would leave the Bratva. He would no longer be a soldier, but a free agent. He always wanted to own his own businesses, not just for the Bratva. But he could still help. They had a problem coming. They had too much cash and more coming in every day. Thanks to Vasily's success a majority of the money was legit, but they still struggled with evading authorities and turning bad money into good.

Vasily would leave the Bratva. He would go to California, something he'd dreamed about since his earliest days. Despite the Cold War propaganda and Russian civic pride, California seemed like nirvana with its bikini-topped women, sun-drenched beaches, wide freeways and cloistered mansions.

He would leave the Bratva, but he would remain an investor on their behalf. He would make Sergei wealthy and establish a core of legitimate businesses in the US for the Bratva. He would continue to be their money magician, only freelance. They shook hands on it. That signaled the full faith and credit of the empire they'd built. Vasily was a free man. The Bratva was now his client.

Chapter 7

"I don't need any of that calculating and studying crap. I've got a guy who never misses," Milt said as he jammed a handful of caramel popcorn in his mouth.

Lennie scoffed and turned back to his pages.

"You won't find anyone better than this guy," Dan said, thumbing toward Lennie.

"You ever heard of Thoroughbred Nostradamus?"

They shook their heads.

"Guy is amazing," Milt said. "He only makes a pick when he has a winner. Doesn't waste time trying to handicap and predict every race. When he's got a lock, he releases it. So I just have to wait for news of his next lock. Course in the meantime, I can keep playing the other races."

"What's his angle?" Lennie asked, still focused on his pages.

"What do you mean?"

"Is it a subscription site, a membership service, pay for pick? How does he make money?" Lennie set down a stack of pages and looked at Milt. "If you are a good handicapper you still have to make money. I make money by keeping my information to myself. My other option is to sell the information, which gives me some guaranteed return, but also lowers the odds on my selection."

"Guy's got a website—inside word dot sh."

"What the heck is dot sh?" Dan asked.

"It's a country level domain," Lennie said. "Rather than dot com or dot org, countries own certain domain suffixes. The island of Tuvalu owns the suffix dot TV. It's a hot domain if you're in the entertainment industry."

"So dot sh stands for sshhh." Dan said, with a finger to his lips.

"I guess." Lennie poked his smartphone and waited a moment. "Sh is St. Helena."

"That's a country?"

"Yes it's a country," Lennie said. "Off the coast of Italy. It is best known as the place where Napoleon was incarcerated following Waterloo and his downfall."

"Whatever," Milt said. "All I know is when this guy gives you a horse, you cash tickets. Take a look at this." He pulled his smartphone out and prodded it with pudgy fingers. He turned the phone so they could see. "Check this out."

Dan could see a guy with his back to the camera. The person was standing at a mutuel window. He spun around holding wads of bills in each hand. "Thank you T-Nost." Another image showed a horse crossing the finish line. A group of people jumped up and down. One of them turned to the camera and said, 'Thank you T-Nost, another winner.' Then a talking head filled the screen. 'If you're tired of losing bets and uncashed tickets, you need Thoroughbred Nostradamus. If you are sick of losing days at the track, that can all end right here."

Dan and Lennie exchanged questioning glances.

The video continued. "Using state of the art mega-computers to crunch the traditional numbers, plus physio-biometric data on every contestant, Thoroughbred Nostradamus can separate you from the losers. His patented model to determine peak performance blends the known numbers with inside information and proprietary modeling to give you the greatest edge in investing.

"The other thing unique about Thoroughbred Nostradamus is he doesn't call every race. He doesn't even call one race per day. It may be a week before he announces a lock. He waits for the optimum time, where his picks are true locks.

"In the past year, T-Nost has identified thirteen locks. Eleven were winners, one placed and one showed. The average mutuel over the past year was over eight dollars. One winner at the Oak Tree meet paid twenty-two dollars.

"For a limited time you can become a T-Nost member for an annual fee of one hundred twenty-five dollars. Once you sign up, you just wait for the e-mail from T-Nost, then head to the winner's circle. It's as easy as that."

The picture changed to another horse race and a close finish. Fans cheered, throwing their arms in the air. Again, one person turned to the camera. "Thank you T-Nost." The screen faded to black and Milt pulled back the smartphone beaming with pride.

"Bunch of crap if you ask me," said Lennie.

"What do you mean?" Milt said. "They document his picks, he's had eleven winners out of thirteen picks."

"How long have you been a subscriber?" Dan asked.

Milt looked down sheepishly. "Not that it matters, but about a week."

Lennie laughed and Dan shared a smile.

"What? You think it's bogus?"

Dan held his palms toward Milt. "I'm not saying that, but it feels like these random newsletters I get from stock pickers. If you invested with me, you'd be up one thousand percent. Milt, anyone can go back in time and spot something, then claim credit for it. I don't want to burst your bubble, but tread lightly, my friend. This could be a scam. You know, just to sign up a bunch of people. It doesn't mean his picks are any good."

"Well, we'll find out soon enough, nonbelievers," Milt said.

"What do you mean?"

"T-Nost has a pick at Santa Anita today. And because I'm a kind and generous friend, I'm going to let you in on it. I'm not supposed to. Rules say I can't tout the horse or give information to any non-members, but I want to prove to you this guy's got the goods."

"Who's he got?" Dan asked. He had to because Lennie wouldn't ask for a tip on a horse if he was waterboarded with hydrochloric acid.

Milt unwrapped the silver coating covering his hot dog, then stared at Dan. One word came from his lips. "Zaqualina."

The name shot through Dan like an electric current. She had won the Breeders' Cup Filly race last year and was named Two- Year-Old Filly of the Year. Undefeated and boasting an average margin of victory of seven lengths, she was the current princess of the thoroughbred racing world.

"Going out on a limb, isn't he?" Lennie said. "She'll be less than even money."

"Only one position pays to win. I plan on having the

winner and cashing a fistful of tickets," Milt said sitting upright in his chair.

Dan mumbled under his breath, "If Aly makes it to the Oaks, we may face her."

"You mean if she doesn't go in the Derby," Lennie said. "According to her connections, Zaqualina might skip the Oaks and opt for the boys. No standouts yet on the Derby front. She might be a fit for that race. And might be good enough to win it. I take nothing from the horse. She's a freak, but Milt, your tout just predicted a virtual walkover. She'll win here, but won't pay enough for cab fare to the next bus stop."

Milt would have had a catchy rejoinder, but his mouth was occupied with the first half of a bratwurst with German mustard and jalapenos. His eyes watered as he chewed vigorously trying to reply.

Dan opened a page on his form carrying a story on Zaqualina and her connections. The owner, Tad Stapleton, was also a lawyer. Like Dan, he owned his own shop. Probably makes a hell of a lot more than me, Dan thought. In the photo accompanying the story, Stapleton was standing next to Chick Mangold in the winner's circle following the Lady Barbara Stakes. Stapleton appeared to be in his thirties, tall, lean and tanned. The consummate California kid. Where did he get the money to buy Zaqualina for one point five million? Must have a heck of a law practice. Or a silver spoon.

Mangold, Zaqualina's trainer, was a loudmouth media whore, known to all who followed the sport. Seemed like every year he had top derby prospects and live Breeders' Cup entrants. The article recounted the recent stake.

Zaqualina had won easily at a mile and a sixteenth, not a hair out of place as she crossed the finish line.

Jesus, Dan thought. She's gigantic, sleek black with a long flowing tail. She has to be seventeen hands high, and built like an NFL running back. Black was a rarely used official color for a thoroughbred. Due to small white markings on her forehead, she was by rule a dark bay, but good luck finding a color other than coal black in her shiny muscular coat.

Dan stared at the article—frozen, his eyes out of focus. *Maybe I should take the million.*

Lennie noticed his friend's lock on the photo. "No disrespect, buddy, but *that's* a racehorse. Would be no dishonor in running second to her."

Chapter 8

Jake Gilmore peered down from the second mezzanine above Gulfstream Park. His six foot two frame meant he always had an unobstructed view. With most of his bulk carried above the waist, he was rarely crowded by others.

A tarnished rodeo buckle and cracked leather belt separated his blue jeans from his Western shirt like a bow on a Christmas ribbon. An off-white cowboy hat was tugged down low over his eyebrows. Thirty years of training had created habits he would never break. His fashion sense was one of them.

From his perch the inter-coastal canal beckoned and eventually the Atlantic Ocean. Closer in, the town of Avalon stood silent. Although present, none of this was within Jake's focus.

His binoculars were locked on Aly Dancer and Kyle Jonas warming up on the far side of the track. Five minutes earlier he'd saddled Dan Morgan's filly and given Kyle a leg up.

She looked brilliant with her neck arched. She tugged on the bit and pulled to free herself from the lead pony. Kyle stood, legs locked and bent over from the waist. Everything looked perfect and that scared Jake.

Aly Dancer was the favorite in the Magnolia Stakes. Having the best horse in the race made Jake the envy of the other trainers. That was normal. But given that they were entering the Spring of her three-year-old season, it hoisted additional pressure on Jake. The Kentucky Derby Derby focused the racing world on the newest crop of three-year-olds. Even the fillies were drawn into the spotlight.

Jake had never played poker at this table. He'd never had a horse that could come close to this performance level. And now, they were supposed to win. If they won, they broke even. If they lost, there would be questioning and criticism. He'd dealt with favorites his entire career.

This was different.

This was his entry to the big time. If she won, they kept advancing. If she lost, it would be his fault. In order to climb in this business, get good horses, get wealthy owners, he had to win—right here and right now.

He was betting his career on Aly Dancer. His stable at Gulfstream was only six horses. The remainder of his clients' horses he'd left in Virginia. They couldn't win at this level. So he'd fast-talked, and placated his other owners—that the horses needed to be freshened and they'd have a great season at Fairfax or Laurel or wherever he decided to go from here. It was a risk, but a calculated one.

If Aly Dancer was what he thought she was, he'd make more money and garner more attention playing at the highest level of the game. This was his shot at the bigs. This was the moment. She had to win.

The offer to buy the filly was something he was compelled to communicated to Dan Morgan and he'd done that. They didn't need to speak about it. They both knew the outcome.

If he sold, she'd move out of Jake's barn and make another trainer rich. He'd get a commo on the deal, but that was a pittance compared to what he could make managing her career. If she won today, Dan would believe the price wasn't high enough. That might end it, but he couldn't be sure the buyer wouldn't chase harder.

She had to win today.

He sensed someone standing nearby. He didn't lower the binoculars.

"We got a deal?" the man said.

Jake kept his eyes on the filly. "No word."

"Better hurry. I might lose interest."

Jake paused, hoping the man would walk away. He didn't. After several seconds of silence, Jake replied, "Not my call."

"We need to get this deal done. And done fast."

Jake grunted. He turned away from the voice, watching. Aly Dancer stretched into a canter. She looked lean and powerful, stretching with her front legs and driving from the rear ones. Her coat glistened in the late afternoon sun. Aly Dancer pranced like a boxer in a pre-fight routine.

"If we don't, I might have another opportunity for you."

"I don't need any opportunities. I got a race to watch if you don't mind. I know how to find you."

"Don't worry, I find you."

Jake could feel the presence move away. He peeked out the side of the binoculars. Bastard. Jake had checked him out. Anton Nikotin. Owned a bunch of cheap claimers, mostly moving down in value. He had no business buying a horse like Aly Dancer and offering that kind of money. It didn't make sense. But he'd learned in this game appearances were often phony. This deal was wrong on so many levels. But in the end, it wasn't his call. She had to win today. That made him nervous.

~

Kyle Jonas was in Florida for one reason and one reason only. He was riding it. Kyle had picked up the mount at Fairfax Park when Aly Dancer was an unraced maiden. He had Jake Gilmore to thank for that shot.

With one powerful surge of those hind legs, Kyle knew he was never getting off of this horse—not without a fight. If Jake took Aly Dancer to Florida, Kyle was going to Florida. If Jake took Aly Dancer to Kathmandu, Kyle was going to Kathmandu. It was that simple. Aly Dancer was his ticket.

He left everything behind. A steady flow of mounts and morning works at Laurel Park in Maryland. Many trainers for whom he was first call to ride had to take a back seat. He traded it all for this. An opportunity like this was once in a lifetime. Kyle wasn't going to miss it. At this stage in his young career, Aly Dancer could be a game changer.

~

"She looks great," Lennie said as they watched the horses approach the gate. A small round of applause went up in Tycoon's when Aly Dancer was shown on the screen in the post parade. "She looks like a million bucks."

Dan swallowed trying to get his heart out of his

throat. You have no idea, he thought. Lennie didn't notice the reaction as his attention was focused on the television monitor.

Maybe he should have sold her. If something happened to her, if she took a bad step, if she tore a suspensory ligament—

Put it out of your mind.

He rubbed his face and stood, drawn to the monitor by some unseen gravitational pull.

Run well Aly. Run well baby.

~

Aly Dancer calmly stalked toward the gate. Kyle pulled his knees in and up and she was in the gate. Jake breathed a small sigh of relief. He hated the one hole. Give me anything but the one hole. Going a mile and a sixteenth, there would be a short run to the first turn. From the one hole she had to break well and hold ground or outside speed would bury her. Jake held his breath.

Why's it taking so long to load?

Get them in there. Aly Dancer stood calmly, casually glancing right as the rest of the field slid into place. She looked serene and confident.

Just run your race.

Somewhere above him he heard the crackle as the PA system was keyed.

~

They're all in line. And they're off. Tambourg fires to

the front from the middle of the track, Nanquette on her outside. Pico Pico's next and Aly Dancer inside that one…

~

"Damn it," Jake muttered. Just what he'd feared. She broke a step slow and two speed horses got the lead and the rail. Though she was still on the rail, she was in a box with horses ahead and to her right. She was eager and Kyle had to put her under a slight restraint to keep from running onto the horses in front of her.

Just my luck.

~

Down the backside Tambourg continues to lead three parts of a length, Nanquette on the outside. Aly Dancer stalks in third on the rail…one back to Gateholder, Pico Pico, a break of two to Stalwart, Princess Gail and Cloudchaser… Symbianna trails. Opening quarter in twenty-three and two.

~

"Sensible fractions," Lennie said.

Dan nodded, still glued to the TV monitor. If he tried to speak he wasn't sure any sound would come out. Aly was tugging on the reins. Kyle's arms were jerked forward with every stride, his elbows tucked into his sides.

"She wants to go," Lennie said in a low tone.

"Get after her, Kyle," Milt yelled. "Get her up there."

~

Kyle tracked the leaders, checking behind to make sure no one was trying to sneak along the rail to his left. As they entered the far turn, he'd have a decision to make. He could go wide, pushing the horses alongside him even farther outside, he could try and get through on the rail or he could split the front runners if they separated.

A clean shot on the rail was the best option, but if he waited too long, runners would sweep past him on the outside and he might never get through.

He shushed at Aly Dancer to try to calm her. She had her ears pinned and wanted those front runners. Kyle had to be patient.

~

Nanquette moving up to challenge Tambourg. Six furlongs in one ten and one. Aly Dancer edging closer. Pico Pico moving strongly on the outside and Symbianna has gotten in gear, she trails the leaders by five, moving up sharply. Out of the turn…Tambourg holding a slight lead… now Aly Dancer splitting horses…three of them across the track. Symbianna trying to move up from the rail.

~

Kyle snapped Aly Dancer with his whip. She was surging forward strongly. He prepared to throw a cross with the reins when they were bumped from the outside. Aly Dancer bounced sideways into Tambourg. Kyle gathered her and Aly Dancer continued to roll. Tambourg took a left hand whip and veered toward the middle of the track. Tambourg pushed Aly Dancer back into Nanquette. She was like a ping pong ball between them. Aly Dancer dug down, lowering her head and put on a burst of speed. She was a half-length in front, but Tambourg continued drifting to the right. Symbianna was moving through on the rail.

~

Aly Dancer takes the lead.

Tambourg running a gutty race is second. Nanquette still there in third. Symbianna comes through on the rail. Four of them, anyone can win. Aly Dancer holds sway Symbianna gaining on the inside.

~

"Come on" Dan shouted. The whole room was screaming, except for Lennie.

He calmly stated, "She's a winner."

Get 'em Aly, get em," Dan shouted. "Watch the inside, watch the inside. Hold on baby."

The cheering grew louder, all pulling for Dan's horse.

Suddenly Aly Dancer veered left.

"Whoa." Dan's insides lurched. "Whoa. What the …? Look out."

~

Kyle went to his right hand with the whip. As soon as he hit her she ducked left, knocking Tambourg into

Symbianna. Both jockeys shot upright and gathered their mounts. Aly Dancer hit another gear and shot away, crossing the finish line a length ahead of Nanquette.

~

Jake knew what was coming. It only took a few seconds. He watched Aly Dancer finish and stride out. Seconds later the inquiry sign went up. He didn't know what happened, but he knew one thing. Her number was coming down.

~

Aly Dancer strode out powerfully. Kyle stood up in the stirrups and eased her.

To his inside Tambourg galloped up.

"What the fuck was that?" Jimmy Cancere shouted from Tambourg's back.

Kyle looked over, then looked down. The move had scared him, nearly tossing him from her back. What happened? She was moving easily to win. What caused her to veer? He shook his head.

"You're coming down," Cancere yelled as he pulled past. "That was bullshit. Fucking rookie."

~

Dan stood in front of the monitor; hands on his head as they replayed the stretch run over and over. The head-on shot drew groans from the crowd and caused Dan to wince.

Aly could have tumbled. She could have ended in a heap on the track. She nearly knocked over two other horses.

He closed his eyes, breathing deeply. Sweat trickled down his back. "She's safe. I don't know what happened, but she's safe."

A million dollars. I almost witnessed the loss of a million dollars.

God, this is crazy.

"She just shot left," Dan said, speaking to himself.

"Something spooked her," Lennie said. "But she straightened and ran on." They stood quietly watching the replay again. "She won Danny, but you won't get the money. We both know they've got to DQ her."

Dan nodded. "I know. It's just...I don't know."

Chapter 9

Beth DeCarlo led Aly Dancer along the outer rail. Jake trailed her watching every step the filly took, looking for any anomaly, any difference, any deviation that would explain it. She knew Jake wouldn't find it. He wouldn't discover the explanation in her physical form.

Beth walked with energy. Most grooms slid along or slumped like walking was a punishment. Beth's gait was upbeat, hopeful—like whenever she got to her destination, there would be a party or ticker tape parade. Her gait never changed. She made the basic task of ambulation look like a celebration. The men lined up along the outside rail did not fail to notice.

She reached up and scratched the filly above the ear. "It's okay baby," she whispered. "It's okay." Aly snorted and tossed her head. She knew what happened, of that Beth was sure, but she couldn't know the significance. She couldn't know what it meant.

The inquiry sign had come down minutes earlier. The number one had dropped from the top of the tote board to fourth. Kyle had pled his case to the stewards, but they would hear none of it. Though it wasn't his fault, Kyle might get days. A suspension was the way stewards demonstrated control over the uncontrollable. Certainly some jockeys deserved days when they interfered with competitors. In this case, who knew? Who could have seen it coming?

Nanquette was declared the winner. Groans from the grandstand ensued. In some pockets shouts of joy erupted. That was the common result when the order of finish was altered by humans. The groans were loudest when the favorite was the number coming down on the board.

Jake walked up alongside. He pulled off his cowboy hat and scrubbed the top of his head. She knew what he was thinking. Losing favorite, unschooled horse, gifted animal, in another trainer's hands it never would have happened.

"Wasn't your fault," Beth said.

Jake pulled his hat down firmly, tugging it down over his eyebrows.

"She's okay." Beth said, patting the filly's neck. "She just got pissed off." They walked several strides in silence. "She moved between horses and got joggled between them. Got bumped from both sides repeatedly, then when she had them beat, she just wanted to get in their faces to prove her point."

"Shouldn't have happened," Jake said, staring at the ground.

"She'll get over it. She's still learning. That bouncing around was a new experience." They walked several paces. Beth stroked the filly's mane. "She's an athlete. She's a proud athlete. Why do guys spike the football in the end zone? Why do basketball players flex their muscles when they dunk over someone? Why do they pound their chests after making a great play?"

Jake walked in silence. They turned off the track and down the chute toward the backside.

"Because they can't help themselves," Beth said, throwing her arms up.

Aly Dancer turned to look. Jake didn't.

"Everything builds up to that point and explodes out of them. Most don't remember the antics. Their pride in accomplishment has to come out. Hers came out today. Heck, somebody in a bar bumps into you, then does it again, then bumps you again, eventually you bump back. That's all."

"I know you're trying to help," he said. Seconds passed. "We just can't let her become a rogue horse. She has too much talent. We have to help her stay in focus." He paused. Beth and Aly Dancer stopped walking. "And Beth?"

"Yeah?"

"You spike the ball *after* you reach the end zone. Do it in the field of play, you become the laughing stock of the league."

Beth smiled. The fact that he had said "we" was all she needed to hear. That was Jake. He took all the pressure, all the criticism, but he acknowledged that they were a team. "We."

"We'll get her head right." Turning to the filly she whispered, "Won't we girl?"

Chapter 10

It was a crazy dream.

In quiet moments like this drive home, the dream would overtake Dan's thoughts and attempt to hijack him.

Put it out of your mind.

His stomach ached as if he'd swallowed a scorpion. Even though he knew the stewards were right to disqualify Aly Dancer, he'd run memories of more egregious events that didn't result in a horse being disqualified. He'd looked to Lennie and Milt to agree—to be enablers to his wishful thinking. Neither played along.

There was always an exception. The lawyer in him ached for an exception that would change the result, but like a guilty verdict, the jury had spoken. And from this, there was no appeal.

Just to highlight his day, he'd stayed to watch Zaqualina race at Santa Anita. She won by five or six lengths, just toying with the field, a few ticks off the track record. Milt was ecstatic and danced a jig as though he'd won the lottery. It was no financial haul. She paid three bucks for a two dollar bet, but you'd have thought Milt turned wrought iron into gold. He praised his new messiah, T-Nost, and made a show of his superior intellect by being a paid subscriber.

The filly looked unbeatable and maybe that was the salvation. She was so good her connections might take on the boys and skip the Oaks.

On the phone Jake was his usual reserved self. Somewhere east of disappointed and north of embarrassed, he gave Dan his take. She seemed sound, didn't have a scratch on her. She cooled out well and seemed no worse for wear.

Kyle never saw it coming and was damn lucky just to stay on her back. He was sick like everyone else and had no explanation. Jake was uncharacteristically speechless. He was always a man of few words, but tonight Dan could tell that not only were there few words, there were fewer thoughts. Jake had no clue what caused her to bolt into those other horses.

If there was a positive to all this, barring something unforeseen they were still headed for the Oaks. They'd take it day by day.

Dan decided to call Beth after he got home. Calling Jake first was the code. Owners never talked to "the help" about troublesome situations. Always the trainer first. Beth would likely have little to add, but he wasn't calling her on matters of equine behavior.

At least one issue was resolved today. The offer to buy Aly Dancer was gone. A million dollars was a heady price for a horse that looked more suited for a demolition derby than a horse racing derby. He should have taken the money. No. Maybe.

His internal debate did little to soothe the scorpion

in his belly; in fact with each stab there was the "I told you so" after effect.

Dan rubbed his face and changed lanes. Thinking of Beth brought the dream back.

It would never work. Even if he ran extreme success scenarios, even if the longest shots on the board ran one, two, three, it would never work. Their lives didn't intersect. That's all there was to it.

He was a lawyer. His practice was a love, but one that had a geographical ball and chain. He lived where his clients needed him, where he was admitted to practice.

She lived where the races moved her. Since she'd been a toddler, Beth was on the move from one racetrack to the next. Growing up as a trainer's daughter, the family followed the money and moved to locations where her dad's horses could compete and win races.

He'd war gamed it out. What if his practice became highly lucrative and he bought that training farm? Beth could run the farm for him. Her touch with animals was magical. They could settle down and be together.

But it would never work.

It was merely a justification—a rationalization that he couldn't make true. She needed to be on the circuit. She gave horses confidence. She nurtured that will to win. She brought the best out in them, their very best. And in reciprocal fashion, they brought out the best in her. Her pride in their performance was the payoff. He saw it in her smile, in her walk, in the way she managed her charges. No, she was born to be on the backside. He couldn't take that from her, no matter what.

Success for her would take her farther away—perhaps California, New York or Kentucky. Racing in the Mid-

Atlantic States was a solid career for some, but the highest levels of the game weren't in those places. Success for her would be a very permanent separation from Virginia.

They'd never spoken of it. It would be the buzz kill of all buzz kills. Their relationship was in the moment, and they both knew that was the only place they could experience it. Speaking of it would begin the death spiral.

Why couldn't he just accept it? Why couldn't he be content to live in the moment?

If he sold the filly, they could still be together—couldn't they? No, it would be like ripping her heart out. She knew the business, that's what she would say, "It's just business." But they'd both know it was a lie. Even if he showered her in gifts from the sale price, it would never replace the hole. They would never be the same.

Their loves kept them apart. Their love for each other could never bridge the gap.

But why not this time? His marriage to Vickie was supposed to have been perfect. Two top grads from the same law school class. How could their lives not be more connected and intertwined?

He'd found a way to mess that up.

Two years before Vickie had shattered him with one word. *Selfish.* The truth from a loved one tasted the most bitter.

He wasn't selfish. Never had been. How could she say that? She was just being vindictive. She wasn't serious. Me? Selfish?

But it haunted him. Is my relationship with Beth doomed because I'm selfish? I'm not selfish. Is that why our lives can't intersect? Because I'm selfish with my new life? Is that why I can't sell Aly Dancer, because I'm selfish?

Vickie just didn't understand me. Our relationship was just wrong from the get go.

Maybe the long odds on his relationship with Beth were better than the chalk bet his first marriage had seemed. He'd cashed on longer odds before. Why not this time?

Selfish?

Put it out of your mind.

Chapter 11

Monday, April 23

Dan had been in the office for two hours when the front door rattled open. Being a one-man legal shop, he'd been mired in the least glamorous of necessary evils—billings and receivables. Grabbing a stack of receivables, he headed to the outer area where Mindy was settling her purse and canvas shopping bag, which was a sign of the new age working woman.

"Thanks for the flowers."

"Oh, no problem. Thought they'd brighten up the place," he said. Dan dropped the pages on her desk. "Some receivables. You make the good cop calls, I've got a stack where I'll be the bad cop."

"Aly win?" she asked, slipping off her tennis shoes to trade for more fashionable, yet sensible office footwear.

It was an innocent question, but he was still stinging from Saturday's race. "Ran fourth, long story, another time. I left some dictation as well."

"Tommy has a doctor's appointment this morning, so I'm going to take my lunch break early."

Having grown up with a single mom, he knew the routine and the difficulty in keeping hours while raising a child alone. At least his mom had a sister and brother-in-law who took up the slack for her when she went back to work. "Take him and take your lunch break too, no problem. Heck, take him to lunch. No appointments until later today and I've got a brief I need to work on. Take your time."

No sooner was he back at his desk than the phone rang. Mindy raced around her desk and the ringing stopped. She was a pro on the phone, able to ask the right questions to send persistent salesmen packing, but savvy enough to divine whether a potential client was searching for representation, particularly one who could pay.

"Judge Riley's bailiff on one," she shouted. It was their Italian intercom system. Dan Morgan and Associates had the most basic of telephone equipment still available on the market. No caller ID, no screens, just buttons and handsets. Though he could certainly afford an upgrade, it wasn't a priority. Their intimate system worked the best.

Dan picked up the phone and announced himself.

"Mr. Morgan, Janice from Judge Riley's office. I've got Grady Cohen on the line as well."

"Grady," Dan said to his opposing counsel.

"Morgan," came Grady's whiney voice. Jerk, Dan thought. What's up with the last name? The guy was always angling to get under my skin.

Janice took control of the conversation. "Judge wants to pre-try Jones v. Gabrelli case on Monday, April 30. Two o'clock, in chambers."

Riley was a stickler, one of the tougher judges in the fourth district. He could have just sent an order in the mail. Judge Riley worked his docket like he was still in the JAG corps.

"Good by me," croaked Grady.

"Fine," said Dan.

"He wants all exhibits marked and ready, no hiding or he'll strike them at trial."

"What about rebuttal exhibits?" Grady asked.

What a slime bag, Dan thought. Grady Cohen was known for blind-siding opposing counsel with undisclosed exhibits and secret witnesses all conveniently protected under the guise that it was rebuttal evidence. Dan had experienced it firsthand.

"I think she said all exhibits, Grady," Dan said.

"I'm talking to the bailiff, Morgan." What a prick. Guess he hasn't had his cup of coffee this morning.

"Mr. Morgan's right. All exhibits. You've been warned. You can try and bring up something on rebuttal, but take your chances. You know how the judge can be. He wants all witnesses identified, including address and phone numbers."

Grady groaned like he'd been stuck with a shiv.

"Proposed jury instructions," she continued. "Points of law, motions in limine—"

"We don't even have a trial date." Grady said. It was one of his more intense whines.

Pathetic.

"You will on Monday," she said. "Bios on experts, expert reports if you intend to offer them, and one other thing." She paused as if checking her notes. "Come with settlement authority. You don't have to bring clients or reps, but have authority." This brought another animal sound from Grady.

Since Dan represented the plaintiff in the action, it meant Grady had to come with an offer of settlement. He had no high expectations that it would settle, but was glad the judge was forcing the conversation.

"Thank you Janice. Anything else?" Dan asked in his most polite voice.

Good relationships with bailiffs were critical to a trial practice, heck any practice. They were gatekeepers for the judge and no doubt shared their impressions with the robed one. It made no sense to act like a pouty teenager when dealing with them. That would be Dan's advantage against Grady Cohen.

"I may have a conflict, I think I have a hearing with Judge Senser that day. I'll have to check my calendar." Grady was now back pedaling full force.

"Monday, two o'clock," she said defiantly.

"Thank you, Janice," Dan said just to drive the knife in further. He smiled and ended the call.

Judge Riley wasn't the best draw he could have gotten for a personal injury case. He was an old defense attorney before going on the bench. But one thing was to Dan's advantage. Riley ran his courtroom with Swiss precision. He was known for forcing settlements through the sheer will of protocol. Lawyers who were unprepared or in need of continuances received no quarter from Judge Riley.

Dan had good medical evidence and damages, but liability would be the sticking point for the case, especially with a defense-oriented judge. A settlement would be the best alternative and Riley was the man to make that happen.

"Mindy, call Clara Jones and let her know we have a pre-trial on Monday," Dan shouted through the imaginary intercom. "She doesn't need to be there, but I'll need to talk to her later in the week, so set a time. I'd like to have her come in."

It was always best to talk settlement in person. Clients had courage on the phone, less so in person. Although he was ready and prepared to try the case, a fair shot at settlement might be the best outcome for Clara. It was a good case, but if they got hung up on liability, the case was worth nothing.

"Jake on line one," Mindy shouted.

Dan snapped up the phone. "How's she doing?"

He could hear Jake clearing his throat on the line. Whipsawed from his conversation with the bailiff, Dan was entering a different communication dimension. The legal conversation was staccato and precise. Jake's conversation would be slow country western.

"She's fine." The words from Jake flowed like molasses. "Ate up well."

"What do you think? We going to the Oaks?"

"That's your call boss, but no reason I can see not to try it."

Dan fist-pumped the air, but displayed no emotion in his voice. "Let's do it then. When do you pack up? The meet starts in a week."

"We'll pull up stakes here in a day or so and shuttle the horses. Beth will be with Aly," Jake said.

He didn't need to say it. There was no way that horse was going anywhere without Beth.

"You see Zaqualina? Think she'll go in the Oaks?" Dan asked.

Jake harrumphed. "Not my call. We don't get to

decide. We just show up with the best we got and see what happens."

Dan knew he was lying. Jake had been thinking about the race for months. He down-played his thinking in front of owners, but Jake wouldn't take the challenge if he didn't think Aly was up to it.

"One other thing we got to talk about," Jake said. "The guy who made the offer came by today."

"I imagine after Saturday he's not interested."

"Oh he's interested. He offered one point two for her."

"What?" Dan grabbed his forehead. "Why would he offer another two hundred? I thought being DQ'd and running fourth, that would be the end of it."

"She didn't run fourth," Jake said. "She was placed fourth, big difference. She ran first. But anyway, I can't tell you the why. I can only report an offer."

"Don't tell me who it is," Dan said.

"Gotcha."

Dan didn't want to know who the potential buyer was because it might influence his decision. If he knew, he could figure out who the new trainer would be, what the owner's silks would look like, and he couldn't bear to think of Aly Dancer in another barn. But this was business. He only wanted to think of the offer, not the result. For that reason Dan never wanted to know who made the offers.

Mindy appeared in the doorway and gave him a wave. She was heading out. Dan waved back.

He leaned back slumping in his chair. "Jesus, one point two," Dan muttered.

"One condition," Jake said.

"What's that?"

"You have to sell her before the Oaks."

It hit Dan like a George Foreman punch to the gut. Dan had always been a small-time owner. He'd had success, but nothing like Aly Dancer. No matter where an owner started in the horse racing game, there was one common desire—race on TV. The Triple Crown, the Breeders' Cup, the top Graded stakes in the country were televised races. Dan longed for that dream. Aly Dancer was going to race on TV. The only question was whether Dan would be the owner when it happened. One point two, he thought. This is crazy.

"Let me know what you want to do," Jake said sullenly.

Dan thought for several seconds, then sat forward. "Take her to Churchill Downs, Jake."

"Do I tell them no?"

"Don't tell them anything." He needed to keep his options open. That was a lot of money. "Take my filly to Churchill Downs. They got a race for us coming up."

"You got it," Jake said, more spirited.

"And say hello to Beth for me," Dan said. It was unnecessary. Jake knew what was going on between them and Dan wanted it in the open, without actually saying it.

Dan hung up. With elbows on the desk, his face was in his hands.

One point two million.

Not only was the buyer not frightened off by Aly's performance, he came with more money. Dan ran after-tax scenarios and threw mental blocks of cash at his wish list. There was still money left over.

God that's a pile of money. But what's she worth if she actually wins the Oaks? Can she win it?

The specter of Zaqualina thrust into his mind. *Can Aly beat her? Am I crazy?* Beth would never forgive me.

Jake would be pissed, that's for sure, but it's business to him. Beth would never get over it. Never.

The phone rang, jarring him back to the present.

"Dan Morgan?" The voice was foreign, not Spanish which he recognized in many of his clients, but something else—less musical sounding accent, more mechanical.

"Yes, who's this?"

"Is about your filly." The "is about" rather than "it's about" was a tell, but he couldn't nail it.

"Jake Gilmore is my trainer. Talk to him." If this was the buyer, Dan didn't want anything to do with him.

A heavy breath pushed through the phone line. "If you know what's good for you, you sell the horse."

German? No. Dutch? Have I even heard Dutch? No. Something eastern European. Slavic?

"I don't deal direct. If you want to talk to someone see Jake—"

The line went dead.

Chapter 12

"We got a deal?"

Jesus, Jake thought, give me a break. He turned and looked over his shoulder down the shedrow. They'd just off-loaded Aly Dancer and six other horses. Beth and Jorge were busy hanging feed tubs in the stalls and kicking straw to smooth the bedding.

It was Jake's first visit to Churchill Downs, and although the racing officials were astute, due to the backlog of trailers through Gate G it took them nearly an hour to drop papers and get stall assignments. A track liaison directed them to Barn 11, which Jake would share with three other trainers.

The backside was controlled chaos with the meet opening on the following day and only eight days to the Kentucky Oaks. Trainers from all over the country converged on Louisville, soon to be followed by well-heeled owners in private jets and over one hundred thousand fans for the Derby on the day after the Oaks.

"No word," Jake said, waving the man off and turning back to stand in front of Aly Dancer's stall. She had traveled well from Florida, but something wasn't right. He peered into the stall, looking for any sign of discomfort or unusual behavior. Jake sensed the unease, but couldn't see it.

Two days after the Magnolia Stakes she'd gone into a funk. She was eating up well, holding her weight, and showed no adverse visible signs, but he knew. He'd honed his intuition on such matters over the years. It was a hard-won skill of seasoned horsemen. She wasn't right. He needed to get her to the track, stretch her legs, build her confidence. She needed her fire back.

Jake pushed his baseball cap back and scratched his head. He sensed the man approaching down the shedrow. With a glance he realized there were two of them, one extra-large and the other economy-sized. Anton was the extra-large. Jake was not about to let them near his horse.

Moving quickly Jake intercepted them halfway and motioned to step out of the shedrow and into the grassy area fronting the barn. A whitewashed rail fence framed the grassy area, separating it from the gravel road splitting the barns. This would be home for a while, familiar and foreign at the same time.

The barns were white and framed in dark green. Eighteen stalls on each side, back to back, covered by a large green sloped roof. As was customary, the roof extended eight feet beyond the stalls to provide a shaded walkway for hot walking around the barn.

Beth's blonde head poked out of a nearby stall. "Everything okay?" she asked.

"Yeah," Jake said, without looking toward her.

Churchill Downs' backside was abuzz with new horses being settled and reporters flashing in and out of barns, searching for a scoop. Fortunately for Jake, their interest was in the Derby prospects, less so with Oaks participants. Despite twenty years on the mid-Atlantic circuit, not many of the reporters could identify him on sight. They'd figure it out later, but for now he liked the anonymity from the circus followers.

Anton Nikitin put a foot up on the lower plank of the fence and leaned his elbows on the top of the railing looking away. The bulk of his six foot frame leaned against the structure. His teeth were yellowed by routine unfamiliarity with a toothbrush and his nose bore the bumps and shifts of a boxer or a street brawler. His tight-cropped crew cut made his forehead appear massive, like the cliffs of Dover resting on white bushy eyebrows.

Anton thumbed toward the other man. "Sergei Cheskov."

Jake nodded toward him.

"Works for me," Anton said.

Sergei didn't raise his eyes toward Jake. The man was occupied with kicking a chunk of gravel into the road.

"I get impatient," Anton said, also not making eye contact.

Jake stood with his arms crossed, his feet wide apart. "Don't know what to tell you. I passed your offer onto the owner. It's his call."

"You need to be more persuasive."

"He has all the information he needs, all your conditions, timing, everything. When he's made a decision, I'll let you know. Til then, stay away from my barn."

Anton smiled and raised his eyes to meet Jake's. "That a threat?" he asked.

Sergei shuffled away from the fence, stepping behind Jake.

Too close for comfort, Jake shifted his feet. "Take it however you want. You've got no business being around my barn. I don't train for you. Go hang out with whoever you want, just not here."

"You don't like it when I get impatient," Anton said, the smile quickly gone. "I been told I got anger issues."

"I don't have any information for you, so run along." Jake turned and took a step away. "You, too," he said to Sergei.

"I got another idea for you," Anton said.

Cocking his head toward Anton, Jake said, "I don't need any ideas from you."

"You might like this one." The smile returned to Anton's face as Jake stopped in his tracks. "What you get for winning Oaks. Fifty thousand? Trainer share?"

"What are you some math wizard? It's standard rate. Figure it out yourself."

"How you like fifty if she don't win?" Anton said, nodding toward the barn.

"Are you bribing me?" Jake asked. "'Cause that's a nonstarter, pal. I'll take you to the stews right now."

"Nothing to take to stewards, Jake. I'm just suggesting business deal. You can't beat Zaqualina anyway. Hear she's going to the Oaks. Going to pass on Derby. She win anyway, why not make the money?"

"Don't like the sound of it," Jake said, walking away. "And if you haven't noticed, let me just say it—I don't like you. Stay away from my barn. Last time I'm telling you guys."

"She can't win, Jake. We both know it." Anton said. "Don't be stupid."

Jake stalked toward the barn, tugging his ball cap down.

Chapter 13

"Call Q," Vasily said, exiting the elevator and leaving Mickey in the hallway.

Mickey wasn't allowed to enter Vasily's apartment. No one was. Since Vasily's wife had died from breast cancer three years before, no one had entered his apartment. Mickey knew it wasn't a personal issue. It had nothing to do with emotional privacy. It always had to do with money. Everything Vasily did had to do with money.

Mickey knew that Vasily had several safes in his modest apartment off Arroyo Seco Parkway. In order to retrofit his third floor apartment, Vasily bought the whole building. Since that time, rent was always paid on time. Serious construction was done to install vaults and reconstruct the walls of his unit to make them bulletproof.

Hell, the place was probably bombproof, Mickey thought.

Without entering the unit, Mickey knew that Vasily would be on his knees opening the floor safe and pulling out stacks of hundred dollar bills. Mickey made the deliveries, many times from the import export business

Vasily owned on Fremont Avenue. He would have to be an idiot not to know what was inside the Russian pottery and artwork that they hauled to Vasily's apartment complex.

It was okay. Mr. K took care of Mickey. A fair salary, always paid in cash. Wherever they went together, Mr. K paid, with cash—lunch, dinner, strip clubs, the track, everywhere. On frequent occasions, Vasily would slip Mickey an envelope and tell him to make sure the Caddy always topped off with fuel. These envelopes, routinely with twenty-five crisp hundred dollar bills, ensured the fuel gauge never dipped below three quarters.

Mickey dialed his phone and leaned against the door frame.

After three rings, he heard "Hi."

Dumbshit, Mickey thought. Who answers the phone with hi? Anyone from this country knows to say hello. Only a Thai numbers freak talks like that.

"Q, need a pick. Mr. K wants one for Saturday," Mickey said, without emotion.

"Oh, Saturday. Too early. Too early. Is only Thursday. No form yet. Not 'til Friday."

"I know what day it is, chopsticks," Mickey said. He shifted his weight and scratched the stubble under his ear. "We'll start running it Thursday and will need the pick Friday before midnight."

"No possible," Q said, agitated and struggling for words. "May not be no pick on Saturday. May like nothing."

Q was formally known as Trihn Duc Quang. In elementary school he was deemed a math prodigy. Algebra, geometry, fuzzy math, it all came easily to Q. He scared his teachers because, even with the use of their advanced math books, they couldn't keep up.

Mickey met him at UniSoft, the IT start-up where they both worked. Mickey was a whiz at website development; Q could do all the math and algorithms to create customer measures, buyer intentions, and Internet tracking. They both were heads and shoulders above the unwashed, unshaved geeks who slaved for these on-line rip-off artists.

Mickey figured the scam out quickly. Get a boatload of cash from eager investors, blow through the cash on bullshit personal expenses, and do a second round. In the meantime, grunts like Mickey built websites that dazzled the money men. If all went right, the company got bought out and the founders made millions. Guys like Mickey got nothing, but promises of "next time." Right, next time they'll make sure guys like Mickey made out, not just the MBA rich boys who founded the pieces of crap.

He didn't match the other software geeks. Mickey's frame was that of a power lifter. As the endorphins kicked in from power reps and bench presses, Mickey could see the technological solution. His peers munched on free cream-filled donuts and lattes, pondering life's imponderables over a game of foosball or Pacman. They were putzes in black rimmed glasses. They were lucky anyone paid them for their time—for anything. Mickey learned that he was being used. He wouldn't stand for it.

Mickey quickly latched onto Q. The rail-thin, ninety-pound Thai had a thing for horse racing, as did many Asians. Q would work sixty hours a week programming dynamic software gizmos and another sixty hours a week handicapping Santa Anita, Del Mar, and Hollywood. Mickey visualized the greasy, unshaven, and disheveled Q plugging away at his computer. The barren apartment was unlit, save for the glare from the monitor. Mounds of racing forms littered his feet.

Ever the businessman, Mickey taught Q that he could make far more money selling his tips than actually betting on them. At the very least he could make extra cash and bet his tips as he wished.

Missing everything that might help Q from a marketing standpoint, Mickey stepped in. It was easy money. Q did the handicapping, Mickey built the business, which included a group of thugs and hangers-on who could distribute the tip sheets.

Mickey finally had it with the software start-ups and Mr. K made everything cash flow. In a conversation with Vasily about Q, the light bulb went off. Mickey couldn't see it at first, which was the beauty of Vasily's business mind.

Vasily suggested a new business. Mickey and Q could continue with their tip sheet business. He wouldn't interfere with that, but for a nice wad of cash, Vasily bought rights to the picks, and specifically to Q's best picks, whether it was one per week or one per month, didn't matter. Vasily just wanted the best pick. With the infusion of cash, the web empire of Thoroughbred Nostradamus was born.

Mickey built the site and commerce features on the back end, Q just identified his strongest pick and Vasily's first Internet venture was born. It was odd for Vasily to be in an Internet business. He didn't have an e-mail account, didn't surf the web, and had never actually touched a computer keyboard. He just knew how to make money and how to wash money. Thoroughbred Nostradamus was the perfect venture.

"Saturday, rice boy. Need the pick by Friday night,"

Mickey said. "And by the way, don't freaking miss. Dead solid lock. Got it?"

Chapter 14

Saturday, April 28

Alone in the office again, but Dan didn't mind. After slogging through a few years in a big law firm and working as a prosecutor, he was proud to run his own shop, even if that meant long hours and weekends. In his situation nothing happened unless he did it. There was no momentum without his effort. That was fine with him.

He put down the dictation recorder and stretched. He was the legal workhorse, the marketing director, the accountant, the chief executive, and the guy who made the coffee.

His cell phone jostled him out of his moment of peace. It was Milt.

"You coming out today?"

"Can't do it, got too much work," Dan said.

"You need to talk to your boss about that. Can't even get away on the weekends to get to the track," Milt said.

"Yeah, I'll talk to him about that."

"Just wanted you to know that Nostradamus has a pick today. Thought I'd tell you about it, being the honest broker that I am," Milt said.

"That and I'll bet Lennie won't care so you call me."

"Whatever. Word to the wise. Mistral's Image in the feature at Churchill."

Dan tapped his computer to life and pulled up the daily racing form site. "Mistral's Image," he said, scrolling down on the morning line entries at Churchill Downs. "Quite a stretch, they didn't have enough earnings to get into the Derby, so he's going in the Derby Trial. Hell, Milt, he's six to five in the morning line. You'll be lucky to get him at even money. Some pick."

"This guy doesn't miss, I'm telling you. I'm happy to double my money on a sure thing," Milt said, defensively. "You want me to put anything down on it for you?"

"There are no sure things Milt. You know that. I'll pass. But good luck and be careful. Don't go crazy on this guy's picks. He's bound to miss one and probably when you've passed a boatload through the windows. Thanks for the call."

Dan pulled up an article on the Derby Trial. This looked like a walkover for Mistral's Image. They couldn't get in the Derby, although he'd have been a contender. His connections must be aiming for the Preakness after today's race.

He clicked off the Internet and turned back to his notes on the desk. Just as he picked up the Dictaphone, the cell rang again.

"Jake, how you doing? How's our girl?"

"Gotta talk," Jake said. Dan could sense the urgency in his voice.

"Something wrong? What's up?"

"Yeah, something's wrong. Don't sell the filly." It

sounded like he was winded, but maybe he was just walking on the backside, Dan thought.

"Jake, I—"

"I'm serious, don't sell her. I know I got no right to tell you what to do, but it's a scam. The whole thing's a scam. I've got a meeting with the Stews tomorrow. Gonna lay it all out for them. Get the sons-a-bitches ruled off, maybe thrown in jail. Bastards."

"What do you mean? What's a scam?"

"I gotta go. Just don't sell her. If you want I can find another buyer in a heartbeat. Just don't do this."

"Jake—" The line went dead.

Should I call back?

He held his phone, looking at it. What the hell? For the past week he'd tried not to think about the offer, yet it came rushing in whenever his mind wandered. He hadn't told Jake about the mystery caller from earlier. It would do no good for anyone.

He hadn't told Beth either. That bothered him more, but he couldn't risk her reaction and the possibility he might sell. He leaned forward, elbows on his knees. Jake knows what he's doing. He's the trainer. Leave it to him. That's how the business works. Don't mess with it.

What's the scam?

~

Rain streamed down the living room window. Lightning flashed, illuminating the apartment, followed by the inevitable crack of thunder. The air conditioner chugged in the background, ceaselessly attempting to rid the air of humidity. Uppermost branches of the pin oak tree bobbed, swayed, then head-butted the window.

Dan set his beer on the end table, the place the beer always rested, within easy reach from his spot on the plaid couch he'd borrowed from his mom. A freshly microwaved plate of spaghetti was balanced between his knees. He snapped on the sports channel.

He was living through that awkward time, too old to hang out in bars and too confident to log onto a dating service website. Another Saturday night with the remote control. Beth was all he needed from a romantic standpoint, but even she hadn't returned his call from an hour earlier. Where was she?

Mistral's Image had won the Derby Trial. He ran off by five lengths and returned $3.20. Dan smiled as he thought of Milt dancing around the OTB because his three to five shot had won. It didn't take a genius to figure that horse, but then again, playing chalk was a sure way to lose money. They were called bridge jumpers for a reason. Bet big, then cash or jump, those were the options.

No, thanks.

The phone jarred him from the middle of a pitch in the middle of an inning of the middle of a baseball game that no one would remember.

Beth.

He punched his Blackberry. "Hey, was wondering about you."

Silence.

"Beth?"

That was when he heard the snuffling sound.

"You okay?" he said, sliding the plate onto the couch.

He heard her inhale, then choke as she tried to muffle her sobs. "Dan," she said, barely audible.

"What?"

She inhaled and gasped. "It's Jake." It was all she could get out, then her voice collapsed and the crying filled the void.

"What is it? Jake okay?"

"He...he's...dead."

"What?" Dan shouted. The crying returned full force and it sounded like she had moved the phone away from her.

"Beth," he said softly. "Beth, where are you?"

She choked and calmed the concussive sobs. "At the barn."

"Are you safe?" he asked. No response. "Anybody there with you?" No response. "You okay? What happened?"

"I found him...," she said, then the crying burst forth again.

"Take a deep breath." He could hear her trying to comply, her breathing chugging in opposition to her compulsive reaction.

He let her take some breaths, then continued. "Tell me what happened."

"I came back from dinner..." several more breaths. "to check on Aly."

"Okay," Dan said slowly.

"The light was on in Jake's office and the door was partly open. I just figured he was working late." Two deep breaths came quickly through the receiver. "I pushed the door open and there he was." The last two words came out as a high-pitched squeak.

"What do you mean there he was?"

Nothing.

"Beth?" He stood and leaned, his forehead against the wall.

"He—he was hanging from the rafter. He hung himself." She broke down again.

Hung himself? No way.

Dan had to concentrate to bring air into his lungs. "Beth, who's there with you? Somebody there?"

"The police, the track police. I didn't know what to do. I just screamed and security came. They called the police. They just left with Jake's body. I don't know what to do."

Dan ran his hand over his face. More than anything he just wanted to hold her, but six hundred miles prevented that.

"Okay, just calm down," he said. "Do you have a vehicle? You need to get away from there for a little while."

"I can't."

"You have to."

"Jake's truck is here, but I don't have the keys. They were probably—" Then she broke down again.

"Is Jorge there? Anyone?"

"No," she said, snuffling. "He left this afternoon. I don't know where he is."

"Can you call him?"

"He doesn't have a phone."

"Here's what I want you to do," Dan said. "Walk over to the track security office."

"I can't," she mumbled. "I can't leave Aly."

"Aly will be fine. Go to security. There'll be someone there. You don't want to be alone right now. Tell me you're walking there right now."

Silence.

"Beth?"

"I'm walking."

"I'm going to call you back in twenty minutes. You stay there until I call. Twenty minutes. Okay?"

"Okay."

"I love you," he said.

He couldn't tell if she said anything. The line went dead. Maybe she didn't hear him. It was all right. He did love her, damn it—just an odd time to say it out loud for the first time.

He spun through the contacts on his phone and engaged the line.

"Hello?" The voice sounded half asleep.

"I need a big favor," Dan said. "Really big."

"Yeah? What's that?"

"I need you to drive to Louisville tonight."

Chapter 15

The sky lightened in the rear view mirror. Dan took a slug of his coffee. It tasted like it has been strained through sweat socks and bat dung. He choked down the remnants which included grinds for him to chew on. What did he expect from truck stop coffee? He wasn't drinking it for the taste, only for the caffeine.

Lennie had been sleeping since they pulled back onto the Interstate. He'd spoken with Beth twice since they'd hit the road. She was better, but still dazed. Word that he was on the way had settled her.

He'd downloaded everything to Lennie and they spent the first two hours pondering the scam. If something nefarious was going down around a racetrack, Lennie had the best mind to crack it. So far they had nothing.

Lennie stirred. Dan turned the radio up a notch.

"Want me to drive for a while?" Lennie said, rubbing his eyes.

"I'm good."

The passenger sat upright and lifted his cold coffee from the cup rest.

"Jesus, I've had some bad coffee in my day, but this tastes like three-day-old sewage." He took a big swig anyway.

Traffic was light, had been since they'd escaped the city. Dan blinked and refocused his eyes. Two red lights guided him. A smattering of white lights defined the oncoming traffic from across the interstate divide.

"Where are we?"

"About halfway."

"What state?" Lennie asked.

"Beats the shit out of me. Tennessee?"

"Got no use for Tennessee." Lennie said. Dan looked over. Lennie shrugged. "No racetracks."

This brought a chuckle from Dan. It surprised him. He thought he'd forgotten how to laugh. That's what made Lennie such a good friend. Well, that, and getting into a car at midnight to drive halfway across the country.

"By the way," Lennie said. "If we're in Tennessee, aren't we going the wrong way?"

Dan exhaled loudly. "Hell, I don't know. Maybe we're in West Virginia."

"I'm okay with West Virginia. They got racetracks."

The tension in Dan's shoulders lightened. It had been several hours since he'd had any thoughts other than Jake and Beth. He rubbed his face. The radio crackled with some indecipherable song. They rode in silence.

Lennie took another sip and grimaced.

"Jake give you anything else?" Lennie asked.

"Nope."

"There are a million scams on the racetrack, but they all have one thing in common," Lennie said. Dan looked over without speaking. "Cashing a ticket. Some kind of score."

"Why would someone offer a million two for a filly. It has to be something major." Dan said. "That's a lot of tickets."

"The horse is worth good money. No disrespect, but that's a ton for a filly, especially one that hasn't won a graded race."

"Yet," Dan said, staring straight ahead.

Lennie stretched and yawned.

"Could be a ringer," Lennie said.

"I thought about that."

"Somebody's got a filly with the same markings, they forge a lip tattoo and you can't tell them apart."

"But usually the ringer is the faster horse," Dan said.

"Yeah, that's the way it usually goes," Lennie said. "Run the horse up the track several times, then bring in the ringer when the odds are high. Are we sure the guy who wanted to buy the horse is the same one running the scam?"

"Has to be," Dan said, pausing. "Jake was fired up about not selling her because of the scam. Wouldn't make sense otherwise."

"You know I gotta ask you," Lennie said, pulling up his ball cap and scratching his forehead. "You sure Jake was okay?" The statement hung in the air. "I mean, these guys get in tough spots, stress, money problems, could be a lot of things."

"Jake didn't kill himself," Dan said, looking straight into Lennie's eyes. "Not a chance."

Lennie leaned his head back against the headrest. "Okay," Lennie said. A pause released some of the tension.

"Most betting scams involve getting a favorite to run out, finish out of the money. It's easier to hold a horse or impede their performance than to make one perform above their normal level. Sponging, which can be done by the trainer or buying off a jockey. Still happens. But with drug testing of all winners, there's little chance to scam a horse into running first. Unless it's a ringer, but again, that makes no sense. Are we sure it's a betting scam?"

"What else could it be?"

"I know," Lennie said. "But if the Oaks was the target, she won't be the favorite, probably second or third choice. Sorry man, but Zaqualina is the nuts in that race."

"If she goes," Dan said.

"Well, that's true, but either way, it's a tough race. No sure thing. A betting scam in a Grade One race? That's crazy. There's too much scrutiny. Money's too big. Jocks, trainers, everyone—they want to win. Plus, too many eyes on the participants. And let's say Aly Dancer is four to one or five to one. Getting her to run out is no big deal."

"It's no big deal and maybe no one notices," Dan said. "Unless they worry they can't beat my filly."

Lennie shrugged. "True, but I think they're confident. Should be anyway. Sorry, man." They rode in silence, then Lennie spoke. "There has to be a financial impact. That has to be the motive—more than just scamming a win. Why risk it? Makes no sense."

Dan nodded. They were where they started. Nowhere.

The night sky lifted slowly, filling the car with daylight. They were less isolated, part of a caravan rather than souls illuminated by dashboard bulbs. Dan noticed how scruffy they looked. It had been a long time since he'd pulled an all-nighter. With Judge Riley on Monday, he was destined for another one soon.

"You got her insured?" Lennie asked.

"Yeah, after she won the stake at Fairfax Park."

"Maybe they're going to take out a big policy and kill her."

"I thought about that, but there's nothing to be gained, and why does it matter that I sell her before the Oaks?"

"She wins the Oaks, they can bump up the insurance value, then take her out. If you're right that they killed Jake, they won't bat an eye at killing a racehorse."

"Yeah, but like you said, she's no lock, even without Zaqualina in the field," Dan said. "Hell of a gamble to rip off an insurance company. If she runs out, they overpaid for her and the whole thing's a bust."

"True." Lennie reached down between his legs and pulled up a racing form. "Not much of a card today. But I know one thing."

"What's that?"

Lennie snapped the paper open. "Looks like we've run flat into Godel's Theorem."

"Huh?"

"Godel's Incompleteness Theorem."

"Look Lennie, I've been driving all night. I'm barely functioning. How do you even think this stuff up?"

"Try getting a math degree from Princeton and not have this stuff floating in your brain."

Dan took a deep breath, then shook his head. "Okay, hit me with it."

"Godel's Theorem says that if an axiomatic system can be proven to be consistent from within itself, then it is inconsistent."

"You make my head hurt. So what does that mean?"

"Well my math profs would set their hair on fire, but it means no consistent system can have all truths, but no falsehoods."

"Means to me we don't know shit."

"I'll accept that answer," Lennie said, turning a page in the racing form. "We don't have enough information to form any reasonable hypothesis. I need a diversion. And I have a better chance figuring out these races right now than I have figuring out what Jake was onto."

~

Beth stood with her head leaning on Aly Dancer. The filly's feed tub was still half full. Tears slipped from Beth's eyes and blended into Aly Dancer's coat, darkening the once vibrant sheen.

She snuffled. "You have to eat, girl. You have to." The filly's head bobbed up and down, but didn't approach the tub.

With no sleep and the haunting image of Jake's feet swinging above his desk seared into her, she was a ball of crippled emotions.

Jorge had shown up. He'd heard the news of course—everyone had. He had enough honor to help Beth muck out the stalls and fill the feed tubs, but then he was gone. Probably already picked up by another trainer, she thought.

As the backside awoke, Jake's death was the buzz. Many hands walked slowly past the barn, looking and pointing, but not stopping to talk. That was okay with Beth; she didn't want to talk to them anyway. Thirty minutes after Jorge left, a guy from the racing secretary's office appeared. He handed her the papers allowing all of the horses to be moved from Jake's barn—all of them but Aly Dancer. A group of unwashed Mexicans led the horses away.

Damn vultures. Jake wasn't even cold yet and the owners were moving their stock to other barns. *Jesus, how early did these bastards start calling the owners?*

The vet rolled by wondering how he was going to get paid. He was followed by the feed man. Beth just shrugged. She had no answers.

The chalkboard next to Jake's office still showed the training regimen for his horses today. Jake had no idea that when he'd chalked that up, it would be the last time.

Her shoulders chugged and she cried quietly. Aly Dancer's hind quarter shivered as if shoeing flies. The filly raised her back leg and pawed the straw.

"I'm never going to leave you Aly. Never." Beth leaned away, rubbed her face, and snuffled. "It's going to be okay, girl." She stroked the filly's mane with parted fingers. Her voice was barely audible. "We're going to be okay."

She leaned back against the rough wood wall. *How did I get here?*

All she knew was caring for horses. From before she could remember, she worked the backside with her father. Three months in one town, then on to the next. She never had friends—not in the traditional sense. During her school years she was permanently the new kid. Though mature, friendly and outgoing, there was no need for others to invest in a relationship with her. One day she was in school, the next she was gone—another track, another backside. Her life was that of a nomad.

Vince DeCarlo was a journeyman trainer. He'd hitch up the trailer and move to whatever location he could win a purse. When she turned eighteen, she knew it was time to leave. Her dad still squeaked out a living on the northeast circuit. He'd taught her the nuts and bolts of training, but he'd never had a big horse. Beth knew he never would. Save for a few phone calls on Christmas and Thanksgiving, they rarely communicated. No hard feelings, just the nomad's game of moving on, ever moving on.

She was alone again. That didn't scare her. That was common. What bothered her was not knowing where she was headed.

Her father knew how to prepare a horse to race, but what Beth learned from Jake took the art to a new level. In Vince DeCarlo's world the trainer created the athlete. The trainer molded the athlete into his regimen—days for works, days for rest, days walked, feed, everything was scripted, everything uniform.

Jake was light years beyond that. Jake taught her that horses were individuals. You had to get into their heads and understand them in order to get the best out of them. At Jake's barn nothing was standardized, everything customized. He'd often said "we don't train *a* horse to race, we train *this* horse to race."

Beth was never the same. Training was not about managing an assembly line of equines, it was about psychology and physiology. It was about "training in" potential, not "training out" uniqueness. "The horse will tell us what it needs," Jake would say. "We just have to be listening."

At the moment, Beth was listening, listening intently, but she didn't know what for.

Lead ponies clip clopped past the barn with horses heading to the track. Aly Dancer lifted her head and peered at them. Beth knelt down and began unwrapping the covering on Aly Dancer's front legs. "I don't know what's gotten into you. You've got to tell me...show me. Whatever it is, I'll fix it, but right now you've got to eat."

Beth banged on the feed tub with her fist. Aly Dancer stuck her nose in the tub, pushed some feed around, then removed it. The filly looked down at the girl swiftly undoing the wraps. Kernels of feed stuck to Aly Dancer's nose and chin. The filly exhaled loudly and shook. The feed particles scattered; several caught in Beth's hair.

"I don't know what that means," Beth said. "But at least it's something." Before she realized, a smile appeared. The muscles of her face noticed it before her heart. Beth looked up with tightened lips and ran her hand over her hair. "That's right, girl. You and me." Beth went back to the wraps. "You and me."

~

Road weary and blurry eyed, Dan and Lennie had arrived at Churchill Downs. Lennie stared slack jawed as they approached the twin spires from Main Street. The Kentucky Derby Museum stood at the foot of the massive white entrance leading to the grandstand. This was hallowed ground. The parking lot was nearly vacant and they made their way around to the entrance of the backside.

An hour of waiting in line, first in the car, then in the racing secretary's office. Dan had to get his license, as did several dozen others who had assembled. With the

Kentucky Derby in six days, combined with the opening of the meet a few days before, the backlog for certification was tedious. Lennie was allowed on the backside as a guest, an accommodation that wouldn't be available as Derby Day approached.

Eventually they navigated the backside towards Aly Dancer's barn. Work was in full swing as grooms and hot-walkers paraded horses through the equine village. Some were going to the track for training, many were simply being walked. The air was alive with activity as trainers, jockeys, agents, vets, and of course reporters intersected in a commotion to get the day's work done.

Lennie pointed out the well-known trainers he spotted and called out the best runners in each person's barn. The man certainly knew the game. He was like a kid at a free carnival. Salve and wet leather filled their nostrils, along with the ever present aroma of manure and straw dust.

The green barns seemed to stretch to infinity as they negotiated the crossroads and gravel paths of the backside. To their right, the massive grandstand stood like a sentry bearing down on the racetrack where several horses strained and tugged against their riders, flexing their muscles.

Riders in t-shirts, jeans, and flak jackets shot by in pairs, as horses worked in company. Steam misted and rose off the backs of horses as they were washed down following workouts. The athlete's heads bobbed in rhythm, yanking on the shanks connected to a groom's hand. The coolness of early morning was giving way reluctantly to the sun as it broke through the clouds beyond the twin spires.

Spanglish was the predominant language of the backside, especially among the workers at the lowest rungs of the game. Few were fully bilingual, but all could communicate in the hybrid that dominated this community.

Dan spotted Beth from the roadway and yelled. She ducked under the webbing on Aly Dancer's stall and rushed toward him. As they embraced, the tears returned. He held her shaking in his arms as though she were a small child awaking from a nightmare.

He tried to soothe her with words of reassurance, but the physical contact spoke louder and more persuasively. She sobbed thank yous and oh my gods. He ran his hand over her hair eventually out of words.

When they separated she rubbed her eyes as she'd done a thousand times in the past several hours and stood tall inhaling to fight off the sobs.

Lennie stepped up and rubbed her arm. "Hell of a deal," he said.

"Okay, tell me everything," Dan said.

She retraced the events with arms gesturing as though exorcising a demon. Occasionally she had to stop to get her breathing under control.

Beth had returned from dinner in the café to check on Aly. The light in Jake's office puzzled her and she pushed open the door to find Jake hanging above his desk, tied to the rafters.

Stable hands rushed to her following her screams, eventually followed by track security and Louisville police.

"Did you get the names of the police and security?" Dan asked.

She pulled two business cards from her back pocket and handed them over.

"Where are all the horses?" Lennie asked.

"Gone." She gulped covering her face.

"What do you mean gone?"

"This morning someone from the racing secretary's office came by with papers to move the horses to other trainers. All but Aly Dancer. Owners must have called first thing." Then the tears came again.

"Jesus," Lennie said. "Word spreads fast."

"I don't know what to do," she said, squeaking out the last words.

Dan had to distract her, like redirecting a kindergartner.

"What's the schedule today?"

She gave him a puzzled look.

"For Aly. What's her schedule?"

"Jake was going to work her six furlongs today, but—"

"Okay, let's work her," Dan said. "Kyle here?"

"I don't know if we should," she said, crossing her arms and snuffling.

"What do you mean?"

"I don't think she's right. She's off her feed, her energy is down. I don't know. I didn't know if you wanted to—" she stopped and looked down.

"What?"

She shook her head staring at Dan's feet. "I don't know. Just didn't know which trainer you were going to move her to, that's all." She lifted her head and locked on his eyes. "Wherever she goes, I go with her. That has to be part of the deal. I can't leave her."

Dan stepped forward grasping her shoulders, their

eyes still locked. "Beth, you are my trainer. I don't need anyone else." Her hand quickly rose to her face and she covered her eyes as though the weight of the comment crushed her. "Beth, I trust you." Then with a lowered voice, "I love you." This caused her to drop her hand. "Aly needs you. I need you. Nobody knows her better than you. You've been at this game since you were out of diapers." This brought a reluctant chuckle. "This is your job." He paused. "If you want it that is."

The stunned look on her face dissolved as the words sank in. Her shoulders rose and she took a deep breath. She shook her head as if wiping away cobwebs.

"Okay," Dan said. "Like I said, what's the schedule today?"

She stepped away and crossed toward Aly Dancer's stall. She checked the feed tub, stepped closer and examined the horse as if for the first time. Her head nodded slightly. From her back pocket a phone snapped open. She punched it and listened. "Kyle, get over here, you've got a horse to work right after the break."

Chapter 16

It would have been funny if the situation weren't so sad. Lennie made his money knowing horses, thoroughbreds. He knew about performance, speed ratings, days of rest, pace, energy distribution. There was likely no issue on the topic of horse racing he didn't know or over which he held no opinion. Yet here he stood timidly holding Aly Dancer's shank. She'd move her head slightly and he'd two-step away. She'd lift her head and he'd two-step to the side. Lennie's head bobbed side to side like a boxer avoiding a jab. The filly just looked at him, blinking. Any movement by the filly and Lennie's reaction was to move—not for safety, not for the horse, just a nervous tick.

"Hold her still, will you?" Beth yelled, as she sponged the soap suds off the filly's back.

Kyle stood two paces behind her, his arms occasionally raised, palms up. He was trying to keep the conversation going, but Beth had talked enough. Kyle turned to walk away, then spun back.

"It was cuppy," he mumbled.

"Yeah, you said that," Beth said hosing the filly's hind quarters.

"She might need different shoes," Kyle offered.

Beth didn't turn to look. She shook her head and continued washing Aly Dancer down.

Kyle threw his arms out again and turned. This time he walked away, but drifted like a falling leaf. He had no place to go. His only reason for being at Churchill was Aly Dancer. Now he might not have that, Dan thought.

Beth finished the rinse cycle and gave Lennie instructions on how to hot walk her around the barn. Lennie began moving. He gave the shank a gentle tug and Aly snapped to attention, causing Lennie to stumble backward. Beth grabbed the shank and began walking the filly. She yelled and Lennie ran up. She handed the shank to him and said, "Keep going, left turns only, around and around." She twirled her finger to indicate he should circle the shedrow. Beth dusted off her jeans and walked toward Dan. Over her shoulder she yelled, "Might talk to her. She likes that."

"Hey," Dan yelled. "Tell her about Gordo's Incompleteness Theorem. She may understand it better than me."

She shook her head with disgust as she approached.

"Don't worry about it," Dan said.

She huffed. "Right, I've been a trainer for about an hour and you should fire me." Beth walked past him and entered the trainer's office.

"You're being too hard on yourself."

She stared at the chalkboard that held the training schedule for Jake's horses. Of the six horses, five had been erased. Only Aly Dancer's name remained. Jake's hand had scrawled "Work-6f" next to her name. "I know better," Beth said.

"She didn't go that bad," Dan offered.

"She went terrible," she said, meeting his eyes. "I never should have led her over. I knew something wasn't right. I made her look bad, might have compromised her. I made me look like an idiot, so good luck getting anyone to let me train. I got Kyle chirping at me, like he's some freaking horse expert." Lennie and Aly Dancer paraded past the door and turned up the shedrow. She scoffed. "I got a degenerate gambler as a hot-walker. Man who's never touched a horse. And I got you." She gestured weakly toward Dan. "And you oughta fire me, cause I don't know what the hell I'm doing."

Dan stepped forward and put a hand on her shoulder. "Forget about the work. Forget about the race. Focus on her. If she needs time, we'll give her time. Take the pressure off yourself. Get her right."

"I'm just so angry with myself. Jake wanted to work her six. I didn't think we should work her at all, so what do I do?" She asked, shrugging. "I work her four. Nice compromise. Like an idiot. Fifty-one and four."

"Forget about it."

"She's not right, Dan. I've known it and yet—" She threw her hands in the air.

"Okay, enough with beating yourself up. Let's move forward." Dan sat on the edge of the desk. "When did you first notice?"

"Aly?"

"Yeah."

"Was just after the Gulfstream race. Then she seemed to just lose interest. She just hasn't been herself."

"Did Jake have her checked out by a vet?"

"When we first got here, Jake had them give her the once over. Couldn't find anything," she said.

"Well, get the vet over here. We need to check again."

"Dan, I don't have any money," she said quietly. "It's not like I got a bunch of savings. I haven't even opened a trainer account."

"Don't worry about it, that's what owners are for."

She looked up with a sheepish laugh.

"We'll get you all set up. You probably need to get over to the secretary's office and get your license and all that stuff," he said. "You need to set up your accounts with the feed guy, the farrier, heck everybody."

"We're good on feed," she said.

"What do you mean?"

"Jake bought for six horses. Now I got one. We got plenty of feed."

Dan considered her remark and looked down at his shoes. It was possible, he thought. He crossed his arms.

"Throw it all out," he said.

"What?"

"The feed. Throw it all out. Every bit of it." He looked out the door down the shedrow. "Throw out everything. The feed tub, wraps, liniment. Throw it all out."

"You think someone's putting something in her feed? Poisoning her?"

"I don't know. I'm no scientist, but something's not right, so let's start off fresh. Change her stall. Change everything."

"Why would someone try to poison her?" Beth asked, the innocence shining through. "Who would do that?"

Dan watched Lennie and Aly Dancer slide by and cross out of sight. He folded his arms and leaned back against the bare wood wall. He had a notion, but not one he could share with Beth. Not right now. If you wanted to buy something badly, one strategy was to depress the seller's opinion of the value. Gets the seller off the hump. Might think what he's got is going down in value, so better take a deal than ride the price down.

He turned and locked eyes with Beth. "We need a new start anyway," he said, gesturing out the doorway. "I mean, I got you new help. Heck, what else do you want?"

~

Kyle had walked back to his pickup. Dejected and frustrated, he filled his faded Big Gulp cup with iced tea crystals and water from a garden hose. He sipped the tea slowly. Make it last, he thought. The slower you drink, the more it will fill you up.

His regimen to make weight forced a strict calorie intake. Iced tea was empty calories. He survived on empty calories.

Aly still wasn't herself. She lacked the fire he'd become accustomed to. It seemed like she was sightseeing rather than running today. The track was cuppy, but he knew better. Something wasn't right.

Since following Aly Dancer from Gulfstream Kyle had struggled. A few exercise mounts, many forced introductions, but few rides. His agent, TP Boudreaux, hadn't even made the trip. Boudreaux's other riders were back at Laurel Park and he worked to keep their books full. TP had made a few phone calls to try to get Kyle some rides, but nothing worked out.

Kyle had promised himself he'd never give up the mount on Aly Dancer, not after that surge bringing her to her maiden win and the gutty stretch drive to win the My

Lassie Stakes last year at Fairfax Park. He'd go wherever she went. Simple as that.

Kyle wouldn't risk that his phone wouldn't ring before a race or that they'd put someone else up for a training exercise. No, he'd sleep in his truck like he'd done at Gulfstream.

Save money. Stay close.

He visited Aly Dancer every day, mostly because he didn't have anything else to do.

Kyle sipped the tea again, slowly. He'd get a jog in later, keep the pounds off. He needed that Oaks purse. That one race could make up for three months of grinding it out back home.

This would be his breakthrough. Despite advice from Cyndi and friends, he had to hold out. He was so close, like a moth to a flame. Would the flame keep him alive or would he be eaten by the fire?

He needed that purse.

Chapter 17

Dan yanked open the glass door and confronted the reception desk behind a five-foot wall. Typical police protocol, he thought. Make sure the civilian seems as small as possible and has to crane his neck to see the duty officer.

The request for Inspector Banks was answered with a bored finger pointing down the hall. There was little activity in the station; a few blue shirts getting ready for a shift sat on metal desks swapping stories.

One office was occupied. The glass partition identified him as Inspector Shefford Banks. Dan poked his head in. Two cowboy boots were propped on the desk. The owner was nearly reclined in his standard issue metal green and gray office chair. He could have been sleeping, but for the pages of reports he held up to his face. The pages dropped and an eyeball appeared between the pointy toes of his boots.

"C'mon in."

"I'm Dan Morgan. Understand you're investigating the murder of Jake Gilmore."

"Murder? That's a heavy word."

One bushy eyebrow heaved upward. His face narrowed to a V at his chin, making his mustache look like the ice cream on a cone. His eyes were steady and inquisitive. He pushed his cowboy hat back and scratched his forehead.

"You mean the suicide at Churchill last night?" Banks said. "Pardon me if I don't get up," he continued, with a wave of his hand. "I got a bad back and this is the only thing that gives me any relief."

"Wasn't a suicide," Dan said stepping in and pulling one of the client chairs to the side so he could eye Banks.

"And you know this how?" Banks tossed the stack of pages onto his desk. He reached over and grabbed a note pad and pen.

"Cause I knew him. Known him for years. And in a week he was going to send a horse in the biggest race of his life. Not exactly a suicide scenario."

"Let's start with who are you?" Banks said, pen at the ready.

Dan gave him the upload on himself and his relationship with Jake. Banks scribbled notes feverishly. Despite his reclining posture, the inspector was writing down everything, flipping the page to continue. When Dan had finished, Banks lowered his feet and sat upright at the desk. A noticeable groan was emitted and he grimaced.

"Good to see you working this case on a Sunday." Dan figured he'd build a little rapport with the guy. "I have a small law firm and Sunday hours are part of my life too, unfortunately."

"Well, criminals don't take weekends off, I don't play golf, and my wife hates my guts, so what the hell? Here I am."

He scribbled some more notes and tapped the point of the pen.

"So Mr. Morgan, you figure the guy who wanted to buy your filly killed Gilmore?"

"The last time I talked with Jake, he told me not to sell, that the whole thing was a scam. I think he was going to spill the beans on them, said he was going to the stewards. They got scared and killed him."

"But you don't know who the buyer was?"

"I didn't want to know."

Banks shook his head. "Somebody wants to give me a million bucks, I guess I'd just want to know the check would clear." He tapped the pen on the note pad. "We got no prints, other than Jake's and—" Banks flipped back several pages. "Beth DeCarlo. Guess she worked for the guy."

"Well she sure as heck didn't do it."

Banks cocked his head, looking out of the corner of his eye. "How can you be so sure? Wouldn't be the craziest thing I've seen."

"She weighs about a hundred pounds soaking wet. Jake was at least two-fifty. How you figure she could hoist him to the rafters?"

"Like I said." He shrugged and waved his hands palms up. "Wouldn't be the craziest thing I ever saw. Older man, young girl, you'd be surprised what a guy will do for a pretty thing. Once in a while those pretty things get pissed off. You'd be surprised what an angry woman is capable of. I live with one." Dan stared in silence. "Interviewed a woman several years ago—cute as a bug. Twenty-something, flashy smile, real personable, you know. Anyway, came to find out she stabbed her husband to death, froze him in the freezer in the garage, then ran his body through their wood-chipper out back. Sweet gal."

"What? Why?"

"The guy liked to sit on the couch and watch football. Kinda got caught up in the game. Apparently he wasn't a good listener."

Banks cleared his throat. "But I digress. Let's assume you're right, just for kicks. What do you suggest we do? We got no prints, no witnesses, no evidence, no nothing. Now, supposing the buyer contacts you, let me know, we can bring him in. But we don't have a hell of a lot to go on. These horsemen get in financial jams, have a run of bad luck, make some bad bets and poof. Wouldn't be the first time." Banks gazed toward the ceiling. "Course usually it involves a handgun."

"What about his cell phone? Did you check to see incoming and outgoing calls?"

"Didn't have a cell phone on him."

"He always had his cell phone. That's the only way he could communicate with clients, employees, vendors, whatever. Never saw him without it."

"Didn't have one when we found him. Checked the office, the desk, the barn area, his truck. Nada."

"Don't you think that's a little strange?" Dan said, holding his Blackberry out so Banks could see Jake's phone number on the screen.

"I'll run it, see what we get."

"One of his last calls in or out had to be the buyer. Get me the numbers and I'll call." Dan scribbled down his cell number for the inspector. "I'll tell him Jake gave me the number and I want to make a deal."

"Hold on there, Rambo. Let's see what we get first. In the meantime, stay in touch. And I don't want this DeCarlo gal leaving the area. Told her myself, but she wasn't listening real good last night."

~

Thirty minutes later Dan was back at the barn. The second race of the afternoon had just been run. Lennie was like a cat tied to a tree. Although he had his racing form and pens aligned on the desk in the trainer's office, he dared not leave the barn area to get a bet down. Head down and glasses hanging from his nose, Lennie translated the seemingly random numbers into reality.

"Beth back?"

Lennie's head snapped up. "Not yet." He glanced at his watch. "Should be about ten minutes."

Dan leaned against the door frame. "I have a surprise for you." Lennie's brow furrowed, but he didn't speak. "As soon as she's back." He crossed to the desk and admired Lennie's handiwork.

"You like anyone today?"

Lennie scratched the back of his head and nodded. "Like a ten to one in the sixth. Got a vulnerable favorite in the feature. Not bad for a Sunday card."

Dan addressed the elephant in the room. "Thanks for hanging out today. I know you'd rather be on the grandstand side. Probably didn't expect to be babysitting a filly on this trip."

"You're a little light on help. No problem." He smiled. "Beth's going to be all right. If she runs her stable like she does her employees—"

Dan chuckled and let the comment hang in the air.

Beth skittered through the door. "Okay," she said and took a deep breath. "License in progress. Account will be opened tomorrow. Confirmed that she's nominated for entry. Talked to the feed guy. Ordered some new supplies."

She crossed her arms and looked at Dan. "And I'm going to need a healthy advance on training fees."

"We'll work that out," Dan said. "Right now I've got to run over to the grandstand. Lennie's going to tag along. You okay here?"

She nodded.

As he started toward the door, she grabbed his bicep and whispered, "You staying tonight?"

The question froze him. It wasn't about protection. It wasn't about timing. It was about them. His thought drifted back to those early mornings in the hotel at Gulfstream. Though grown adults, he felt like someone playing hookey from high school or sneaking out after Mom was asleep. The comment energized him and crushed him at the same time. He hadn't told her.

Dan grasped her shoulders and looked down at her sapphire eyes. "I have to go back. Got a pre-trial tomorrow and I can't postpone." He could feel her slump.

Her eyes closed for a moment, then lit back up. "Okay, just checking."

"I'm on a flight tonight and I'm planning to be back tomorrow night. Promise."

She nodded, putting on her best face. Lennie had strolled out of the office and stood in front of Aly Dancer's stall.

Dan leaned down and kissed her. She gripped him tightly. Dan could sense the desperation and passion at the same moment. She could go from hard boot trainer to innocent little girl to passionate woman in a matter of heartbeats. And she could live them all incredibly well.

As he pulled away, Shefford Banks' admonition about Beth not leaving town shattered the emotion. He wouldn't say anything. He couldn't. With Aly Dancer here, she wasn't going anyplace. No need to upset her.

She looked up through soft eyes, an expression of longing and uncertainty.

"Take care of our girl," he said.

Still in his embrace, she sucked in her breath and nodded. She blinked several times.

"I'll be back before heading to the airport."

She pushed away and inhaled deeply. "Got to find a new groom anyway." She paused, smiling. "I love Lennie, but—"

"Enough said."

Chapter 18

Dan and Lennie crossed Longfield parking lot and entered the grandstand. They moved easily through the sparse crowd. Any racetrack in the country would love to have the number of fans that Churchill had today, but because the paddock and grandstand were so massive to accommodate the numbers on Derby Day and Breeders' Cup, the area felt eerily empty.

Leading the way, Dan moved toward the paddock and cut under the grandstand to a bank of elevators. Lennie sleepwalked behind, taking in the enormity of the structure and absorbing the historical significance to his chosen occupation. When he stopped, he locked eyes with Dan. "No way."

"Way."

A black woman in a red short-jacketed uniform awaited them in the elevator. Dan stepped in and said, "To the top."

She smiled and punched a button. Seconds later the elevator doors opened. A bank of ticket sellers stood across the narrow entry. Tables with gold and white silk were packed in sets of fours and eights with small numbered stanchions. The room was barely half full, but it was a Sunday after all. Forms and programs were spread on tables and waitresses in black and white mock tuxedos shuffled among the patrons. Banks of televisions were positioned to give each seat an unobstructed view.

After checking for their names on a clipboard, a woman in a black cocktail dress strapped a black band around their left wrists. Total access, Dan thought.

It wasn't the fanciest club room he'd ever entered, but the attraction wasn't inside. To their left a series of sliding doors along the far wall beckoned them. Lennie was pulled toward the doorway as if drawn by an alien force. Dan joined him at the railing. Far below the entrants for the fifth race entered the track through the tunnel under the grandstand. From this point, they could see the entire racetrack, the backside and half of Louisville.

"Jesus," Lennie muttered, breathlessly.

"Nice spot," Dan said.

"This is Mecca." Lennie paused and inhaled. After a moment he whispered, "I've heard about this place. Never thought I'd actually be here." He pointed to the racing surface far below them. "Do you have any idea how many racing greats have traveled this way? How many champions? Secretariat, Cigar, Man o War, Northern Dancer. All the greats, they all made their name right here. Right below us." He leaned forward, elbows on the railing. "Alysheba and Ferdinand, Sunday Silence and Easy Goer."

"Alydar and Affirmed," Dan added.

"Unbelievable."

Dan smiled. It stunned him too, but for Lennie, this was the pinnacle.

Lennie turned. "So how'd you score tickets to Millionaire's Row?"

"Don't worry about it. You just have a great time. I've got a meeting."

As he spoke a man approached them from their right. He had a blue and white striped seersucker suit. Tall and lanky, he moved like melting butter. Although probably in his late thirties, his hair was salt and pepper, turning to a permanent gray. His mustache was similarly flecked with white. A megawatt smile flashed as he neared.

"Mr. Morgan?"

Dan turned and extended a hand. "Bradford Bennett?"

"Please, call me Brad," he paused. "Or Tripp. When you are dubbed at birth with a tag like Bradford Bennett the Third, nicknames are more comfortable."

Dan knew the Bennett family had been the center of the Kentucky thoroughbred industry since the start. Their prestigious Sunrise Farms had produced many of the greatest thoroughbreds through the ages. His grandfather, the original Bradford Bennett, had been one of Colonel Matt Winn's closest friends. Winn had turned the Kentucky Derby into the greatest two minutes in sports.

One of the greatest marketers of his generation, Winn single-handedly created the tradition. Sunrise Farms had been responsible for nearly one hundred entries in the Derby over the years, winning three and siring two others. Sunrise stood the country's finest stallions, which covered Graded stakes winning mares year after year, creating the privileged class of thoroughbreds.

When Dan called the steward's office, he was connected with Bennett III. Given his quick turnaround back to DC, Bennett agreed to meet in Millionaire's Row. Dan was not one to object. After introductions with Lennie, they stepped inside to a corner table.

"Your friend going to be okay?"

"Believe me," Dan said, turning and smiling toward Lennie who was still perched on the railing. "Around a racetrack, he can definitely take care of himself."

A waitress mysteriously appeared and Tripp motioned toward Dan.

"Iced tea, please."

"Arnold Palmer for me, thanks Donna." Tripp leaned forward across the table. "So you're a lawyer?"

Dan nodded.

"Me too. Well, never actually practiced. Graduated from UK law school. Guess someone in my family thought I could take all the legal work for the farm in-house. That it would be some big cash coup for us. Bennetts are horse people. Always have been. I had no interest in it, though I thought the classes were interesting and it's come in handy in my role as a steward, but a life in the law was never in the cards for me."

"Funny, I work my butt off in the law so I can pretend that I have your life. At least the breeding and racing side. Not sure I'd have any interest in being a steward."

Tripp set his smartphone on the table and spied a monitor. "Fair warning. If this race requires a photo or there's an inquiry, I have to skedaddle downstairs," he said, thumbing behind him to a stairwell beyond the bar.

"Understood," said Dan, leaning forward on his elbows. "Jake Gilmore trained for me."

Tripp nodded. "Aly Dancer. Nice filly."

"Thanks. Anyway, he was getting offers for her. Seven figure offers." This caused a bushy eyebrow to rise on Tripp's face. "It was all too suspicious, but heck, it's a lot of money." Dan paused. "Jake called me and said it was all a scam and that he was going to the stews about it. Then he's murdered."

Tripp's head bobbed along as if nodding at a story told at a cocktail party. Very politically savvy, Dan thought. When the 'murder' word was uttered, Tripp froze.

Donna set the drinks down and disappeared. Tripp leaned in. "I thought it was a suicide."

"Someone wanted it to look that way. But there's no way."

Tripp took a long sip, then said, "We've had some sad situations around here, usually involves tapping out on money, run of bad luck, drinking."

"Jake was going to start his first Grade One race. Hell, even if I sold, he was going to get a nice commission. Not exactly suicide material."

Tripp scratched his moustache and whispered as if to himself. "Sure don't need the bad pub this week of all weeks."

There it was, Dan thought, bad time for a friend to be killed when it might cause a PR stir. As if being murdered was something a guy scheduled like a haircut or a dental appointment. Was it impolite to refuse to apologize for the unfortunate timing of a friend's death?

"I'm just looking to figure out what happened," Dan said. "Find out who killed Jake and why. Can't help but think it's got something to do with my horse." Dan took a long drink of his tea and placed the glass down exactly on the ringed doily. "So I'm trying to figure out if Jake told you or one of the stews about what he found."

"I never spoke with Jake. Never had the pleasure. Have to say he seemed like a solid trainer and an honorable man." More political correctness, Dan thought, as he nodded. Tripp continued, "When you called this morning I did some checking. We have an intake process when a non-racing complaint is made. Non-racing meaning something that doesn't happen during a race. Honestly it is usually some bullshit argument between competing stables. His gelding isn't eligible for non-two, so and so is using some prohibited substance. I wanted that barn. You get the picture."

"Not much fun."

Tripp's eyebrows bounced up and down like a needle on a seismograph as if to say no kidding. He continued, "So we have a few layers of folks who do intake on the calls. Just to weed out the crappy stuff. So Janey Parks comes to me—she does intake—and said there was a potential scam being set up. As you can imagine, that gets our attention."

"Like a heart attack in an emergency room."

"She'd set us up for a meeting ten o'clock this morning," Tripp said. "Course he never made it."

"I need to know what Jake told Janey. Every word."

"We can set that up for you, but it was a bit strange."

"How so?"

"To make sure we aren't being run around on some bogus claim, she takes info to allow us to do some background. In fact we want all the info up front, but Jake wouldn't offer it."

"What do you mean wouldn't offer it?"

"Jake told Janey that it was too hard to describe on the phone. He had to show her the math."

"Show her the math? What scam would be so hard to describe? What math?"

"We never found out." Tripp sipped his drink. "Had

me wondering was 'show the math' an expression that Jake used. You know like 'let me paint you the picture.'"

"No. Never heard him say that. If he said show the math, that's exactly what he meant. Just don't know what the hell that might be. But somebody damn sure targeted him for fear that he might tell."

Chapter 19

The wheels hit the tarmac and jolted the plane sideways. Dan's head snapped forward. He was awake. From the moment he buckled himself in, he'd been out. The fatigue had become too much. Good thing, he remembered, regaining his senses. He was in the middle seat of the last row. Perfect, he thought, but at least he'd gotten a seat.

In desperate need of a toothbrush and a shower, he stretched, much to his seat mates' dismay. Like everyone on the flight, he had his phone out and was downloading messages and plugging for voice-mails.

Shefford Banks had left a voice message that he'd gotten the numbers from Jake's incoming and outgoing calls. Banks provided three phone numbers that were called and received most recently. Banks asked for a call back to narrow down others that Dan might recognize. He'd be available in the morning.

Tripp had called, first commenting on how nice it was to meet Dan. Southern charm, never turned off, Dan thought. Tripp had also spoken with Janey and she'd agreed to speak with Dan by phone. The cell number was provided along with Tripp's cell and e-mail address in case he could be of any further assistance.

The third voice-mail was from Mindy. She'd stopped by the office tonight and there was a voice-mail message from Rachel Compton. The name didn't ring a bell. Mindy continued, Rachel was Jake's sister and the funeral was planned for West Lake Baptist in Lexington on Saturday.

Funeral on Saturday, Derby Day, Dan thought. In a perverse way it made sense. A lifetime hard boot who never ran in the Derby would be buried on Derby Day. He made a mental note to have Mindy send flowers. The funeral would be a short drive from Louisville. Maybe they could send Jake off with a win in the Kentucky Oaks. That would only be fitting.

Mindy also found an envelope outside the door from Grady Cohen filled with exhibits and pre-trial materials. Sewer service as it was known in the trade. Cohen was supposed to serve the documents on him by before the weekend, so of course the documents were marked "hand delivered" with Friday's date and left outside his door on a Sunday night. What he had come to expect from Grady Cohen.

As passengers climbed out of their seats to stand in the aisle waiting to exit, Dan hung his head, shoulders slumped. In the adrenaline rush of the past twenty-four hours, the reality of Jake's death had not hit him full force.

It just did.

A funeral made the event permanent, not something that could be fixed. Jake had never spoken about family. Just that he grew up in the business. He'd been married at an early age, but as with many backside marriages, divorce was the outcome.

Just like me.

Events and emotions crushed him from all directions. Dan had a tremendous filly who was on the fritz, a dead friend, an unsolved murder, a new trainer with no cash, and an upcoming trial against an unethical lawyer.

What could possibly go wrong next.

That's when his phone rang.

Chapter 20

Beth was in tears again. He could barely make out her voice, but the caller ID identified her number.

"What is it?" Just sobbing on the other end. "Are you okay?" Beth's sobs remained constant. She hadn't reacted to the question, so it wasn't her that was in trouble, he thought. "Beth, is it Aly? She okay?"

After several sniffles, she spoke. "It's not Aly. Well, not really." The tears came in choking torrents.

"Is Lennie there?" More sobbing. "Is Lennie with you?" He could hear the phone being jostled and Beth sniffling. More jostling. "Beth?"

"Dan?" It was Lennie. "Dan. Just came back from grabbing some dinner and Beth had some visitors. Guys said if the filly wasn't sold, she wouldn't make it to the starting gate come Friday."

"Who were they?" Silence. "Lennie, who were the guys?"

"She doesn't know. Didn't recognize them."

"Put Beth on the line, and don't leave the stall tonight. I'll make it up to you somehow."

"No worries. I'm not going anywhere."

He could hear the phone being passed back to Beth. She sniffed hard and a weak voice came on. "Dan?"

"What did they say? What exactly?"

"Said they had a deal with Jake and they were coming to get the horse. I wouldn't let them near her. Aly wasn't too happy about it either."

"Beth, she's not for sale."

"You can't sell her," Beth said, sniffling. Then the anger came. "You just can't."

"There's no deal. Never was." This seemed to calm her somewhat. "I'm not selling and I never told Jake anything like that. What did they look like?"

"Two guys. The one who talked was a big guy in a suit. The other looked like a jock or hot-walker. Didn't say anything."

"Anything unusual about them? Accent?"

"Yeah, the guy had an accent. Not Spanish, couldn't make it out. Kind of choppy. Kept saying he had a deal with Jake. Said they were taking the filly and there was nothing I could do to stop them. He said if not tonight, then tomorrow. I screamed. I think the one had a gun, but it was dark. A couple guys ran over from the other side of the barn. They left, but they said they'd be back and if I tried to stop them it would be the last thing I did. Dan what's going on?"

Dan exited the jet way. "I don't know." He rubbed his face. "Did you call security?"

"Yeah, they said they'd post an agent outside the barn, but the kid looks like he's sixteen. He's just sitting in a pickup out front."

"It's better than nothing."

"I'm not so sure," she said.

126

Dan thought standing in the terminal, his hand over his eyes.

"Okay," he said finally. "Here's what I want you to do. Leave Lennie there and go get some sleep."

"Sleep? I can't sleep."

"Just go. You've been up for nearly two days." We both have, he thought. "You need to get some rest. Leave Lennie with Aly. I'm going to make a few phone calls. I'll call Lennie as soon as I have things set up. Everything's okay." He wished he could believe that himself. "You go get some rest. I'll take care of things from here. Do you have a hotel room somewhere?"

"No, I was just going to stay here."

"Go get a room. Take my car."

"I can't," she whispered. Dan knew what that meant.

"Lennie will give you some cash, just go. Get some sleep, get a hot shower. I need you wide awake tomorrow morning. I'll have everything handled by the time you get back. I have to make some phone calls. Now, go."

Dan sat in the nearly vacant terminal. The pilots and flight attendants trudged past him. Despite the hour he had three phone calls to make. The first was to Bradford Bennett the Third, the second was to Shefford Banks and the last one was to Ginny Perino.

Chapter 21

Monday, April 30

Judge Riley positioned himself behind his massive maple desk. He adjusted his wire rims, lifted a set of pleadings and looked at the two counsel.

"I assume you've exchanged pre-trial memoranda."

"Yes, your honor," snapped Cohen.

Dan gave Grady Cohen a steely-eyed stare. "Yes, your honor." It would do no good to whine about Cohen's behavior. Unless he had more than a tardy exchange of documents, he would come off as weak.

"Good." Riley scanned the pages. He was five feet tall on his luckiest day. His bald head glistened in the morning light that poured into his chambers. Tufts of hair ran from his ears and around the back. He was in his mid-sixties and had been on the bench for the past twenty years.

Riley was a stickler. He was not one to lose his temper or raise his voice, yet he commanded respect with forceful decisions and a penchant for economy in the judicial system. Early on in his tenure he'd begun scheduling routine hearings at six am. If there was an abundance of motions in a given week, he'd hear them during motion calls beginning at four thirty on Friday afternoons. It was good for litigants and taxpayers, but lawyers were the victims of his efficiency.

Jury trials were often scheduled to run from eight am to six pm with a half-hour lunch and mid-morning and mid-afternoon breaks. Bench trials often went as late as nine pm, since there were no jurors to worry about. Cases rocketed through his docket and many attorneys scrambled to avoid trials in his court.

Several anonymous lawyers filed a grievance with the judicial standards council. As there was nothing inherently wrong with longer judicial days, and as long as jurors were not unduly burdened, there was little that could be done. The heightened security in the wake of courthouse shootings and terrorist threats forced Riley to contain his schedules to the hours set for public access to the courthouse. It was a win for the anonymous group of attorneys, but merely forced Judge Riley to speed up the process in other ways.

Once he'd heard enough argument, he'd point to the door and call the next case. Complex legal arguments that ran nearly an hour in other chambers were disposed of in mere minutes.

The word on Riley was he didn't want to try your case, he wanted to try the case behind yours, so he would put extreme scheduling pressure on his docket which not surprisingly caused cases to settle.

In most courtrooms, being the fifth or sixth trial on the list for the two-week jury session meant it was safe. The case would not be called to trial that session.

In Riley's courtroom, counsel with cases as far down as tenth or twelfth on the docket received unexpected calls to come over and pick a jury. His docket dissolved like an avalanche. The farther down the list, the less prepared. Without preparation there was greater urgency to settle. Cases flew off the list.

Riley was fair and had a knack for knowing which party to push. Dan had often joked that good judges were quick to figure out which party was crazy. Sometimes both parties were crazy, but if he determined that your client was the crazy one, pressure would be applied.

Routine motions would be denied, time lines shortened, pre-trial rulings would be adverse. The practice was never proven, but pressure on the crazy party led to settlements and settlements meant the next case on the list was up.

"Stipulations?" Riley asked.

Dan jumped in before Cohen could respond. "There are many matters in my statement of facts to which counsel could stipulate. Could shorten the trial considerably." He knew he was singing Riley's favorite tune.

Cohen cleared his throat. "Your honor, you know that in the typical case stipulations would be easy to achieve. This case is unique."

"It's a hit and run, what's unique about that?" Riley said.

"Yes, your honor, but there are controverted issues of ownership."

Dan leaned in knowing Cohen was on the ropes. "Grady, can't we stipulate to ownership of the vehicle. Do you really need me to prove it's your client's property? Seriously."

"He makes a good point," Riley said. Dan could sense the needle of the crazy meter leaning toward Cohen.

"I'm sure we could reach some agreement, given the opportunity to discuss."

Riley flipped a page on his legal pad. "Let's do that right now. Mr. Morgan do you have matters on which you are seeking a stipulation?"

Dan pounced. "My statement of facts would make a good starting place." Cohen exchanged the cold-eyed glare.

The judge drug Cohen through each statement and pushed for agreement. On matters where agreement wasn't reached, Riley told Dan to submit those as part of a motion in limine. Riley couldn't make Cohen agree, but it was a signal that those issues might go against Cohen on the morning of trial.

They hurriedly reviewed witness lists, exhibits and jury instructions. Riley hit a buzzer on his phone and his assistant entered. He handed her the pages. "Type up this pre-trial and counsel here will be happy to sign before they leave today." It wasn't so much an instruction to his assistant as it was a threat to counsel. No changes, no delays.

Dan quickly checked his watch. He'd be out of here in thirty minutes or so, then head back to the office before his seven pm flight back to Louisville. All had been quiet since this morning. He wasn't sure if that was good or bad.

"Where are you on settlement?" Judge Riley said.

This was what Dan had hoped for. As the plaintiff's counsel, his objective was to get a cash settlement. Cohen, representing the driver and insurance company, wanted to soft-pedal any settlement allowing his client to keep the cash and Cohen to keep sending legal bills.

"We made a demand several months ago, just after

depositions had been completed," Dan said, turning to lock eyes with Cohen. "We haven't received a response."

Cohen squirmed in his seat and puffed his chest preparing to respond.

"That true?" Riley said, not pleased.

"More of a communication error than anything else. We, um. You see—"

"Enlighten us, Mr. Cohen," Riley said. "Now's your chance to communicate."

"I haven't received information from the claims rep. He's been traveling and—"

"You got a phone number for him?" Riley said, reaching for his phone. Dan smiled inside, but didn't dare flinch or diminish his poker face. He'd been on the other side of this equation before and though it was fun to watch Cohen in the pressure cooker, it could be him someday.

Cohen leaned forward palms out. "I-I-uh. I'm sure I can have a reasonable counter in say three days. Close of business Thursday."

Riley leaned back. "That will be a little late."

"A little late? What do you mean?" Cohen said, sputtering.

"I had a case settle this morning. I've got an opening on my docket. Figured we'd pick a jury on Thursday."

"What?" Cohen shouted.

Riley was unfazed. "Your offer will be a little late because we'll be one day into the trial."

Dan felt like he'd been hit in the face with a shovel. He had to get back to Louisville. The Oaks was Friday. Jake's funeral was Saturday, both more than 600 miles away from the courtroom.

Cohen was in full backstroke mode. "Your honor,

I have a conflict. I have motions in Judge Becker's courtroom."

"I'm sure Judge Becker will understand," Riley said.

"I have witnesses that I have to bring in. I'm not sure I can be ready in two days."

"I'm sure you can," Riley said. "Since you're representing the defendant, you don't have to go first, that gives you more time. You have, what, a few dozen lawyers in your firm. I'm sure someone can cover for you."

Cohen spun toward Dan searching for a lifeline. "I'm sure Mr. Morgan has matters scheduled this week as well."

Dan extended his arms. "Wide open, Judge. Seems like a good time to try the case." The thought of trying the case this week crushed him, but had sworn to act in his client's best interests at all times. An early trial was to his client's advantage. He also took some pleasure in yanking the life raft from Grady Cohen. And it was true, he was wide open. But he'd planned to be at Churchill Downs, not Courtroom Six.

"Good. It's set." Riley scribbled notes in his time planner.

"But, but, your honor, I uh—" Cohen sputtered. Dan studied his opponent twisting in the wind.

"Have your settlement offer to Mr. Morgan by noon tomorrow," Riley said, ignoring Cohen. "If this case is going to settle, I don't want it to be on the eve of trial." The judge leaned back indicating we were done. "No other business before us, thank you, gentlemen. Please ask Sharon to send in the next motion. And sign the pre-trial statement before you leave. She'll have it ready for you soon. See you Thursday morning."

As the door shut behind them Cohen whispered,

"This is bullshit." Dan remained silent as Sharon was sitting a few feet away typing up the final pre-trial order. They were in the judge's anteroom which included Sharon's workstation and two blue leather chairs and matching couch.

"He can't do this," Cohen said.

"I think he just did," Dan replied, this time a smile erupting.

Cohen stomped out the door and down the hallway.

"Mr. Cohen, you have to sign the order," she shouted after him.

A harrumph and clicking heels were all that could be heard.

Dan turned toward her. "Judge seems a bit frisky this morning."

Sharon rolled her eyes as if to say, it's like this all the time.

He took a seat and waited for Sharon to complete the document. *Where to start? God, it's the Oaks, the freaking Kentucky Oaks and I won't get to see my own horse run.* He held his forehead, staring at the floor. One word found its way into the fortified shell of his mind.

Selfish.

God, I hate that word.

Where to start?

He dialed the phone. "Mindy, we're in trial this week. Thursday. Jones case. Call Clara, get notice to Dr. Jankowitz, we'll need to get out some witness subpoenas. I'll need you to stay late tonight."

Here we go, he thought. *Damn it.*

Chapter 22

Tuesday, May 1

The day was a whirlwind of activity.

Aside from actually trying cases, the final stretch of trial prep energized Dan like nothing else. Setting his litigation themes, deciding on order of witnesses, and planning witness testimony engaged him.

He wrote his closing argument, which became the framework for trial presentation. The opening statement would flow smoothly once the back end work was completed.

He spent three hours prepping his client and acclimating her to the judicial process. Two other fact witnesses were briefed on the phone. Another half an hour was spent with his medical expert. The case was coming together nicely.

Shortly after three o'clock he finally settled down with the lunch Mindy had brought in hours before. Witness subpoenas had been delivered. The rest would be him. That's the way he wanted it.

He'd broken the news to Beth and she was predictably disappointed. The good news was that Aly was eating well and seemed alert for the first time in a week. Dan had convinced his banker to set up an account for Beth guaranteed by his personal credit line. Obviously he was on the hook financially, but relieving the economic pressure had brightened Beth's disposition.

A vet had checked Aly from head to toe, run blood work and could determine no ailment. The fact that she'd been off her game for a few days leading into the biggest race of her life was unsettling, but her general condition had improved.

Dan leaned back and rested. Visions of Jake hanging in his office blurred his mind. What was the woman's name? In the steward's office? Janet? No, something softer, more casual. Janey. Right, Janey Parks. He brought up the Churchill website and found the main telephone number. After a minute Janey was on the line.

The voice didn't match the name. Rough and gravelly, it was a voice that certainly passed cigarette smoke for decades. She had a personality to match, impatient and testy.

"Mr. Bennett said you took the intake call from Jake Gilmore."

"I take 'em all."

She didn't sound like a Janey. She sounded like a Gus.

"So you spoke to Jake."

"If I take 'em all, then I did. Make sense to you?"

"Okay. Do you remember Jake's call?"

"Jake who?"

"Jake Gilmore."

"Nope. Don't remember."

"Jake called to set a meeting to discuss some kind of a scam that was being planned."

"Oh yeah, now I gotcha." Her tone settled. Perhaps she suddenly realized she was the last person to talk to him. "Kinda cagey fella. Said there was some plan afoot, but didn't want to tell me about it. Guy killed hisself, dint he?"

"He turned up dead, yeah. What do you remember him saying? Exactly."

Dan could hear the smoke being dragged through the cigarette as she paused. Kentucky was tobacco country after all. "Said he needed to show the stews how it was being planned. I asked him and he said it was too hard to explain on the phone. Kinda felt like he didn't want to tell me, since I wasn't a stew and all. I said I gotta have more than a plan in order to set the meeting. He says it involves betting." She coughed and took another drag. "Like there's another kind, least around a racetrack."

"Did he seem frightened or nervous or anything?"

"Not so that I could tell. Mostly angry. Course, they all are."

"Hmmm. Anything else you remember?" She paused. Well at least she's trying to remember, he thought.

"Something about buying a horse. Some tough guys. Figured it was the same group as running the con. He wanted a background check on some guys, but wouldn't give me the names. Like he'd only speak to the stews about it."

"What happened?"

"I told him I'd set the meeting. Seemed like he was a straight shooter, ya know, not some guy just pissing and moaning. Probably gave him the time and room number. That's what I usually do anyways."

"Anything else?"

"Nope, that's all I remember."

Dan thanked her, gave her his contact information, and asked her to call if she thought of anything else.

He scanned his cell phone as he set it down to pick up the sandwich. Dan remembered the voice-mail message from Shefford Banks. In the frantic moments since he'd arrived back home, Dan had nearly forgotten about it. He replayed it and scribbled down the phone numbers relayed from Jake's cell phone.

None of the numbers were familiar, but some of them made sense knowing where Jake's other owners lived.

He dialed one and got voice-mail for a Dr. Jespin. Probably a vet, Dan thought. He took a big bite of his turkey sandwich and dialed another. It was answered on the first ring, catching him off guard.

"Mr. Morgan," said the man. "I know you'd be calling."

Dan choked down the sandwich, chewing frantically. Was this the same foreign accent as the one who had called on Saturday? He couldn't be sure. Two seconds later he'd have bet his life on it.

"We know you'd come around," said the man.

"Come around?" Dan asked, gulping down the remainder of his mouthful. "What do you mean?"

"The filly. We buy your filly."

"She's not for sale," he said, defiantly. "Who is this?"

"She for sale. Everything for sale."

"Who are you?"

"We talk when you change your mind."

"I'm not changing my mind."

"You change your mind, eventually. It good for you. It good for your girlfriend, too."

Dan sat bolt upright. *Be calm, get some information.*

Don't get angry. "Tell me. What's the scam?" He paused. No response. "It might change my mind." This brought harsh laughter through the receiver. "Tell me the plan. Tell me what you told Jake."

The remark drew a prolonged silence. Finally the man spoke. "I don't need to tell you. You not involved. Is my deal. You can't stop it. You only get hurt."

"Maybe I'll be interested if I knew more."

"You can't stop it."

Dan stood, forcefully motioning with his unoccupied hand. "Tell me."

The line went dead.

Dan stared at the phone. What the hell was that, he thought. He replaced the receiver, then a second later snatched it back up and dialed another number.

"Banks? Dan Morgan. I got a number you need to trace. It has to do with Jake's murder."

Chapter 23

Wednesday, May 2

The plane's wheels softly kissed the tarmac and the engines reversed, eventually coasting to a stop. The six am flight from Dulles was half filled with sleepy-eyed passengers. Dan had not slept a wink. His trial notebook was on his knees as he tinkered with the cross-examination of the driver. The driver who ran down his client. He'd also reordered the cross for the defense's medical expert.

Cross-examining a physician was always a challenge. Medical school, internships and years of experience were hard to pick apart for someone with no formal training. Most medical issues at trial were fact specific. He would know the facts better than the expert, but could never be sure when his limited medical knowledge would be skewered at trial. Crosses of opposing experts were akin to defusing a bomb. All the right moves could be obliterated by one careless question. But the courtroom was his domain. And as the trial attorney, he controlled the scope of cross and therefore could build barriers to protect his case. Like boxing, throw a few jabs, get in get out. Don't alienate the jury and don't give the witness the opportunity to throw a haymaker.

He'd gone online and bought the ticket at eleven pm. It would be a quick trip. A day trip to Louisville. Though he would miss the race on Friday, he wasn't going to miss the draw. Two days before a race, the racing secretary would draw the post positions for coming races. For nearly all races this meant that the entrants were assigned post positions by drawing the names randomly and shaking a pill from a bottle that carried the post number. Although open to trainers, most draws were done with the secretary and a few obligatory witnesses.

Churchill Downs had made the post position draw for the Kentucky Derby a media event. Being the little sister of the Derby, the Kentucky Oaks had followed suit.

The odds were stacked against Dan ever having another horse entered in either race, so he jumped a plane to attend, then would jet back to DC that night to be ready for trial Thursday morning.

Sleep had evaded him. His mind rambled with issues from the trial, constantly interspersed with thoughts about the race. Jake's death and visions of Zaqualina running alone through the stretch battered his brain like flashing lights on a cop car. With a task in front of him, like trial prep he could fight off the visions. In the quiet of the moment the images rushed in like the tide.

Thirty minutes later he was showing his owner's ID to track security and again on the backside. Beth spotted him and came rushing out to embrace him. Not exactly owner/trainer protocol, but there was no protocol for their situation. She kissed him and held him around the neck standing on tip toes.

Although being midway through morning works had created a flurry of activity in other barns, Beth's was all quiet. Ginny Perino sat sentry on a folding chair outside Aly Dancer's stall. The filly's head bobbed above the webbing to her stall as if to welcome Dan. Lennie was doing what Lennie did best, reading a racing form while sitting on two sacks of feed. Images of him sashaying with a live racehorse brought a smile to Dan.

Beth's exuberance was tempered when Dan told her he was just in for the day. Just in for the draw.

"Better than nothing," she said, still smiling.

With his arm around Beth, they walked to Aly's stall.

Dan extended a hand. "Ginny."

"Dan."

"How's she doing?"

"All good," he said.

Ginny wasn't much of a conversationalist.

Ginny Perino was a farrier by license, a loan shark by reputation, and an enforcer when the cause interested him. Rumors of his quick temper and savage beat-downs preceded him wherever he went in the business. He was not particularly big, probably five eight, but all of the strength was centered in his arms and chest. Handling thoroughbreds with one hand and hammering shoes with the other had endowed Ginny with an upper body that would make power lifters swoon.

Dan owed his life to Ginny.

Not because Ginny much cared about Dan, but rather because Ginny wanted to rearrange the face of a guy who was harming racehorses. That guy just happened to be an eyelash away from ending Dan's life. Serendipity one might say, but Dan earned Ginny's respect by covering for him when the cops investigated.

Ginny and Dan weren't friends. They weren't business associates. They weren't even acquaintances. They were simply guys who could nod at each other with respect.

Dan needed muscle. Ginny could provide it—for a fee, of course. That was the extent of the current relationship.

Dan leaned in and scratched Aly behind an ear. She moved forward, bright-eyed and engaged. "Hey, girl. You doing okay? You look great. Ready to kick some butt?" The filly's head shot up and down as if responding. "What time is the draw?"

"Eleven," Beth said. "In the Derby Museum."

"Never been," Dan said.

"Amazing place," Lennie said joining them. "Got over there yesterday. After chores, that is," he said casting a glance at Beth. "They got this three hundred and sixty degree theater that will just blow you away. Interactive place, you can call up all the prior Derbies and watch them. Well at least those since they invented moving pictures anyway. It's nirvana for a racing geek like me."

Dan's phone buzzed and he stepped away to take the call. It was Mindy.

"I've got Grady Cohen on the line."

"Put him through."

The last thing Dan needed was Grady Cohen knowing he was in Louisville. Thank goodness for Mindy and the magic of call transfer. He owed her one.

The line engaged. "Grady?"

"Morgan."

Prick.

"Do you have some time to get together today?"

"Not a good time, Grady. Got a trial I'm preparing for."

"Yeah, yeah. Want to talk about an offer."

"So talk."

Grady was silent. Probably trying to choke out the words, Dan thought. Let him talk, all I have to do is listen.

"We don't think there's any liability in this case."

Dan laughed.

"But since we will expend resources trying the case, bringing in witnesses, experts, what have you, my client has decided to make an offer." He cleared his throat. "No admission of—"

"What's the number, Grady? I don't have all day."

"Seventy-seven thousand, nine hundred."

Nice round number, Dan thought. Typical insurance company tactic.

"Not even close.."

"It's not your call. It's your client's," Grady said.

"We both know my ethical obligation and I will relay your offer to my client, but you need to know that the next words out of my mouth will be 'you'd have to be crazy to consider taking this offer. It is an insult.'"

"I'm just making an offer."

"You've done your job," Dan said.

"You need to know my client is at the upper end of where it values this case."

"Good to know. See you tomorrow."

Chapter 24

A roar erupted after the racing secretary, Dave Hannah, announced that Zaqualina drew the four post. Cameras swung toward their connections, reporters swarmed in leading with pointed microphones. Dan recognized Tad Stapleton, Zaqualina's owner from the presentation following the filly's win in the Santa Anita stake. Stapleton nodded confidently, though appearing a bit overwhelmed by the reaction. His trainer, Chick Mangold, stood with arms extended taking in all the attention. Media whore, Dan thought.

Six names hung on the board behind the racing officials. Nine horses were entered. Aly had not been drawn. The one, five and nine posts were still available.

Dan leaned over to Beth and whispered, "Anything but the one hole." Starting on the rail could be a death sentence for a horse, especially one like Aly Dancer who liked to lead. If she broke poorly or outside speed got the drop on her, she'd be pinned behind horses. At a mile and an eighth the race was long enough that a horse could overcome it, but it was a risk. One that Dan desperately wanted to avoid. To beat a field like this and a horse like Zaqualina, everything had to go perfectly.

She stared straight ahead. "I want the five. I want Aly to look her right in the eye."

Hannah drew a piece of paper from the bowl on the table. He read it and announced Pinnacle Penny. An assistant shook the pill bottle, poured a marble into his hand and stated, "Nine."

Soft applause rose to their left as their connections seemed pleased. Reporters who could drag themselves away from Mangold turned to get comments from Pinnacle Penny's connections.

Shoot, Dan thought, I would have loved the nine hole. Now it's fifty-fifty. He turned to look at Beth. She hadn't moved as if she was willing the racing gods to give her the post position she wanted.

From behind, Lennie whispered, "She can win from the one hole, Dan. She could do it against this field."

Dan trusted Lennie, but knew he was just being kind, softening the blow. We don't want the rail.

Hannah reached into the bowl, raised his eyes to the assembled mass. "Aly Dancer."

Dan tensed. Everything went to slow motion. The pill bottle shook. "Five, please five," Dan muttered. The marble dropped into the waiting hand.

"Please, please. Gimme a five."

The assistant slowly twisted the marble, showed it to Hannah. His head rose. One word was emitted. "Five."

Dan shot from his seat, thrusting his fists in the air. "Yes." He turned to hug Beth, but she was still sitting, emotionless. Lennie pounded Dan's back. Ginny's powerful hands slapped together like punches to a slab of beef.

Hannah chuckled. "You wanted that one, huh?"

Polite laughter skittered through the crowd. Two rows ahead of Dan, shoulders were slumped. The connections for Abelito had drawn the remaining slot, the one hole.

"Ladies and gentlemen, the field for this year's Kentucky Oaks," Hannah said. A chill scurried down Dan's back. This was the real deal. This was big time. The room dissolved in applause.

Track announcer Ben Binfield stood holding a piece of paper. He stepped to the board and wrote his morning line odds. Zaqualina was made the favorite at six to five. Aly was second favorite at four to one. Pinnacle Penny was nine to one and all others were significant double digits.

Dan felt a nudge on his shoulder. "Skip Wilson, Daily Racing Form. Appears you're happy with your draw."

Dan turned to him. "Just didn't want the one hole," he said, with a relieved laugh.

"Weren't sure you were going to enter. You know with Jake and all."

Dan nodded. "We're here."

"Who's training for you?"

Dan stepped forward and extended a hand toward Beth. "Beth DeCarlo is Aly's trainer."

Wilson reached forward and shook her hand. "Tough situation."

She nodded.

"Aly Dancer's move in the stretch kind of bothered me," Wilson said. "What happened?"

"She won," Beth said, blood rushing to her face. "She won, didn't she?"

"That's not what I mean. She seemed spooked by something last time. Got that worked out?"

"She's all right. She'll be fine," Beth said, defiantly.

"Her work the other day was a bit uncharacteristic, wouldn't you say?" A slight smile creased his lips.

"She's fine," Beth said.

The room was moving. All were standing now. Folding chairs slid on the tile floor. Some were filing out. Others congregated in small circles. Lennie shook Dan's hand. "You really didn't want that first post," he said, smiling. "Would have been a killer."

Wilson leaned in toward Beth. "Come on. Something's up with your horse. She looked rank in the Gulfstream race. Something's wrong."

Dan stepped between them, softly putting an arm in front of Wilson. He could tell Beth was about to explode. Despite being around these creatures and this industry all her life, the media attention was totally foreign to her.

"She said the filly's fine." Dan said. "She's fine. Thanks."

"Why don't you want to talk about it then?" This guy wouldn't give it up.

Beth pushed forward. "She's never been beat."

"She's never faced a horse like Zacqulina. Think Aly Dancer can beat her if she's not on her game? Not at her best?"

Beth's hair shook and her teeth were gritted. "She ain't never been beat. Got it?" Beth shouted. "She ain't never been beat."

Chick Mangold swung around behind Wilson and extended a meaty hand toward Beth. "Good luck little lady. Big race, welcome to the club." Dan wasn't sure if he was sincere, but now wasn't the time to call Beth a little lady.

She spun away, leaving Mangold's hand hanging. Wilson stepped back. Beth took a step and turned back, her lips pursed and visibly shaking. "Four races. Never been beat," she screamed. All heads turned toward their group.

"She just got DQ'd once," Mangold said, chuckling.

Beth locked eyes with him. Breathing heavily through her nose.

Wilson started to say something, but the words never made it out. Dan eyed Beth, ready to put an arm out and leave the area. A flash of blue went past him and Mangold was airborne backwards over a jumble of folding chairs. The blue flash was Ginny. Mangold stumbled backwards. Folding chairs slid, but didn't break his fall. All Dan saw were brown snakeskin boots flying through the air.

Mangold was on his back, one leg over a downed chair. He scrambled to get out of the tangle of tan folding chairs. Ginny stepped toward him and leaned down. "You should be more careful." Mangold's hands were up, not sure if Ginny was done with him. The room froze. Dan hooked an arm around Beth's elbow and moved her toward the exit, Lennie in tow.

Once outside they stopped. Beth was fuming. "Idiots," she sputtered.

"We're going to have to give you a little media training," Dan said, trying to lighten the mood. It didn't work.

"I'm serious. What's the matter with these people?" she said.

Ginny strode through the glass doors and joined them. "Fella needs to work on his manners," Ginny said with a wry grin.

Dan and Lennie burst into laughter. Beth's head shook. A reluctant smile slowly bloomed. Her blonde hair swung as her head twisted side to side, then a laugh erupted. She high-fived Ginny. "Nice assist," she said.

"Never been to one of these draws before," Lennie said. "They're kind of fun."

Laughter burst forth again.

Beth was trying to stifle hers, but she couldn't contain it.

Dan put his arm around Beth. "Let's get out of here."

"Yep," said Ginny. "I think our work here is done."

Chapter 25

The door was locked.

Mickey Soldatov shook the knob. He pounded on the door. No sound. He pounded again. Only the sound of the pool circulating behind him. Mickey gazed around the courtyard.

The one-level apartment building surrounded a small kidney shaped pool. Patches of dirt, a kid's tricycle and a pink flip-flop littered the sparse green space to his right.

The pool was probably a big selling feature for the leasing agent, Mickey thought. But once you saw it, unless you were crazy, you'd never put a body part in it.

Dust blew up from an uncovered barbecue grill to his left. Maintenance didn't appear to be a priority for the super.

He pounded his fist on the door again. Nothing. He deftly pulled a curved blade from his back pocket and quickly popped he lock.

The stench hit him first. It was an arid, eye watering aroma of body odor, sweat, and rotted food in no particular order or percentage. Housekeeper must be on strike, Mickey thought.

"Something wrong with your hearing?" Mickey said

to Franco Wolletti. "V broke your leg, not your eardrums. Come on, man."

Wolletti's eyes expanded like balloons at a kid's birthday party. He sat in a brown plaid overstuffed chair. Rips in the lining exposed yellowed foam rubber in multiple locations. His right leg was propped on a matching ottoman. Two crutches leaned against the wall. His sweatpants covered the cast on his leg, a pitted Dodgers t-shirt stretched over his protruding belly.

"Franco," Mickey said in a tone meant to shame him. "Be a mensch and offer your friend a drink."

Franco didn't move. The Dodgers logo rose and fell. At least he was breathing.

"Well thank you, Franco. So kind of you to offer." Mickey crossed the narrow hallway into the kitchen. He could be heard opening and slamming cabinet doors. He held his breath from the fumes that poured out of the refrigerator. "Jesus, Franco. Cure for cancer growing in your Frigidaire? Hard to tell if that's mold or a new life form." His voice trailed off as oxygen was expended, but not replaced.

Moments later he emerged. His fingers extended into two short glasses, and a bottle of Cutty Sark was in the other. He spun the cap with his thumb and quickly poured two glasses up over the knuckles on his submerged fingers. He set the bottle down, handed a glass to Franco, licked his soaked fingers, and sat on the edge of the ottoman.

"So, how are you doing?"

Franco rubbed the stubble on his cheek, but didn't answer.

"Oh come on Frankie. Don't be like this. Have a drink." Mickey hoisted the glass to eye level and downed half of the glass. Franco returned a halfhearted toast, then set the glass on the end table.

Mickey exhaled his disappointment. "Frankie, we're pals. Pals need to enjoy each other's company. Don't make me drink alone. That's not cool."

Franco stared, took a deep breath, but said nothing.

"I know. V kind of hurt your feelings. I get that. Well and your leg." Mickey tapped lightly on the cast. Franco tensed, but then relaxed.

"You know V. He can get kind of emotional, but he loves you. He gets paranoid sometimes, but he's always taken care of you. He had me go to the hospital and pay your bill in full. They won't be sending you any bills."

Franco's eyes said "big deal," but his lips said nothing.

"Are you working?"

Franco nodded.

"Good. Work is good. Helps the healing process." He paused and swallowed the last of the scotch. "Speaking of work, Vasily has a job for you." Franco pushed back into the chair like he was oozing into quicksand. "Easy job. Potentially very lucrative."

Mickey scanned the inside of the apartment, nothing on the walls but chipped paint, everything on the floor, including the twelve-inch TV set. He motioned around. "Might be enough to get you an upgrade or even a new place." He stared into the man's eyes. "Just need to know if you're in."

Franco closed his eyes. Two teeth came out and curled over his bottom lip.

"Franco. This your chance. Mr. Big wants to make amends. This will get you back in his good graces. Will be easy. No weapons. No violence. I promise. Nobody gets hurt. A very simple thing. Piece of cake."

Franco breathed deeply, then his eyes fluttered open. He looked at Mickey, then quickly looked down. His head nodded slowly.

"That's my Franco. Vasily will be so relieved to know he can count on you."

Mickey stood and brushed his hands on his jeans, then clapped them to say "we're done."

"Thanks for the hospitality." Mickey walked to the door. "Good talk, Franco. I'll be in touch."

Chapter 26

The euphoria had evaporated by the time Dan, Beth, and their cohorts had reached the backside. Getting to the race was always the objective. Now that they were officially in it, could she win? The theoretical had given way to reality. Could they beat Zaqualina? Could anyone? Although Aly Dancer appeared better and was back on her feed, the question remained. Was she good enough? Could she perform on this stage?

Jake always believed she could, from the first days of training. Aly Dancer was special.

Just being here was a rush for Dan. Racing on national TV. A Grade One race. The half million dollar winner's purse. With a phone call he could have a million two, but it was now like selling a child, selling a dream, selling everything he'd worked for. If she lost, there would likely never be an offer like this again. If she won…If she won…

His phone buzzing in his hand jarred him from the dream. When he saw the caller ID, he felt like he was sucked into vortex. Pulled from his equine thoughts and slammed back into his job. He fell behind the group and told them to go ahead.

"Grady?"

"Hi, Morgan."

What a jerk. "You can call me Dan."

"Whatever. You talk to your client?"

"You seem edgy, Grady. Client pushing you to settle this?"

"Like that's any of your business," he said. "I'm about to put the hammer down before we start tomorrow morning. Just want to see if your client has come to her senses."

"She's lucky to have senses left after your guy ran her down."

"Whatever. We got anything to talk about?"

"I spoke to my client and relayed your pathetic offer. Despite my advice, she wants to counter. We'll take two-fifty."

"That's crazy. I think we're done."

"Probably right. You can think about it while my medical expert is on the stand detailing the injuries. Broken femur, severed artery. She almost bled out there in the street. Near death experiences always seem to get a jury's attention. That and six months in a rehab hospital learning to walk again. I'm going to make the jury cry and you know what happens when jurors cry. They spend your client's money and they spend it in big, healthy chunks. So, yeah, we're probably done."

Cohen was silent. He'd played the game before. "Lost wages are minimal. Specials aren't that much. You're way too high."

"That's what's great about the jury system, Grady. You and I can disagree about the value, but in the end we don't get to decide. Real people do and I like my chances."

"We've got some room, but not much. I'll talk to my client."

"You do that, Grady. Otherwise, see you in the morning."

Dan clicked the call off. This case wasn't going to settle. He felt a million miles away. In less than twenty-four hours he would be in court six hundred miles away. A pang of guilt ran through him. He'd come for the draw and left his case behind. Though he had his trial book with him, the distance from the courtroom seemed generations away.

He was living a split life.

One foot in his passion for law, the other embedded in his love of the sport. He couldn't do just one. In one his love, in the other the occupation he loved. Could they ever come together? He'd resigned himself to missing the race. He would be somewhere in a cross-examination when the gates flew open in the Kentucky Oaks. He'd never missed seeing one of Aly's races live or via satellite. This one he would miss. It pained him, but he couldn't let down a client, that's what paid the bills. More important, that was the duty he owed. A duty he would never forsake.

~

By three o'clock he'd made his round of good-byes. The airport awaited. Lennie had offered to drive him, but he declined. Secretly, he wanted one more walk around Churchill before he left.

Dan couldn't say this was his wildest dream, because everyone in the game had the same dream—run in the Kentucky Derby or Oaks. He'd just never planned on actually getting to the race, then not being in attendance. It was like winning the lottery, but not getting to spend the money.

Dan had spent time on the phone with Clara Jones, and he'd convinced her to stay strong. Trying the case had upside and in his heart he knew the insurance company would make another offer. It was the right thing.

The Derby week crowd was beginning to show, accompanied by TV trucks, camera booms, and plastic tent studios. The infield had been partitioned for the few who had reserved tickets and those who would walk through the turnstiles to party away the Oaks and Derby.

He shuffled by the paddock as the line of jockeys descended to meet up with trainers and owners in the coming race. There were many racing grandstands that drew awe-inspiring gazes. Saratoga Springs, Del Mar, Belmont, but Churchill Downs was the grand dame of them all. It was a monument to racing, a part of the country's history. He could spend hours just wandering the grounds, watching patrons discussing wagers and those who just were there because it was the place to be. Starting Friday, private jets would fill the airport as owners arrived to be seen, to engage in the festival, and ultimately to watch their chosen steed's fate.

He reached the Derby Museum and pulled out his phone. It was time to get back to business. He lifted a hand to flag a taxi cab, then dialed the number.

A blue minivan pulled up to him at the curb. The door automatically opened. He turned slightly as the call went to voice-mail. "Hey Grady, it's—"

From behind he was slammed into the open van door. His cell phone and trial notebook flew from his hands and he fell face first, jammed behind the driver's seat. A knee crushed his lower back, pinning him to the floor. The passenger door slammed shut as the van sped away.

A second knee compressed his upper chest. The van rolled like a ship in heavy waters. The man was knee surfing on Dan's back as the van veered through traffic. His left arm was trapped against the backseat. The other arm could only reach up the back of the passenger seat, virtually worthless. He flailed his arm, but his shoulder socket was not designed to fold in that direction. Dan tried pulling his legs under him, but the weight of the two knees prevented any motion.

He screamed "What the—" His voice was lost below the driver's seat. He couldn't be heard outside the vehicle anyway. "Get off!"

Dan continued struggling, then felt a hand touch him behind his ear and press his head down firmly. "What are you?" Only his feet and his one useless arm could move. A second later he felt a prick on his neck. A cooling sensation spread out from the spot. He grunted and tried to buck the man off. There was no leverage.

Bastard just injected me with something. What's going on? Could be rat poison. Could be anything. Faces? Clothing?

Can't see anyone's face. Have to stay strong. If they let their guard down, I'll jump them. Need to…

Then he slumped onto the floor and struggled no more.

Chapter 27

Clayton Pinkney pulled his eight year-old Honda Accord into the carport. The wheels stopped in exactly the same spot they'd been in when he left seven hours before. The wheels always stopped in the same place.

Everything Clayton did was predictable. In this sleepy Pasadena neighborhood a fully enclosed garage was unnecessary. Mild temperatures and soft breezes allowed cars to live outdoors. The roof on the carport was all that was needed for the occasional rain shower.

Clayton's blue plaid shirt was tucked into his tan chinos. With a kitchen knife, he'd added an additional hole to his belt and it was pulled snug, allowing the leather to flap against his pocket. Clothes fit better on scarecrows than on his withered body. Thin brown hair, unkempt, fell in splotches, except for the back where it stood defying gravity. His eyeglasses were from the Carter Administration, black and thick with equally dense lenses. A slave to fashion he was not.

His wheels had stopped in the same spot six years before when he returned home with a pink strawberry cake on Arlinda's birthday. It was her favorite; that's all that mattered.

She hadn't responded to his shout when he pulled open the kitchen door that day. The cake rested in the shadows of the kitchen counter as he'd searched the house. He found her in the bed they'd shared for decades.

Clayton shook her. No response. He put his head to Arlinda's chest. No heartbeat. He softly tapped her face and called her name. Nothing. Then he crumpled to the floor, hoping to die himself.

Strokes were like that.

They crept in the darkness and took a life without warning. Three weeks to the day after he'd retired from his position with Pasadena Power. The gold watch weighed heavily on his trembling arm. He was a lifelong worker bee, never an executive, merely a steady, reliable accountant.

Their retirement dreams were dashed. They were going to travel the country. Childless, they had each other and a lifetime of memories to create. Their lifetime of retirement together was all of three weeks.

Suddenly he was alone.

Well, there was Mitzi, Arlinda's Pomeranian. Clayton never had much use for the mutt, but now they were bound by fate. Slowly his heart had opened and Mitzi, like all dogs was ready and willing to enter in.

Phobic and not much of a joiner, there was no room for new friendships or clubs or, god forbid, dating. Mitzi was the singular outlet for his emotional needs. It was the only way to reconnect with his wife of thirty seven years.

In his seven decades he'd never dealt with police officers, coroners or EMTs. Not until that day he came home with the strawberry cake.

He couldn't stop shaking. Tears flooded down without embarrassment. They poured out of him.

With the coroner's assistance, he selected a mortuary and made plans he'd never imagined. Four hours later, it was just Clayton and Mitzi in the house.

Who dies on their birthday? It wasn't right. It was never right.

He looked at the cake on the kitchen counter. It was his wife's cake. It was a cake for celebrating.

Stupid pink cake.

He stared at it in anger, in resentment, in frustration. He wanted to eat the whole damned thing. Eat it until he vomited. Shove it in his face. Make it disappear. Make it all go away. Devour it like a raccoon tearing into a roadside deer. Eat it like he'd never eat again.

Clayton stared at the cake. Tears streamed off his face and dropped onto his shirt. He gulped, calmed himself, and wiped his hands across his face. Holding the counter top in his trembling hands, he breathed, eyes closed, pain creasing his heart. He picked up the cake, and walked out the front door. Clayton trudged across the perfectly manicured lawn, rang the doorbell, and handed the cake to Mrs. Bradley without a word.

She seemed to understand with sad eyes and a shake of the head. Silently she accepted it, giving him a shoulder hug. There weren't the right words.

The Bradleys had four kids. They'd appreciate the cake, he knew.

Clayton shoved his hands deep into his trouser pockets and walked back across the yard, back to Mitzi.

Then he'd cried some more.

~

On this day, six years after burying Arlinda, Clayton Pinkney carried a sack of groceries through the kitchen door and whistled for Mitzi.

He'd gotten her a new chew toy—a silly white bone with a squeaker in it. The noise was sure to be annoying, but she'd treasure it. She'd create sound, a proxy for joy in an all too quiet house.

Mitzi would wriggle all over in excitement. Clayton would get on his knees and scrub her ribs. She'd jump and lick his face. She always did. That was one good thing about dogs. They never had a bad day, always celebrating, always happy.

That kooky dog had helped him limp forward after the loss of Arlinda. Mitzi had gotten him through everything. It was the two of them against the world. Just a man and his dog.

He'd give her toys. She gave him hope. They needed each other, but Clayton needed her more.

"Mitzi, hey girl. Come see what I got."

No response.

She always met him at the door, wiggling and prancing, her toenails slapping the linoleum like rain drops on a metal roof. Mitzi just wanted to share her love.

He called for her again and whistled. Nothing.

Setting down the groceries, his heart tightened. It brought back that nightmare of six years before. No, not Mitzi. No. Arlinda was counting on him to protect her, to care for her. No, not her.

He yelled and raced to the living room. Mitzi was on

her side next to the couch. Dead, sleeping, or unconscious? That wasn't the primary issue, though.

Clayton's problem was with the man sitting in the darkness. The man aiming a gun at him.

Chapter 28

A bolt of lightning shot up his neck. Dan's head snapped forward. The pain seared up into the back of his skull. His eyes scrunched in futile response. There was no light behind the blindfold. He was secured in a seated position with his arms pinned behind him. The only sound was his own breathing. At least he was breathing, he thought.

He rolled his head to dissipate the shot of pain up his neck. It did little good. His back was sore and his feet were tingling from whatever connected him to the chair. He arched his back, then leaned forward. There was little give in the bindings. He was able to make fists, but whatever held his hands was unlikely to provide freedom.

What day is it? He bolted and tensed. *Crap, what day is it? I'm supposed to be in trial. His breathing came in gulps. My trial starts Thursday morning.*

My client. The judge. Damn it. The judge is going to kill me. My client will fire me and probably sue me for malpractice.

Flying to Kentucky the day before trial, God that was stupid. Hard to argue it's not malpractice. Judge Riley will sanction me. Hell, he'll have me disbarred. Crap. The word 'selfish' started to weave its way into his consciousness. He forced that door shut. No time for that now. He tugged with his arms, but they were useless.

Think.

Calm down. Think.

He stopped struggling and slumped. He listened. Nothing. Just his own breath shooting through his nostrils. He listened some more. Though disorienting, he knew the blindfold was a blessing. They didn't want him to see their faces. That meant he might survive this.

Death or disbarment? Right now, the disbarment seemed more certain and troubled him more.

The moments before his capture ran through his mind. How could he have avoided it? What was his mistake? What color was the van? Blue, he thought. What kind of van? No clue. They all looked the same. He didn't see anyone in the van or out. The guy who blind-sided him must be big, at least the pressure on his spine seemed that way, also the force of the hit.

"Hey," he yelled. No response. He yelled again.

A door creaked ahead of him. "I don't know what you want, but I need to make a phone call," he said in as forceful a voice as he could muster. "It's urgent."

This only brought laughter. Sounds like two guys. The door shut. He waited. No footfalls, no shuffling. No voices, no breathing, nothing.

"Hey," he screamed. "Listen to me. Do what you want, but I need to make a phone call." His chin fell to his chest. A stab of pain brought it back upright. He leaned back, breathing heavily.

He was alone again.

Chapter 29

"Mitzi!" Clayton shouted. The dog didn't move. The man just looked at him. His first instinct was to rush to the dog. The second was not to get shot. The conflict resulted in Clayton sprawled on his knees halfway to Mitzi with his arms spread like an Alpine skier landing a jump. With eyes on the intruder, he slowly brought his arms in trying to discern who the man was.

"Wh-what do you want?" Clayton asked.

The man didn't speak.

"I-I don't have anything," Clayton said, his voice trembling. "I don't own anything worth taking. You can have my watch," he said, lifting his arm.

The man waved his gun, indicating for Clayton to sit. He slid to a chair across from the man, palms on his knees.

"She's okay," the man said. "Just taking a little nap."

"What did you do?"

"Just relax," the man said, placing the gun on the couch. He leaned back. "You're asking all the wrong questions."

"What do you—? What questions? What do you mean?"

"Take a deep breath," the man said. "I'm in no hurry. You need to relax. Not good for your heart."

Clayton took his advice. Nearly a minute passed.

The man smiled. "That's better. Now start over."

Clayton's brow furrowed and his head cocked slightly. "Go ahead. Ask me a question."

"Who are you?" Clayton stammered.

"Good!" the man said as if speaking to a child. "See, that's a good question, Clayton. I'm Mickey."

Clayton swallowed hard and shook his head. "Mickey what?"

"Now, there you go again. Not a good question. Okay, I'm going to have to take this over. Let's start with what did you do to my dog? Well, I gave her a little sedative. She was kind of upset when I came in. Doc assures me it's safe. She'll be okay."

"Why?"

"You're not very good at this, are you?" Mickey chuckled. "I just explained, she was kind of upset."

"You know what I mean," Clayton said, his hands shaking. "What are you doing here? What do you want?"

"I just want to get to know you a little better." Mickey said, smiling.

"What? Why me?"

Mickey scooted back on the cushions and put an arm on the top of the couch. "It's simple. You and I are going to be business partners. Just want to get to know you."

"I don't have a business. I don't know what you're talking about," Clayton said, his tone hopeful. Maybe this guy's got the wrong house. Wrong guy.

"When people become partners, Clayton, it doesn't require a business. Sometimes it just requires access."

Access? Clayton thought. What the heck is he talking about? He blinked and shook his head as if the bad dream would end. "I don't have access to anything."

"But you do. You do, Clayton. You work at Santa Anita, don't you?"

Clayton nodded. "I just work at a mutuel window. I just sell tickets."

"Well, there you are," Mickey said, thrusting his hands in the air in mock celebration. "We're perfect for each other." Mickey sat forward. "You see? You do have something of value. And so do I, so we're partners."

"Huh? What do you have?"

This produced a hearty laugh from Mickey. "It isn't obvious? I thought it was apparent."

Clayton just stared, dumfounded.

Mickey continued, "What I have is Mitzi." He pointed to the dog, motionless except for slight movement in its chest. "So here's how it's going to work, Clayton. I'm taking Mitzi with me. You are not going to do anything. You're not going to change anything about your daily routine. You aren't going to tell anyone. You aren't going to do anything. But mostly, you're not going to tell the police. That would be a bad thing." He paused, locking eyes with Clayton. "A very bad thing. You understand?"

Clayton slowly nodded.

"Good. I'm going to take good care of Mitzi. She'll be fine. Then I'm going to call you and ask you for a favor. A very simple thing. If you do it, Mitzi will come home and you'll never see me again. If you don't do it, Mitzi won't be coming home and as for seeing me again …" He paused as though thinking about what to say next. "Well, you never know, probably will see me again, but I won't be very friendly. Like I am today."

"What do you want me to do?"

Mickey made a tsk tsk sound. "Clayton, another bad question. We're getting way ahead of ourselves. We're partners. Right? We have to build some trust. So, do we have a deal?"

"Do I have a choice?"

"That's a good question. Good one." He clapped his hands and chuckled as though pleased. "Do you have a choice? No, Clayton you don't have a choice."

Chapter 30

Thursday, May 3

Time was a fickle master. When blindfolded and bound to a chair, does time pass faster or slower? What seemed like an hour might only be ten minutes. What seemed like a few minutes might be a day.

Dan sat slumped, yet to confront his captor. His neck pain was lessening; he had full range of motion now. Likely the drug that caused his distress had worked through his system. He was hoping so.

Without sight he focused on his other senses. The air smelled like his uncle's garage—faint smells of oil and dusty grease. The scent of stale cigarette smoke hung in the background. That could be a transient smell. Perhaps his chuckling friends were smokers. The petroleum smell was more definitive—a machine shop, a factory, a warehouse.

How did that help?

He was unnerved and at the same time fascinated by the silence. Nothing from the next room. But with concentration he could make out the faint sounds of traffic in the distance. Still in the city? An industrial area after closing time.

How did that help?

A creak, the groan of wood underfoot. Steps approaching. The slide of metal on metal. Then he heard the door swing open.

"How are you, my friend?"

It was the foreign voice. The one who had called him.

"You the guy who killed Jake?" Dan snapped.

The man burst into laughter. Not laughter of denial. It was a hearty, ground shaking laugh. "You do not understand your situation."

"I know enough," Dan said.

A phone interrupted them. A silly ding dong techno tune signaling an incoming call.

Dan could hear, but not understand. Lots of Ds and Ks and Ys interspersed with grunts and gravelly sounds. He couldn't make out a word. German? No. Certainly not Spanish. Not Asian sounding. They were big heavy sounds, complex utterances of consonants and few vowels. He listened intently, but made no connection. After several seconds a phrase shot through as though a flashing light on a pitch black night.

Mohammed Ali.

Or at least it sounded like Mohammed Ali. What? Were they talking about boxing? Was he going to use me as a punching bag?

The call ended.

"So, my friend. You know why you are here?" said the voice.

Dan opted for silence.

"We have a little business to finish, then you can go."

Don't engage him. Make him talk.

"Your trainer sold me your horse. I need to get a signature, then we are done with each other."

"The horse isn't for sale. Jake didn't sell her," Dan said. "If he did, would it be necessary to go to all this trouble?"

"No trouble. You sign the paper, get a bunch of money, we all go our separate ways."

Dan heard the man approach and put something on the table. Then he felt his hands being cut loose. He rubbed his hands together. They were cold and swollen. He tried to get some blood circulating. He bent his elbows and shook his fingers. The man's footsteps led him back to the front of the room. Dan ripped his blindfold off, which brought another chuckle to the man.

The room was dark; the only light came through the open door. His captor was a round blob of a man. He was over six feet tall and thick, in a suit two sizes too small with a wrinkled and stained dress shirt and a wide orange and blue striped tie. The laughter came from behind a red ski mask.

Dan was still secured to the chair. A small desk was in front of him, containing a piece of paper and a ballpoint pen.

"You sign, we leave as friends," the man said.

"Go screw yourself."

"That's no way for business people to treat each other."

"I'm not signing that, I don't care what you do." His eyes searched around the room for any information that could be helpful. There was none. Just a wood paneled office. Not plush wood paneling, but trailer court wood paneling. The only furniture was what he sat on and the desk in front of him.

"Do not be stupid. You don't know what I would do."

The man leaned his head outside the room and a second masked man entered. This one smaller, in jeans and sweatshirt.

"It's too late," Dan said.

The man considered this for a moment.

"What you mean, too late?"

"You want to buy Aly Dancer and run her in the Oaks under your name," Dan said. "It's too late."

"It's never too late. Can buy a horse any time."

"Not if you want to run her, you can't," Dan said. "She's already entered and a change of ownership is within the discretion of the racing secretary. Even with a signature, it's not a given. They can scratch her and probably would. They damn well will when I tell them my signature came under duress."

"Maybe you won't talk to anyone." It wasn't a suggestion, it was a threat.

"I'm just telling you it won't work. You're too late."

The men looked at one another. The big one nodded and left the room. The smaller one dragged in a chair and sat keeping watch.

Dan could hear the man's voice in the adjoining room. He'd made a phone call. It was short, but the man didn't re-enter the room. Several minutes passed. Dan crossed his arms, displaying his refusal to cooperate. The small man sat tugging on the ski mask trying to improve his vision through the knitted holes.

The techno beat of the phone erupted. The song didn't play long. Dan heard grunts and indecipherable words. More grunts, this time questioning. The call ended.

"You sign. We take our chances with the secretary," he said re-entering the room.

"Not happening," Dan said, thrusting his chin forward.

"You make me sad." He tapped the smaller one on the shoulder and whispered something to him. The big man stepped forward and the smaller one left the room.

"I don't give a shit. I'm not signing." *What, are they going to good cop bad cop me? This guy going to rough me up, then the other guy comes in to sympathize—just like the cop shows on TV?*

"You will wish you had," the big man said.

The smaller man returned to the room. The suited one turned, blocking Dan's vision. They spoke a few words and the smaller man walked behind Dan.

Dan swiveled his head trying to watch both at the same time. The big man turned slowly toward him. A sickening grin was apparent through the small mouth hole of the mask. He held a hammer in his hand.

"Sign the paper."

Dan turned his head, trying to see the good cop, but there was no good cop to be found. He was behind Dan. The large man approached, softly pounding the hammer into his meaty palm.

"Last chance, my friend. Will you sign the paper? We all go home. Nobody gets hurt."

Dan's throat tightened; he couldn't swallow. Words were not going to be an option. He shook his head.

"Not smart," the big man said.

The smaller one grabbed Dan's wrist and twisted it behind his back. His shoulder popped, twisting awkwardly behind his back. Dan clenched his teeth, keeping an eye on the hammer. It was methodically pounded into the big man's palm. Dan's left arm, the free one, reached across for his shoulder.

His right hand had been secured behind his back once again. The small man grabbed Dan's free wrist like a hammerlock. He slipped a cord around Dan's hand and yanked it tight. Dan's eyes rocketed back and forth between the men. Neither said a word, just the steady slap of the hammer against the big man's hand.

"What are you—?"

A slap across the face ended Dan's sentence. The small man pulled the cord as he walked to the front of the desk. Dan resisted, but the pain from the cord eating into his wrist slowly brought his hand away from his body and over the desk.

Once Dan's hand was over the desk, the small man pulled down, the cord scraping the edge of the desk and lowering Dan's hand onto the wooden surface.

Dan's eyes locked on the big man. "Are you crazy?" This drew another slap, this time with a closed hand.

"I tell you, you make me sad," the big man said. "This didn't have to happen."

The big man leaned forward. With one hand he pressed down on Dan's forearm, pinning it to the table.

The small man kept pressure on the cord. The big man stared at Dan. "You right-handed?"

"Huh?"

"You write with right hand?"

Dan didn't speak.

"Is okay. I saw you use your right hand to dial the phone. You right-handed. You still be able to sign when we're done."

"No!" Dan yelled.

The hammer whistled through the air, the big man's shoulder rotating to increase the force, crushing Dan's hand. A sickening, slapping crunching sound burst forth. Dan screamed. Nerve endings shot messages to his brain. His brain already knew what was coming. Pain ripped through his fingers and up his arm. The hammer was coming again. More crunching than slapping sound this time.

And again it came.

And again.

Dan's head shrugged forward. He was out.

Chapter 31

Vasily stared straight ahead as the jet engines reversed their thrust. Momentum pushed him forward. Rubber squeaked on the tarmac outside. The small window to his right was smeared with rain. He could see the lights from Standiford Field Terminal. He wouldn't be going there.

The jet taxied for several minutes, then jerked to a stop. The door separating the pilot from the cabin creased open.

Everything okay Mr. Korsakov?

Fine, Daniel. Just fine."

"Welcome to Louisville."

Vasily nodded.

The pilot extracted himself from his seat and stooped forward entering the cabin. Car's here, but let me make sure he's got an umbrella. He released the handle and shoved the door open. "A little nasty tonight, sir."

The cabin filled with damp air mixed with pungent exhaust from jet fuel.

Vasily never flew commercial. That would require him to go through TSA security. With facial recognition coming online, there was no need for the risk. Plus he couldn't stand being in lines. Lines were for *durak*. Fools.

Lines were for people of little consequence. Vasily didn't stand in line.

Officially, the plane was registered to Tad Stapleton, the putz. It was Vasily's money, but like the homes, horses, businesses, cars, it was all in Tad Stapleton's name. Nothing was in Vasily's name.

Well, it was ultimately in Tad's name once intrepid investigators peeled through layers of shell corporations, LLCs and general partnerships, domestic and international. It would take a team of DOJ attorneys a decade to find the bottom. The arrangement was just a thread someone could start pulling on and if they did, they wouldn't find Vasily. To be left alone, don't own anything—officially that is. The world would believe that a Waspy, young JD CPA could build a successful business. It was the story-line of southern California. Tad was good for something, barely. Vasily knew he was a *durak*—just lucky enough to get Maiya to fall in love with him.

Vasily made it work. Sometimes you're working with diamonds, sometimes they are just rocks. Tad was the commonest form of river rock, but big enough and believable enough for Vasily to hide beneath.

Traveling from Los Angeles to Louisville with his name only appearing on his son-in-law's manifest was the best way to fly. He was just an old man, coming to see his son-in-law and daughter's horse run in the Kentucky Oaks. Lucky man, able to fly privately due to Tad's largess.

The thought of that putz being next to his daughter made him shiver. But she was the only family Vasily had. And she'd convinced him that Tad Stapleton made her happy, that she loved him. If that ever changed, Tad would become unnecessary. Vasily couldn't change his daughter's mind, but he could plan. The plan made him smile.

He reached into his leather bag, his hand fumbling amongst the identical flip phones. He secured one of them, powered it up and made sure he had signal.

Vasily dialed the area code for the place he had just left. After two rings Mickey answered.

You got all the relatives invited? Vasily asked.

This brought a chuckle from Mickey. Yes, I've talked to all of them and they are excited.

Good, good. I left some spam in the icebox. Take all you need. Spam was their code for cash. Icebox meant overseas.

You are the best, sir. All of the relatives are in. All set. I ordered the spam for Friday. I should have all we need.

Good, let me know if anything changes.

Mickey was solid. Why didn't Maiya marry a guy like him? He was like a son to Vasily. They were thicker in blood than most families.

He hung up without any ending pleasantries and immediately dialed another number. The bastards in law enforcement can get taps on anyone's phones these days. Vasily didn't have to worry about being tapped. He wouldn't have an operating cell phone long enough for the Feds to apply for a tap. It was important to protect Mickey. The man was integral to Vasily's operations. More valuable than that dog of a son-in-law. Nevertheless, one can't be too careful and the price of throwaway cell phones made it easy to avoid traces.

The line engaged. "You got the horse?"

"Not—not yet, boss." The words came loose

reluctantly, like they'd been nailed to a tree. Then the voice tried to change the topic. "Are you at the hotel yet?"

"What the fuck? What do I pay you for?" Vasily screamed.

"We'll get her. It's—it's just complicated," said the man, trying to make a comeback.

"I don't tolerate complications," Vasily said in a flat tone that was more frightening than anger. "Get it done. Now!"

Again he ended the conversation with the phone flapping shut. This time his face was red and throbbing. *Shit, can't depend on anyone these days. If you want something done, you've got to do it yourself. Durak.*

He eased down the steps. Daniel stood holding the umbrella, arm extended, to protect the passenger, not himself. Once on the tarmac, Vasily opened the cell phone, dropped it on the asphalt, and crushed it with three violent stomps.

Daniel said nothing. His expression did not change.

Vasily got into the waiting limousine. "Clean that up," he said, pulling the door shut.

Daniel uttered a "yes, sir," but it was never heard. The engine roared and the limo shot off along the darkness of the tarmac.

Chapter 32

Ginny Perino sat on a three-legged wooden stool just outside Aly Dancer's stall. Gentle rustling of the straw was the only sound.

Midnight was a quiet time on the backside. No horses being shuttled, no traffic. The help was sound asleep as their workday began in four short hours.

Earbuds cranked a Bob Seger tune directly into his brain. He rolled a fifty-cent piece over his knuckles, flipping it from one end to the other. After flawlessly making its circuit, he switched to the other hand.

As a loner, his needs were simple, his expenses modest. He made enough as an accomplished farrier to sustain himself. His illicit business as a loan shark was where he really cashed in. Money was a needed commodity, either between paychecks or to get out of a jam. Ginny lent.

Like any good money manager, he avoided losses. Threats of violence and a reputation as one quick to engage in physical persuasion ensured that his side business thrived.

He rolled the fifty-cent piece and conducted a mental audit of accounts and receivables. Nothing was in writing. Documents meant evidence. He left no tracks.

Ginny pulled the earbuds and stretched. His biceps rippled in the gloam of the distant halogen lights. Years of physical labor had paid dividends. Dividends that aided his side business as well.

He picked up the footfalls before they could be seen. Back of the barn. Two people, likely men. It certainly wasn't Beth as she'd left only a few hours before. Ginny set his phone down and waited.

Two men swung around the end of the barn and into the brief light of the shedrow. A big guy in a suit. A smaller one in slacks and a polo shirt. Both were too dressy for the backside. Both were completely out of place at midnight on the backside.

They approached with purpose.

"Beth DeCarlo around?" the big one said.

"Who's asking?" Ginny could see them in the corner of his eye. He kept rolling the fifty-cent piece.

"The guy who owns Aly Dancer."

Ginny made eye contact, then focused back on the coin. "I know the owner. You ain't him."

The man pulled papers from the breast pocket of his suit and proclaimed, "This says I am."

"That don't say nothing," Ginny said.

"Read it."

"It's a piece of paper. Paper don't talk."

"We'll just take the horse now."

They edged closer. Ginny stood, blocking their path. "Ain't happening."

Ginny's eyes flashed between the two men. After several seconds of silence, the suit reached into his pocket, pulled a wad of cash, unsnapped a rubber band, and flashed hundreds and twenties.

"You ain't got enough money," Ginny said.

"I can get more. Name your price," the suit said.

"If I want your money, I'll just take it from you. Simple as that. This horse ain't going nowhere."

Ginny sat back on the stool indicating the conversation was over. He heard a distinctive click. The smaller man flashed a switchblade. "My friend says it is."

"You planning on using that?" Ginny said, derisively, to polo shirt.

"We plan on taking the horse," suit said.

"Better get a new plan."

The smaller guy moved in front of Ginny, about three feet away. His blade caught the dim light as he slowly moved it side to side. Hands on his hips, the suit was the same distance from Ginny to his right.

Ginny slowly tucked his feet under the stool, getting weight on his toes. He slowly rolled the coin over his knuckles, eyes on the man with the knife.

"Nobody needs to get hurt here," the suit said.

Ginny glanced at the suit, then quickly returned his gaze to the knife. "Only people who will get hurt are you guys. I'll give you a chance to walk away."

This brought laughter from both men. Ginny switched hands with the coin and kept twirling. He could tell the men were getting irritated. That's what he wanted.

Ginny stopped and held the coin. "Want me to show you a magic trick?"

"No, we want you to get the hell out of the way," suit said.

"Great. You'll love this trick. You see, what I do is make this coin disappear." Ginny's eyes were locked on the knife. He rolled the coin onto his thumb and flipped it high into the air.

The coin spun up toward the pitch of the roof, light glancing off it as it rose. The men's eyes followed the arc of the coin, just as he expected. He only needed a split second. In the same instant he drove forward like a fullback at the snap of the football.

Both hands grasped the wrist. He yanked the man's arm to his left while hurtling into his chest. Knife man flew backward. Ginny lowered his head and drove the top of his skull below the man's chin. They hit the ground as Ginny's momentum jammed the small man's head back. His neck made a disturbing crackling sound, and an emotionless grunt rose from his chest.

The knife dislodged from the man's hand and tumbled to the ground. Ginny looked over his shoulder as the suit rumbled toward him. He quickly propped himself in a bear walk, on hands and feet, keeping his head low. As the suit approached, Ginny lunged his right leg out, catching the big man in the gut.

The suit stumbled back a few steps, but didn't go down. Ginny spun upright, checking for the knife, but he wouldn't have time as the big man came at him.

Ginny jumped into a defensive posture, checking the downed man's condition. He was groaning softly with his arms outstretched on the ground. He wasn't going anywhere for a while.

The big man had about six inches on Ginny and came forward with fists raised. The man's had some boxing training, Ginny thought.

Getting a quick head shot would not be easy. Ginny circled to his left slightly, so his back wasn't to the moaning man on the ground. The kick to the gut should have done more damage. Guy's got some muscle under all that flab.

The man threw a right. Ginny's hand went up and blocked it. The punch grazed the back of Ginny's head. Ginny faked a right. The man's hand went up to protect his face. Ginny leaned in and landed a punishing blow to the man's ribs. Air went whistling out of the man and he stumbled back a step.

Suit was strong and could take a punch, but Ginny had a strategy. Victory didn't go to the strongest, it went to the one with the better plan and the ability to carry it off.

He'd learned that playing chess.

His uncle had taught him and they played well into the night on racetracks throughout the Midwest. When his uncle died, Ginny took over the business, but never played the game again.

Chess taught him business lessons and strategy on that simple board with funny-shaped pieces.

All players knew the moves and simple opening strategies, but that wasn't what allowed a great player to win. It was getting into the other guy's head, making him commit when he shouldn't. Dangling the queen or sacrificing a bishop for ultimate advantage.

At chess you win by making the other guy think he's made the right move, then before he knows it you've trapped him.

Suit could be dangerous in a puncher's duel, but what would give him the greatest advantage would be to grab hold of Ginny. Then his size and weight would be definitive. Nature taught that beasts large in brawn could crush a smaller species, if only the smaller one could be trapped and drawn in.

Ginny had to move his queen into the center of the board, unprotected on all sides. He feigned left and slipped. Suit moved for the kill. He got his left arm around Ginny's head and began pounding on Ginny's shoulder and upper back with his right.

This exposed the suit's left side, where Ginny had already left a calling card. He twisted to his right for greater leverage and gave the man another shot in the ribs.

A wince of pain came from the big man and Ginny knew he'd found the spot. He hammered the rib again and again.

Blows rained down on Ginny, but the nearness softened their impact. The guy was damn strong though. Holding Ginny in a bear hug, the suit tried to turn and wrestle him to the ground. Ginny was able to stagger, keeping his feet under him.

Pain ran up his arm as his knuckles jarred the rib cage. But he wouldn't stop. He thundered more blows until he heard a snap. The man loosened his grip and Ginny laid another one right on the spot, a crack this time.

The man shuffled backwards protecting his side. Ginny launched a haymaker at the defenseless chin. Suit's head snapped with the blow. Before his head recoiled, Ginny dove into the man driving him onto his back.

He pinned the man's arm with his left knee, put his right knee on his chest, and thrust his thumb into the man's Adam's apple.

The suit tried bucking him off, but the injured rib, plus the weight of Ginny kept him on his back. The man flailed at him with his free arm. Ginny batted the blows away. He checked on the smaller man. He was still down and not moving.

"Put your arm down," Ginny yelled. The man kept swatting at him. Ginny rolled his weight onto the rib cage. Suit grimaced. With Ginny's thumb on the throat, there weren't recognizable sounds coming from him.

"Put your arm down." This time the hand flailed, but eventually landed flat on the ground.

"Good," Ginny said. "Now we can have a conversation." Suit tried pulling his head back to clear his airway, but Ginny didn't relent.

"Here's the deal. We can all consider this a misunderstanding, you can pick up your friend and go home or we can continue this dance. Don't matter much to me."

Suit's face turned crimson as he struggled for air. Veins popped prominently on his neck and forehead.

"Do you understand me?"

Suit struggled.

"I said, do you understand me?"

Suit's eyes were terror-filled, opened to the maximum. The struggling stopped and he nodded.

"Okay. If you want to walk out of here with your buddy, nod your head yes. If you want to die here and now, shake your head no."

The suit furiously nodded up and down. "Is that a yes?"

More furious nodding. "Okay, sounds like we got a deal."

Ginny put all of his weight on the man's chest, then bounced up. Suit gasped and rolled onto his side.

Ginny walked past the first man, leaning down to check his condition. After another step, he bent down and gathered the knife. Suit was on his knees and elbows gobbling as much air as he could. Ginny examined the switchblade and nodded with approval at the craftsmanship.

"Pick up your pal and get the hell out of here." He pressed the release and closed the blade. "You won't be needing this."

Ginny flipped it in the air, caught it and slid it into his back pocket. "I'll just keep it as a souvenir of our time together."

Ginny dusted off his jeans and straightened his shirt. Suit had made it up to his knees, leaning back on his haunches. His left arm cradled his side. Ginny shuffled to the shedrow and searched the ground. Seconds later, he bent down and picked up his fifty-cent piece.

"Just be thankful I let you keep the money. Not smart for a guy to flash cash like that. Word to the wise."

Chapter 33

Dan couldn't make out the sound. Some kind of swishing noise. It repeated. He drifted toward it, then retreated. He had no form, just a being, just a spirit, wavering like smoke on an airless night. No form, just presence.

Am I dead?

The swishing returned, heavier this time. He drifted away again, like he was swaying on a swing set. Louder now, with some tapping, then glaring brightness. He locked his eyes against it. Blinking and squinting, he reluctantly let some of the light seep in.

"Hey, fella. About time you woke up."

Dan's head was turned. He couldn't see nor recognize the voice, but he was comforted by the tone. Slowly he opened his eyes. He was elevated somewhere, head cocked toward a white wall. A silver framed window with metal shutters was his line of sight. The shutters were cranked closed, but sunlight filtered through.

Sunlight was good.

"Been out a long time."

The swishing sound had a form now. Rain. A steady rain blown against the window.

Dan turned toward the voice. A shock of pain pierced his neck. He winced and moved in small, punishing motions. With eyes closed and teeth clenched he was able to turn toward the voice.

Lennie.

"How are you, man? Jesus, you had us scared out of our minds."

Dan moved his arm slightly and a wave of tightness and pain rushed up through his shoulder and neck. His hand was a ball of gauze with tubes running out of it. Dan grunted and dropped his hand hoping it would stop the pain.

"Easy there, cowboy," Lennie said. "Your doc is going to be in soon. You had kind of a rough night."

Dan blinked. He was searching for a response that didn't set his body on fire. He took some deep breaths. His mouth was pasty and tasted like mud from a sand pit.

Lennie moved to him holding a plastic glass. He aimed the straw at Dan's mouth. Ice sloshed in the glass. The sound was near deafening. Dan took a sip, then nodded that he was done. He leaned back and closed his eyes.

What the hell happened?

A doctor walked in, glanced at a chart and then washed his hands. He looked like a kid. Probably right out of school. Dan tried to remember of his own doctor's name, but the pain was too much for mental processing.

"Good, you're awake. I'm Doctor Givens." He moved to the bed and lifted Dan's hand. It hurt, but not as much as Dan thought it would. "What did you catch your hand in?" The eyes searched for an answer, but Dan didn't have one. The doctor continued. "You've got three broken metacarpals, one, two and three, two damaged knuckles and I'm sure some nerve involvement."

Dan gurgled to speak. "Hammer," he whispered.

"Huh?"

"Hammer." Lennie pulled closer and Dan locked eyes with the doctor. "Guy busted my hand with a hammer," Dan said, his voice trailing off to nothing.

The doctor's eyebrows spiked. "That'll do it. Not surprisingly, we call it a crush injury. We did Doppler studies to assess vascular damage, then did a closed reduction."

Dan gave him a blank stare.

"All that means is we tried to put the bones back where they're supposed to be. We applied a large soft tissue dressing to alleviate swelling. You're going to want to get checked out for nerve damage. A crush injury like this, it's almost a certainty." He pulled a penlight from his pocket and thumbed Dan's eyelids, flashing the light across his face. "You were out cold when they brought you in. You take anything?"

"No," Dan whispered, then thought about it. "Somebody injected me with something. Neck hurts like hell."

Dr. Givens examined his neck, turning his head slightly. Dan grimaced. A finger pressed on his neck. "Could be right here. Slight edema, puffy area. Know what it was?"

Dan shook his head slowly.

"How soon after the injection were you out? Any idea?"

"Fast. It seemed like. I don't know, couple of seconds."

"Probably Versed," Dr. Givens muttered. "Intravenous, you'd be out in under five seconds. So what happened?"

Dan blinked, but didn't respond.

"They brought you in by ambulance. EMT said they found you in an alley off Piker's Way. Not a great area of town, if you know what I mean. So what happened?"

Dan swallowed. "Got jumped. They gave me a kind of shot. They threatened me. Then they broke my hand, probably injected me again."

"You need to hang out with better company." The doctor grabbed the chart off the end of the bed and flipped pages. "I'm going to give you some pain meds and—"

There was silence, but for the rustling pages. "Your blood work says—I don't see it in the chart. God damn it!" He shouted toward the doorway. "Where's the damn blood work?" He calmed and turned back to Dan. "I think they figured you'd had too much to drink, got your hand caught in something. I may need to draw more blood to look for narcotics or opioids."

Dr. Givens scribbled on the chart, clicked his pen and stomped off, likely looking for someone's butt to kick.

Dan locked eyes with Lennie, then looked down and shook his head.

"Man, we were worried about you. Nobody could find you. Calls coming in to Beth. Hell I even got calls from people looking for you. Thought you were back in DC."

"DC? Shit. What time is it?"

"Little after two."

He looked outside. "Two? What day is it?" He tried to sit up, but collapsed back down.

"Thursday."

"Crap, I need a phone. Give me my phone."

Lennie looked around. "All your stuff's in this plastic bag." He fumbled around with it, pulling out clothes, billfold, keys. "No phone."

"My notebook there?"

Lennie looked up from the bag with a blank stare.

"My trial notebook. Is it there?"

Lennie lifted the items, searching. Then hoisted a battered black notebook.

"Thank God. Give me your phone." Dan quickly dialed. "Come on, come on. Mindy—yeah, I'm in the …uhm." A searing jolt of pain hammered him from somewhere inside his skull. He scrubbed his eyebrows. "I'm fine. What happened?" He listened as she described the frantic search for him. Calls from Judge Riley's bailiff, Clara Jones crying, wondering where he was. He pressed the phone hard to his head and pushed back into the pillow.

Mindy rambled on in a staccato voice. "We called your cell. I finally called Beth," she said. "I didn't know what to do. Client was on one phone, I had Beth on the other. She said you'd flown home. I called the airline. Nothing."

"It's okay. What did Judge Riley say?"

"I never spoke to him, only the bailiff. I didn't know what to say. The judge was really pissed off. The bailiff called back later and said the trial was postponed and a show cause hearing would be scheduled. Client kept calling and wanted to know what happened. I didn't know what to tell her, just that you'd call her as soon as possible. Where are you?"

"Shit," Dan mumbled under his breath. "Okay. Here's

what—Okay, um. Give me. Hang on a sec." He lowered the phone and closed his watering eyes. After a few breaths he pulled the phone back to his head. "Mindy, I'm going to give the phone to someone, to Lennie Davis. Give him the phone numbers for Clara, Judge Riley and Grady Cohen. I'll uhm, I'll call you back in a few minutes."

He held the phone out to Lennie, turned and began vomiting off the side of the bed.

Chapter 34

Dan's eyes fluttered open. No pain this time. Had he woken up on the movie set of a western? The bottoms of cowboy boots were crossed on the base of his bed. Above that he could see a cowboy hat, but no cowboy. He stirred slightly. The cowboy boots dropped to reveal Shefford Banks slouched in an aluminum-framed chair.

"Got banged up pretty good," he said motioning to Dan's arm.

Dan moved to sit up straighter, but didn't respond.

"Ran that phone number. You ever heard of single shot telephones?" Dan shook his head. "Oughta be a law. Fella buys a phone, puts down a fake ID and pays with cash. Traceable, but not to anyone you want to know." He sat up leaning his elbows on his knees. "Line was registered to a—." He checked his notes. "Randall Perkins." Dan shrugged. "Yeah, he thought the same thing. Louisville student. Had his wallet stolen on campus. Happens a lot down there," he said. "Doesn't take long to get a single shot phone. So we got ourselves a dead end there."

Dan cleared his throat. "The guys who took me were the ones who killed Jake."

"Can you prove that?"

"Trust me, I know."

"Bein' a lawyer and all, I figured you knew something about evidence." Banks tipped his cowboy hat back. "Judges round here kind of like that stuff. Not just one guy's opinion." They sat in silence. Banks clapped his hands together, elbows on his knees. "So what can you tell me?"

"Blue or gray minivan. Two guys, one built like a bear, the other a welterweight. Kept me blindfolded until they wanted me to sign papers to sell my horse. Then they had masks on. I wouldn't sign, so they took a hammer to my hand."

Banks winced and shook his head.

"It's the same guys because they wanted Jake to sell. When he figured out what they were up to, they killed him."

"Yeah, I'm tracking. Just missed a few steps between pass go and go directly to jail. They say anything useful?"

"Not so much. But the guys who had me weren't in charge. They had to check in with someone. I told them they couldn't run Aly Dancer. That it was too late and the stews could scratch her. And would, if ownership was disputed. They took that up the chain and came back with the same result. Then they smashed my hand."

Banks scribbled in his spiral notebook.

"Gonna put you out of action for a while," he said, without looking up.

"They figured I was right-handed, so they busted the left one. They're coming back. Want to be sure I can sign with my good hand."

"You right-handed?"

Dan nodded.

"What else?"

"English isn't their first language," Dan said.

"Welcome to America."

"No, wasn't Spanish or anything I could make out."

"Hell, I can't make out Spanish. I'm doing my best mostly to understand English," Banks said. "So we got two guys who speak a language we don't know, drive a blue or gray minivan and like to damage body parts. I guess your horse is the center of all this."

"I don't know what their plan is. Jake thought it was a scam. Not sure if he meant the purchase or some scam dealing with the Oaks. Aly Dancer runs Friday." He paused a moment, still a day behind. "Tomorrow."

"So what's their deal? They going to buy her and stiff her? By what I've read, that filly from California is the nuts anyway. Most folks think she can't be beat anyway. Why buy your horse? Makes no sense."

"She can win."

"Who? Your horse?" Banks paused. "Don't mean no disrespect, just telling you what I hear. "S'pose every owner thinks he can win, don't he? So what's the scam?"

"Don't know, but Jake lost his life trying to expose it. I'll be damned if I'll sell my horse to find out what they have in mind."

Banks nodded.

A tap on the door was followed by Beth and Lennie.

"Hey, you're awake," Beth said. She stopped when she saw Banks in the room.

"This is Detective Banks," Dan said.

"We've met," said Banks, in a cool tone. "I'm gonna let you folks visit. Dan, my card's on the tray over there. Keep me posted. Let me know if you think of anything else." He tipped his hat and slid past the visitors into the hallway.

"How's Aly?" Dan said. "Who's with her?"

"Ginny and some of his boys rotating," Beth said. She cast an eye toward the window where rain pattered against the frame. "Rain and more rain."

'How's the track?"

"Soup," said Lennie. "They'll seal it after the last race today, but forecast is for more rain through tomorrow afternoon, so it'll be a mess. Sloppy track at post time for the Oaks has a correlation of one point zero."

"She okay?" Dan said, turning to Beth.

"Yeah, looks better, acting better, but—" She let it hang in the air.

"They all gotta run on it," Dan said.

"We never even worked her on an off track. Jake wouldn't risk it. Don't know what she'll do."

Lennie moved around toward the window. They were all thinking the same thing—sloppy track. Crap shoot. "How's the hand?" Lennie said.

"Hurts like hell."

"Not sure what the doc gave you," Lennie said. "but it knocked you out in about five minutes. One minute we're talking, the next you're drooling."

This raised a chuckle. Dan's face hurt from laughing, as though his facial muscles forgot how to react.

Beth motioned over her shoulder. "Said they're going to keep you overnight."

Dan sat upright, fighting off the wooziness. "Like hell they are." He peeled the tape off his good hand with his teeth.

"You sure that's a good idea?" Lennie asked.

He bit down on the IV tube and jerked it out. "Hand me my clothes," he said to Lennie. "Let's get out of here."

~

Thirty minutes later Dan's car was sloshing through waterlogged streets of Louisville toward the racetrack. Lennie drove, Dan in shotgun and Beth in the backseat. Once in the car Dan had dialed his client and talked her down. She was angry and frightened.

Dan didn't tell Clara what had happened, just that he knew he'd let her down and he would earn her trust back. He couldn't discuss the case as he had Lennie and Beth who could overhear the conversation, but he promised to call her in the morning and have everything resolved. He promised.

Once at the track, Lennie drove to the barn. "Beth," Dan said. "You stay with Aly. I have a meeting. And since I can't drive, Lennie, you're coming with me." She resisted, but he was adamant. "Keep Ginny's boys as long as you can. I'll pay them to stay the night, but we should be back before too long.

"It's eight o'clock," she said. "What kind of meeting do you have?"

"One where they don't know I'm coming."

He needed to call Judge Riley, but didn't have a home number, and it would have been complicating the mess by trying to call him at home. After a quick stop at a drug store, he gobbled down half a dozen Tylenol with a Red Bull. His hand shouted out with even the slightest movement.

"So where are we going?" Lennie said, backing out of the parking space.

"The Seelbach Hotel."

"Never been there."

"Me neither."

"Which way?"

"Just head downtown. It's on. Fourth Street.

"Okay," Lennie said, shrugging. "Fourth and what?"

"Fourth and Mohammed Ali."

Chapter 35

A top-hatted doorman welcomed Dan and Lennie as they swept up the red carpeted steps into the Seelbach Hotel. The square brown building was like a weathered jewelry box opening up to breathtaking gems inside.

A gold encased stairway led them to the two-story lobby shimmering in ornate marble and Persian rugs. A concave blue skylight ran the length of the reception area giving the impression of daylight. A balcony surrounded the second floor and looked down on the public area below. Flecks of gold and bronze in the marble separating the two floors, combined with dark wood accents screamed genteel moneyed South.

Rich designer luggage and handbags whisked by on carts as well-to-do Derby fans checked into their coveted rooms.

"Mind if I ask what we're looking for?" Lennie said.

Dan stepped to the center of the reception area and scanned in all directions. He stopped a bellhop and asked where the bar was located. Hurried hand gestures provided all the information he would need.

"You stay here," Dan said. "If I'm not back in twenty minutes, come looking for me. I should be okay."

"Yeah, that's what I thought when I let you go to the airport by yourself yesterday."

The Old Seelbach Bar was a sanctuary of dark wood, from the floor to the railings, to the tables and chairs to the actual bar. Dan stepped inside, drew a nod from the bartender, but didn't advance. He scanned the room. *It would help if I knew what I was looking for.* He glanced at each group of patrons huddled among the tables. Nothing clicked. He wasn't sure what he was looking for, but knew it wasn't here.

After a brief conversation with a cocktail waitress and more hand gestures, he was directed to the Oakroom, a five star restaurant on the second floor of the hotel. His hand was throbbing so badly he was sure others could see it expanding and contracting like a cartoon character.

The maitre de turned from his phone conversation as Dan cruised by. "Sir," the tuxedoed gatekeeper said.

"Just looking for someone, be right back."

Dan stepped into the dining room and scanned the tables half-filled with customers.

Nothing.

What the heck am I doing?

After one more visual tour of the restaurant, he turned to exit. There was a flash of recognition and his head snapped to the back corner of the restaurant.

Tad Stapleton, Zaqualina's owner.

He was seated at the end of a rounded bench. Dan couldn't tell who or how many other people were at the table. Tad recognized Dan and gave him a wave.

"Oh my god, what happened to you?" Tad said as Dan stepped near. A stunningly beautiful brunette in a low-cut, jewel-encrusted gown sat next to Tad, along with an older gentleman and another person Dan recognized, Chick Mangold.

"Just got into a bit of a jam, nothing serious," Dan said dismissively as they shook hands.

"Dan? Right?" Tad said. This brought a nod. Tad turned for introductions. "This is my wife Maiya. Her father Vasily and I think you know Chick."

Dan smiled at Maiya and shook hands with Vasily. Their eyes locked, but the man didn't speak. "Yes, I know Chick," Dan said, shaking his hand. "Good luck tomorrow."

Chick leaned forward. "You ever decide to race on the west coast, give me a call. Big purses, short fields."

"I've got a trainer, thanks."

Dan turned to the woman, smiling. "Maiya. That's a beautiful name. Don't run across that one much."

"It's Russian," she said returning the smile and glancing at her father.

"Do you speak Russian?" Dan asked.

She appeared flattered and nodded. "A little bit. Mostly kitchen Russian." Dan glanced at Vasily. The man's eyes were dead and he appeared bored by the conversation.

"Well, I've got to go," Dan said turning away.

"Best of luck tomorrow," Tad called out.

Dan spun on his heels and locked eyes with Maiya. "Hey, I heard a word, I think it's Russian. Let's see if I can say it right. Sounds like *Lawsh Ad*. That mean anything?"

Maiya bounced in her seat. "I know that," she said proudly. "It means horse, doesn't it papa?"

Her father gave her a slight nod.

"Oh, that's great. I was wondering about that. Hey, while I've got you to translate. Here's another one. Do you know this one? Let's see, *Byeaz Oomyets*? Or something that sounds like that?"

Maiya furrowed her brow and pursed her lips. "Hhmm. I don't know." She turned to her father. "Papa, do you know that one?"

Vasily glared at Dan. Time froze as Vasily's laser-point eyes drilled into Dan's.

"Papa?" Maiya repeated excitedly.

Finally he looked at Maiya. "It means fool or idiot," he said tersely.

The accent was similar to that of Dan's captors, but he'd never heard the voice before. Maiya cocked her head back toward Dan.

"Hhhmmm. I was just wondering," Dan said, gazing into space above the table. His expression slowly turned to a smile. He chuckled. "Makes sense." He locked eyes with Vasily. "That's what your partner would say after he'd finish his phone calls with you."

Vasily's expression did not change, but his eyes squinted slightly. "I don't know what you're talking about," he said.

"Your partner, the one who tried to turn my hand into a pancake."

Vasily shrugged.

Tad stood. "I think you'd better leave."

"I'm leaving," Dan said, without taking his eyes off Vasily. "Just got everything I needed. You folks have a nice evening."

Chapter 36

"Have you lost your freaking mind?" Lennie yelled.

Dan rubbed his forehead as he leaned back against the headrest. The rain was coming down in waves as the wipers raced to keep time.

"It's them," he mumbled. Pain locked his jaw and he spoke through clenched teeth. "Where are we going?"

"Pharmacy. I called the hospital," Lennie said. "Your doc was not crazy about your exit strategy, but I convinced him that he was a humanitarian. You know, that Hippocratic Oath stuff."

Dan looked at him.

"He's called in a prescription," Lennie said. "Just told him to pick the pharmacy nearest the racetrack. It's one thing to bail out of a hospital, that took courage, but you need some pain meds, man. Don't be stupid." The car sloshed through cross streets, the headlights being eaten by the shimmering asphalt.

Twenty minutes later Dan ran trying to dodge puddles and re-entered the car.

"What'd he give you?"

"Oxy," Dan said, as he fumbled to open the safety cap against his leg.

"Hillbilly heroin," said Lennie. "Good choice."

Dan threw back two pills and washed them down with a Gatorade. "Let's head over to the barn. I want to make sure everything's all right."

"Only place you're going is to bed."

"Give me your phone, I gotta call Beth."

"Jesus," Lennie said, sliding the phone from his back pocket. "I'll be glad when you get your own back."

"No kidding. Wonder why they took it anyway. Didn't take my wallet, keys or anything else. Heck, they even left my trial notebook alone." He froze, replaying events from earlier. He slowly turned and looked Lennie in the eyes. "They didn't take it."

"What do you mean? Where is it?"

"They didn't take it. I lost it."

"Well, that helps," Lennie said sarcastically. "We can just drive around with the windows down. You can dial the phone and we'll listen for the ring."

"It's on vibrate. Old courtroom habit."

"Oh, that's helpful."

"That's why they don't know they have it," Dan said.

"I thought you said you lost it. Now they've got it?" Lennie shook his head. "How many oxys did you take?"

"I lost it. And they have it. They just don't know it." Dan tugged Shefford Banks' business card from his pocket and dialed.

"Put a trace on my phone."

"Nice hearing from you, too," Banks said, his voice groggy. "Who is this?"

"Shoot, sorry. It's Dan Morgan. Don't mean to call so late, but put a trace on my phone. I was talking on it when those bozos jumped me. It's possible my phone is still in their van. Find the van, find the guys."

"Okay, hang on." Dan could hear rustling noises. Probably getting the guy out of bed. Banks read Dan's number back to him and confirmed it. "I'm on it."

Lennie pulled the car up to the door of the only motel room he could secure in Louisville. The building was pink stucco with turquoise doors. Plate glass windows, covered by drawn gray plastic drapes, separated the doors. A sign out front read Heavenly Inn Motel, No Vacancy. The headlights shone on a bronze placard identifying it as number 38. The placard hung sideways, one of the screws having fallen out.

"Nice place," Dan said.

"Goes for like forty bucks a night most times. Derby week, you're paying three hundred a night. Three night minimum."

"You're a real value shopper," Dan said.

"Pick your poison. Sleep here, in the car or in the barn."

"Did I tell you how much I love this place?"

Dan followed Lennie through the door, threw his pill bottle and trial notebook on the bed, and collapsed next to them.

"I get connecting the phone to the guys," Lennie said, pacing the floor. "But what makes you think Zaqualina's connections are tied to this? It makes no sense. You're trying to prove Heisenberg's Uncertainty Principle with no starting point and no means of measurement. Seriously. You've got a guy who happens to speak a little Russian staying at a hotel on Mohammed Ali Boulevard? That's it? I'm not a lawyer and all, but that seems pretty tenuous to me. And you go right up and accuse the guy. What's that all about?"

Lennie would get no response. Dan was out.

Chapter 37

Friday, May 4

The sun was still buried behind the Churchill Downs grandstand, but it didn't matter. A thick mattress of rain clouds had socked in the structure. Dan spotted Beth sitting on the ground next to Aly Dancer's stall. He could sense her discomfort from a barn away. The oxy had allowed him to get several hours of needed sleep, but the recurring throbbing had him up well before sunrise.

"Where are Ginny's boys?"

She looked up and crawled to her feet, dusting off her jeans. "I sent them home a while ago," Beth said, as she turned to face Aly Dancer.

"Everything okay?"

There was a long pause and she shrugged.

"Beth, you okay?"

She turned her head slightly and he could tell, even in the morning darkness, that she had been crying. "What is it?" No response. He touched her on the shoulder. She turned away, shrugging again.

"I don't know. It's not right, something's not right."

"Is Aly okay?"

She shook her head. "No, she's fine, but—I don't know." Aly poked her head out of the stall, Beth backed up a step and reached for the halter. She scratched the filly behind the ears. "If it wasn't the Oaks, it would be an easy decision," she said.

Dan knew not to talk right now. Beth took some deep breaths.

"Too much rain," she said. "I was over at the track earlier. It's not right." Beth took some deep breaths. "She's worked so hard. Came back from whatever funk she was in and the track comes up like this. We've never even worked her on a wet track. Not once. And with Zaqualina—?" She paused. "Maybe we should pick another spot. I don't know. Pick a day when we know what she can do. When she has her best shot."

Dan leaned against the barn and tried to make eye contact with her. It wasn't going to happen. "You're my trainer. It's your call."

"No," she said, choking back a sob. "I'm not a trainer. I'm just an over-promoted groom. I—"

"Beth, we talked about this in Florida. You were going to get your license. Things happened. Time just sped up. You are my trainer."

She snuffled back some tears. "If something happened to her, I'd never forgive myself. I can't do this—"

"Okay," Dan said. "Here's the deal. If you think she can win, run her. If you don't think she can win, then let's pass."

"I know how much this means to you. It's the Oaks. It's Churchill Downs. It's national television. I just don't know. It's just not right."

"We don't know what's right or not. We don't know.

We just have to make the best decision we can. I can live with that. None of these horses has run on a track like this. They don't know either. Nobody does."

"I just wish I knew."

Dan took some breaths and crossed his arms. He really wanted to run this race. It was a dream, but he held his feelings in check. He had to honor Beth's judgment. She was his trainer and he either had to believe in her or it was all a game. Mostly he had to believe in her as a person and trust her. It was the foundation for everything. Turning down a million dollars, getting his hand pulverized, and ending up in the hospital had to take a back seat. He either trusted her or he didn't. There were no shades of gray here.

"Take her out," he said, finally.

"Scratch her?"

"No," he pointed toward the track. "Take her out, see how she handles it."

She paused and he knew she was going to object.

"We owe it to her," Dan said. "She'll tell us if she can go in it. Then we'll have the information we need. Or part of it anyway."

She turned and locked eyes. They didn't speak. Finally she said, "I don't know where Kyle is, they're only going to open the track for a few hours. Supposed to rain more later today, they'll seal the track until just before the first post."

Taking a horse to the track on race day was a big gamble he knew. Some trainers did it, but it was unconventional and could throw off the race preparation routine. Harder yet with a young horse like Aly.

"I don't want Kyle on her," Dan said. "I want you on her."

"I don't ride works anymore—"

"It's not a work. Just take her around once, get her used to it. See if she can handle it." They were frozen, two feet apart, eyes engaged. "We owe it to her."

"Yeah, I guess we do," she said. Her shoulders shrugged slightly.

Ten minutes later Dan lifted Beth's leg and she was on Aly's back. The filly shimmied sideways and Beth took a firm grip, showing she was in charge. Dan led them to the break. Half a dozen horses were galloping in the muck, none going fast, just splashing through the sealed mud like a four-inch snow. Beth cantered away. Aly's back end dipped as she pushed off in search of hard ground.

"Put some turn-downs on her," came a voice from behind him.

Ginny.

"Just want to see how she handles the going," Dan said.

"I'm telling you," Ginny said, then spat on the ground. "Turn-downs."

Turn-downs were legal on off tracks like today's. The farrier turned down the back prongs of the horseshoe to allow the shoe to dig into harder surface—like cleats on a football shoe.

"Beth's call," Dan said.

They watched Aly move down the backside and into the turn. It was a slow gallop. Dan spied Beth to see if he could sense a reaction. Was Aly sliding? Was she gripping the track? Did Aly want to be out there? He couldn't tell.

After several agonizing minutes, the duo made one circuit of the track and slowly returned. Aly's belly and legs were dripping with brown water. She shivered as they pulled up. Dan grabbed the bridle and clipped a strap to her.

"Well?"

Beth was looking off both sides of the animal, like an avid auto enthusiast scoping a prized convertible.

"How'd she go?" Ginny asked.

No response.

"You want me to put stickers on her?" Ginny followed up.

Beth didn't react. She rode with her head bobbing to each step, staring down at the reins in her hands. Her mind was somewhere else.

They stepped into the grassy area in front of the barn and Beth dismounted. She surveyed Aly's legs, oblivious to everything but the horse.

"I'm telling you Beth—" Ginny started.

Dan grabbed Ginny's bicep and pulled him away. "Give her a minute," he whispered.

They stepped under the cover of the shedrow, as drops started to pitter patter on the lawn in front of them.

Beth held the bridle strap and examined every part of Aly Dancer. She got down on her haunches and felt the filly's legs, scraping wet mud off them. She stood on one side, the bridle strap extended in her arm, then switched to the other side, eyeballing every inch of horseflesh and muscle. Then she pulled the bridle close and leaned her forehead against the filly's neck. Rain softly fell on the woman and the horse. Neither seemed to mind. Beth stood that way, motionless as the world went by. Finally she stood upright and moved directly in front of Aly Dancer. The filly nodded her head shaking the bridle and puffing through her nostrils. Beth just stared as if in a trance.

"What the hell's—" It was Lennie's voice from behind. Dan held up his hand for silence.

Beth reached forward and scrapped some mud off Aly's chest. She abruptly turned and yanked the filly forward pulling on the bridle.

"Lennie," she yelled. He rushed over and she handed him the shank. "Let's get her cleaned up." Then turning toward Dan and Ginny, she said "Get some stickers on the back end. Get moving! We've got a race today, boys."

Chapter 38

Dan dreaded the next item on the morning's agenda. He'd borrowed Lennie's phone again and shut the door inside the trainer's office. He sat behind the desk staring at the ceiling. This was where Jake died. No doubt he had been given a shot of whatever knockout juice they'd used on Dan, then hoisted from the rafters where he died of asphyxiation. Why? It made no sense. Nothing made sense.

He dialed and spoke. "Sharon, it's Dan Morgan. Is the judge free?"

His heels tapped on the floor as he waited. This was not going to go well. He'd replayed versions of opening lines and potential justifications. Nothing was convincing. There was no justification; there was only the truth—stark and uncolored. As crazy as it was going to sound, it was his only option.

Dan heard, "Please hold," then a beep. He drew a breath.

"This better be good."

"Judge, I'm so sorry. I-I, uh, I'm sorry." He waited for the judge to speak, but there was only breathing on the line.

"Okay. I, um, I flew to Louisville—"

"Kentucky?"

"Yes sir."

"Mr. Morgan, since counsel for the defendant is not on the line, we are prohibited from talking about the case."

"I understand, your honor, ex parte communication."

"So tell me why you didn't show up or call or contact the court in any way."

"Okay, I flew out Wednesday morning and was scheduled to fly home that evening and be ready to start the trial yesterday morning." *Just tell it straight out. It's the only way.*

The judge cleared his throat. "Your trip have anything to do with the trial?"

Dan cringed. "No, your honor." More silence. "I own a racehorse—" He paused to see if he got any reaction. Maybe he's a fan. No response. "Anyway, I came out just for the day and on my way back to the airport, I was kidnapped." God, this sounds so bad.

"Kidnapped?" the judge said in a dry tone.

"They broke my hand."

"The kidnappers did?" Riley said, without much interest. It was as if he was listening to a child explaining the formation of the universe.

"Yes. Anyway, I ended up in the hospital."

"The hospital?" Riley said as if uncoiling more rope for Dan to hang himself with.

God this has to sound like it's totally made up. I can't even believe it and I experienced it. "Yes, your honor. There's a detective here, Shefford Banks, he's investigating the murder of my trainer."

"Your trainer was murdered?" Riley said in the same steady tone.

"I know it sounds insane, but the point is I was to be in your courtroom yesterday morning and I wasn't. I apologize and I'm responsible. Hold me accountable, but don't hold my client or the case in the same regard. It wasn't my client's fault and she deserves her day in court."

"She deserves an attorney to represent her. She deserved better."

"I know, your honor. You're right."

"The court deserves better," Judge Riley said. "I had a room full of prospective jurors waiting for voir dire. The defense was here. Your client was here. You, unfortunately, weren't able to squeeze it into your schedule."

"Your honor, I'm sorry."

"Save it for your client."

"It was beyond my control. If there was any way for me to communicate, I would have. I just couldn't."

There was a long and uncomfortable silence.

"Where are you now?"

"I'm, uh, still in Louisville." He could hear a loud exhale. It wasn't a happy one.

"Okay, we can't discuss the case," Riley said, "But I can tell you that I was preparing to issue a show cause order this morning, but I'll hold that for now. I want you in my courtroom at eight am Monday morning."

"Yes, sir."

"I'm going to have the bailiff call Mr. Cohen and confirm with him as well."

"I understand, your honor."

"If you are thirty seconds late, I expect a call. If you are—don't be late."

"Understood."

"I don't know what the hell I'm going to do with you, but by Monday I'll have it figured out."

"Yes, your honor," Dan said. "One question. Do you want my client in attendance?"

"That's your call, counsel. But if she's there, I don't think she'll like what I have to say about you."

"Yes, your honor and again, I apologize. I'm so sorry."

"Craziest damn story I ever heard."

"I know, your honor. But I can give you the number for Detective Banks. He can verify everything I've told you."

"Don't bother. I'll wait for the movie. See you Monday morning. And counselor?"

"Yes."

"Bring your checkbook."

~

Dan leaned back in the chair with eyes closed. Sure as hell he was going to get fined and most certainly censured. A black mark like that on his bar license could cripple his practice. Riley will be fair with my client, he thought, but he'll throw the book at me.

A knock on the door interrupted the personal wake Dan was holding for his law career.

Shefford Banks entered holding a cellophane bag marked EVIDENCE.

"This your phone?"

Dan leaned forward squinting at the evidence bag. "Yeah, that's it." He reached for it, but Banks pulled it away.

"Evidence."

"You find it in the van?"

"Yep. Phone was under the passenger seat. You know a guy named Anton Nikotin?" Banks said, throwing a thigh on the edge of the desk, sitting.

Dan shook his head. "That the guy who took me? Was it his van? You arrest him? Is he talking?"

"Guy's not doing much talking," Banks said. In his relaxed drawl it sounded like a line to a country western song.

Dan jumped and paced behind the desk. "He probably drugged Jake with the same stuff he gave me. You find any drugs or meds on him? I think we can connect him to another guy who's in on this."

"That's going to be tough to do."

"Why's that? You got him right? This Anton whatever."

Banks took a deep breath, then spoke. "Yeah, we got him, but somebody got him first."

"What do you mean?"

"He's dead. Somebody gave him a Colombian necktie." Banks ran his finger across his throat.

"What about the other guy?"

"There is no other guy. Not right now. We got a rental van, a dead body and a cell phone, that's it." He paused. "Well, and a forensics team going over every inch of the van."

Dan rubbed his face. *What now? How do I connect this to that Vasily guy? Hell, was there even a connection?*

"Asked the ME to run Jake's blood work and see if it matches anything the hospital has on yours," Banks said, slumping. "Probably will, but so what at this point? Guy who killed Jake, drugged and beat you. But he's dead now. Hard to connect the dots when that happens."

"I think this is all connected to a guy named Vasily."

"Got a last name?"

"No, but it should be easy to figure out. It's Tad Stapleton's father-in-law."

"The guy who owns Zaqualina?"

Dan nodded.

"Sure you're not just imagining things, running against his horse and everything."

"The guy—this Anton, spoke Russian. I could hear him on the phone speaking it to somebody."

"So of all the Russian speaking folks in the world, you've narrowed it to this Vasily character?"

"The only word I could make out when they spoke was Mohammed Ali."

Banks raised an eyebrow and chuckled. "And you figured they weren't talking about Louisville's favorite son."

"He was repeating back the location of the hotel where he was staying."

"The Seelbach," Banks said, tipping his cowboy hat back.

"Bingo. So I went there last night."

"Whoa, whoa, whoa there cowboy. You bust out of the hospital and go tracking a guy in a five-star hotel. What are you, James Bond or something?"

"Anyway, I found Vasily. Speaks Russian, daughter does a little bit too."

"Not exactly rock solid there, Clarence Darrow."

"I know it's him. I know they're connected. I just can't prove it right now. I think he's the money behind offering to buy Aly Dancer."

Banks leaned forward. "So what's his game, buy

your horse and scratch her, so his son-in-law can win the Oaks?"

"Maybe, not sure."

"Lotta smart folks think his horse will win whether yours is in there or not. No offense, son. Just saying."

"See what you can find out about the guy."

Banks let out an exasperated breath, putting his hands on his knee to stand. "For a guy who don't pay taxes in this county, you sure give a lot of orders."

"Nice. These guys kill my trainer, nab me and bust up my hand and I'm just some bumbling disinterested tourist," Dan said, throwing his good hand in the air.

"I'll see what we can gather on this fella. By the way, you ever decide to go into law enforcement, give me a call," Banks said, slipping out the doorway.

Given what Judge Riley had in mind, a career change might come sooner than you know, Dan thought.

~

Dan was suddenly light-headed. The conversations with Riley and Banks had taken a toll. He shuffled out of the barn toward the track cafeteria. Maybe a cup of scalding coffee would bring him back. The oxy was certainly playing a part in his diminished mental condition, so a brief walk seemed in order.

He considered asking if anyone wanted anything from the kitchen, then realized there was no way for him to carry back stuff with his damaged arm. Just walking had become an ordeal of shooting pain. He figured out that if he hung his arm as if his shoulder was dislocated, the pain in his hand was lessened. So the one armed man crunched the gravel.

This was one of the times of day he liked best.

Grooms and stable hands were hard at work, moving animals, mucking stalls.

Men leaned on the fence posts with their boots providing support.

Jock agents and trainers played their heads-up poker game sorting rides for upcoming mounts.

Vets and farriers hustled to make rounds, making sure they didn't leave any business opportunities available for competitors.

Lennie's phone rang and Dan was brought back to the fact that his phone was now in the custody of the local boys in blue.

"Hello?"

"Lennie?"

"No, it's Dan, Dan Morgan. Lennie's not here."

"Dan, it's Milt. Have been trying to call you. Why don't you pick up? I've tried to reach you for two days. Where you been, man?"

"Long story," Dan said. "You got me now though." The image of Milton Childers brought a smile to his heart. He was always a distraction. This time he needed it.

"Hey, wanted you to know that Thoroughbred Nostradamus is going to come out with a pick today. In the Oaks. Think he's going to tout Aly?"

"I doubt it," Dan said. "Probably like everyone else. Going to pick Zaqualina."

"No way, man. Won't be the favorite. He's already confirmed that. He's going to release the pick at four o'clock eastern. Two hours before the race. I've never seen him so confident. Told us to lock in on the pick and not share with anyone, but I thought, what the hell, if I can't tell my buddies, then what's the point?"

"You know Lennie won't give a damn who the guy picks." Dan stood outside the track kitchen in the drizzling rain, not because he wanted to, but because with the phone in one hand, he was unable to pull the door open.

"I know, but I figure I need to tell him in advance, otherwise he'll think I made it up later. Guy doesn't believe in Nostradamus."

"I don't either, Milt. I think you'll eventually lose your shirt playing this guy's picks. Like all the other schemes and sure things you've bought over the years."

"You want me to tell you the pick or not? Seeing how you got a horse in the race and all."

Dan thought about it. He didn't want to show any interest, but Milt was a friend. Guy's trying to do me a solid, at least in his own mind. Might be good to know. Might have something to do with Jake and this Vasily guy. "Yeah, Milt, sorry. I'd love to know the pick. Call me when you have it."

Sitting alone with his steaming cup of coffee, he tried to piece things together. Was it all coincidence? Jake said the purchase of Aly was a scam. Then Nostradamus picks the Oaks for his premium release. Not the favorite, Milt said.

Were they going to stiff Zaqualina? Is that why Vasily wanted to buy Aly? Hell, he didn't even know if it was Vasily behind the offer. Was he going to buy Aly and stiff both of them? That could unleash a major betting coup. Two favorites running out? He pondered and whistled under his breath.

It made no sense, not in a Grade One race, not an undefeated filly like that. Maybe a nickel claiming race, but not this spot.

Too many coincidences. Jake, Vasily, Thoroughbred Nostradamus, some guy named Anton Nikotin. None of them linked up very well. All he really knew was that his captors spoke Russian and Vasily spoke Russian. Lennie was right. It was weak, damn weak. Jake said the sale was a scam and they killed him.

He twisted his coffee cup in his fingers, staring at the mud tracked onto the kitchen floor by cowboy boots, sneakers and work boots.

Jake fields an offer for Aly. Jake discovers that something's up. Jake gets killed by the guys who kidnapped me. Probably anyway. The guys who kidnapped me had to be linked to Vasily. Maybe. Vasily was the father-in-law of Zaqualina's owner. Online con artist decides to release a pick in the Oaks where Aly and Vasily's son-in-law's horse both were running. Con artist says the favorite won't win.

It didn't exactly line up like a perfect string of dominoes. Con artist might be full of shit. That made sense. Follow the evidence, not coincidence, he told himself.

What was the scam? What the hell had Jake uncovered?

The Russian voice bellowed in his head over and over. *You can't stop it.*

Chapter 39

Mickey Soldatov fanned his fingers and stretched them. He cracked some knuckles on the left side and addressed the keyboard. His clicks brought up the admin site and he entered the password which, after a one-sided conversation, he'd convinced Q to give him.

Q sat slumped against the floor. There was only one chair in Q's darkened apartment and Mickey sat in that. Q pressed an ink-stained hand against his cracked lower lip and looked at the blood. Hand back to mouth, looked at the blood more and put his hand back to his mouth. Mickey had seen this scene play out many times. People who were bleeding seemed to think if they looked at the bloody hand, the cut would get better. Folks were funny that way.

Light from the monitor cast a greenish tint on Mickey. His upper body blocked most of the light from escaping. He was framed by the dim illumination as though standing at a window.

"She won't win," Q said.

"Shut up."

"I tell you. She not win. Zaqualina win."

"I said shut up." He'd started typing. "You don't know shit."

"I know," Q said, repeating the hand to lip routine. "Only horse who can beat her is Aly Dancer. She sick maybe."

Mickey interrupted his typing and turned to face the Thai man. Mickey put his hands on his knees, reversed with his thumbs extending on the outside of his thighs. The move made his triceps pop, displaying the payoff from two hours in the weight room each day. "We going to have to do this again?"

Q scooted along the wall a few inches and drew in his legs. Smaller target, Mickey thought. At least that was smart.

"I know. You wrong," Q said.

"Listen you little tofu eater. I'm done with this conversation. I have some work to do." He turned back to the keyboard. "You get paid well. I set this whole thing up for you. Nobody knows who you are. Let me do my thing here."

"But we tell them wrong. It not right."

"Don't you worry about it. Just keep your mouth shut and let me worry about the business side. We have plenty of options. You still have value." Then Mickey muttered to himself, "Not much, but some value."

He pounded out the note. Mickey was fairly agile as a typist, despite his massive calloused hands. The disparity looked like a man playing with a child's piano, but he whisked out a symphony on the keyboard.

Mickey paused and re-read the note. He nodded as though he'd written a masterpiece. Too subtle? He wondered. Drive home the point, then leave ambiguity for later. This was what he'd learned in his time with the dot com startups. Hit them with the sizzle, but don't tell them where the steak came from. In fact, don't even tell them there is a steak. They'll imagine one anyway. If things don't work out, the wiggle room will stare them in the face. They were all suckers, born every minute and ready to dive into the swimming pool whether there was water in it or not.

He read the note again slowly. He nodded and smiled at his handiwork.

He toggled the mouse, then hit enter.

~

Bits and bytes scattered through the ether. Smartphones hummed, computers beeped and e-mail notices flashed. Working a tout in the old days took connections, months of leg work and a certain snappy, confident style. Working a tout in the new age took an Internet-enabled device, an opinion and the courage to hit enter. He and Vasily had worked six months to get into this position.

It was a beautiful thing.

For a good con the setup was all about arrangement, all about putting wheels in motion. The setup was all about investment. With this gig they found out how to make money in the setup.

It was a beautiful thing.

Make money setting people up. It should be a crime. Then make a huge score when the deal goes down. Shut it all down and start over.

Stick and move, just like boxing.

Stick and move.

~

Milt had a jolt of excitement when he spotted the message on his smartphone. His hands shook as he fumbled with it. Eventually the message opened. It was from Thoroughbred Nostradamus. Milt had been expecting it.

He'd show that math nerd Lennie a thing or two. He'd show him how a gambler made money the easy way.

The message was short. It read:

Kentucky Oaks Special Blowout

Get a bushel basket, cause you'll need it to carry off your winnings with today's pick.

Rain in Kentucky. Off track. Perfect.

Pinnacle Penny will show her stuff today.

Bred for the slop. Reaching a meta-biological peak.

Let the stooges throw money at the favorite.

We will show them. Pinnacle Penny.

Today's Special Blowout.

He read it twice.

Huh?

He shook his head. Don't read into it. Just do it, he thought. Milt clicked off the e-mail and punched up the phone. He pressed the name Lennie on his phone. If he was lucky, Lennie wouldn't answer. Dan would. That would be even better. Now he had a witness, someone other than Lennie.

These guys are going to thank me later.

Chapter 40

Several thousand times per year the activity took place. It was a function of horse racing. Very simply it was bringing the horses from the backside barns to the paddock before a race.

Today was different.

Today was special. On these rare days, with national television coverage, with a grandstand overflowing with spectators, with an infield jammed with enthusiastic, alcohol-induced pandemonium, it was something else. It was a happening, a ticker tape parade, a bottom of the ninth walk-off home run, a three-ringed circus all rolled into one.

In horse racing it was simply called the walk.

All his life Dan had watched the walk, wondering if he would ever participate. For those unique races, Grade One races with wall-to-wall media coverage, the process of bringing the horses to the paddock was a media event.

The call had come over the loudspeaker the way it does on all backsides, alerting the stable hands that the horses for the next race could be brought to the paddock. This time Dan's heart skipped several beats. It wasn't just the next race; it was the Kentucky Oaks.

Beth, adorned in a black pantsuit with a shocking white blouse, looked like a movie star ready to step onto the set. Dan did his best to make his three day old suit look fresh. A new shirt and necktie would draw attention away from the wrinkled and blood-splotched coat, he hoped.

"Let's do this," Beth said, with more than a hint of confidence. This would not be her first walk over, but it was her first walk over as trainer. Dan noticed the change. Anyone who knew her would have noticed the change. She stood straighter, head high, ready to conquer the world. Hopefully Aly would have the same game face.

A gaggle of fans had formed a phalanx of humanity along the pathway to the track. More had congregated at the point where the animals stepped onto the backside for the long walk on the outermost area of the racetrack. From there the warriors would walk toward the grandstand. They trailed through a tunnel and emerged at the paddock behind the spires that defined Churchill Downs. Hell, the spires defined American horse racing.

Lennie brought Aly Dancer out of the stall and into the grassy area. A badge designating her starting post flapped from her bridle.

"Hold up," Beth said.

Ahead, Zaqualina and her connections had stepped onto the path. A flurry of photos and shouts erupted. "Let them go," she said.

Dan saw Tad along with Zaqualina's trainer. They were the very picture of confidence. All smiles, waving to friends and anonymous onlookers. Chick Mangold, ever the PR man, was jabbering something that made others laugh. Guy was always running his mouth.

Aly stood taking it all in. Like a boxer preparing

to leave the dressing room, she tucked her head several times, snorted, but stood calmly. After several seconds, Zaqualina disappeared as she turned toward the track, all heads following. "Okay," Beth said.

Lennie led on the left side, Beth on the right side, each holding a strap connected to Aly's bridle. Dan walked along behind Beth.

The volume rose dramatically as they separated the onlookers. "Good luck, Beth," came one voice, followed by echoes of similar sentiment. "Get her Aly," someone shouted. Cameras and cell phones snapped pictures like paparazzi outside a New York City nightclub. Beth's head was held high. She acknowledged some shouts with a head turn, but no smile. Dan raised his good hand to half mast, his breathing shallow.

As they entered the racetrack the noise increased. Individual voices couldn't be made out. It was like the roar of the ocean drowning out all weaker sounds. Aly's head bobbed up and down as though she sensed the importance of the moment.

They turned left to skirt the outside rail. The grandstand came into view. Dan was sure his heart had stopped. This was it. This was walking onto the Super Bowl gridiron. This was walking to the mound in game seven of the World Series.

The grandstand erupted in blues, pinks, and yellows, like a Leroy Neimen painting. These were not rail-birds in worn trousers and pale shirts. These were fashion's finest. Elaborate hats, push up bras, and flashing diamonds were the order of the day.

"Jesus," Dan murmured.

They slopped along the muddy surface, resigned to

the fact that they would be covered with mud from the knees down. Aly's feet made repeating sucking sounds as she extracted each foot from six inches of mud. Ahead of them each team of warriors trudged forward. Several microphone-clutching reporters circled Zaqualina as they recorded pithy quotes from Mangold.

One reporter broke away from the Zaqualina group like a separating atom and waited for Team Aly Dancer to catch up.

"What do you think of the track, Beth?" the man said, his microphone flashing.

"I hate it," she said without looking at him. A cameraman swung his shoulder gear around to capture them and walked alongside. Aly snorted at him.

"How's Aly Dancer handling it?" the man continued.

"She'll be fine," she said.

Dan smiled and hoped he wouldn't be asked a question. He was sure he couldn't make a sound. His throat felt like it was filled with sand and his jaw was clenched as if his breathing system had vapor locked.

"Can you beat Zaqualina?" The guy was nothing if not persistent.

Beth walked along several strides without speaking. She looked over at Aly.

"Beth?" the man said. "Do you—"

"I heard you," she said. Several more strides, then she turned to him, snapping, "I wouldn't be here if I didn't think we could beat her."

The man quick-stepped up next to Beth. "Are you going to go out with her or lay back?"

"Watch the race," Beth said dismissively, trudging forward.

The reporter turned toward Dan. "Mr. Morgan, your first Grade One race, I understand," he said. "How do you feel?"

Dan tried to smile, but he knew it was stiff and mechanical. His face hurt. He just nodded, no sound.

"Good luck, Mr. Morgan."

They slogged on toward the tunnel. The cameras and reporters hung back. They were alone—Lennie, Beth, Aly and Dan. Surrounded by a hundred thousand clamoring fans, they were alone.

Twenty-five minutes to post.

~

Lennie stood stock still as Beth cinched the saddle. They had developed a workable relationship—Aly Dancer and Lennie that is. Beth was another story. Aly extended her neck and nuzzled toward Lennie. He stepped back, not out of fear, now out of routine.

People were jammed fifteen deep around the paddock and fans collected on the balconies off the back of the luxury accommodations several stories above ground. Most of the attention was focused on Zaqualina and her connections. Philippe Calderon, wearing Tad Stapleton's turquoise and black silks, stood twirling his stick, waiting for the mount. Kyle stood with his back to Calderon in front of the number five stall.

"You ready?" Dan asked.

"Yup." There was more bravado than confidence in his wordy response.

"You walk the track?"

"Two races ago," Kyle said. "Three lanes off the rail is the firmest part of the track. Rail is dead, still soupy."

Beth approached them, her eyes still working over Aly Dancer. She crouched and stroked Aly's front leg, then stood and gave her a complete once over. She adjusted the bridle and gave Aly a strong pat on the neck.

Kyle stepped closer.

"Don't go out with that other," she said, softly. It was obvious to everyone who "the other" was.

"What?" Kyle said, beating Dan to the punch.

"Don't go out with her. Let her go."

"Beth, we can't. Aly has natural speed, this is the only way, we have to be on or near the front. Zaqualina's never been headed. Can't just let her get away with an easy lead. We'll never catch her.

Beth stopped, turned, and drilled Kyle with a forceful look. "You want to ride for me, you do what I say. Let the other one go."

"She's going to eat a lot of mud," Kyle said. "Nobody's won from more than a few lengths back today. Especially with this track."

"He's right," Lennie said. "Front speed and pace runners have won everything today."

"I don't care," she said, quietly looking at Lennie, then back to Kyle. "Get her away and tuck into a nice spot. Long way around today. There's going to be plenty of speed. Grab a good spot and wait. Don't ask her til the five sixteenths pole. We'll run her down in the stretch."

Kyle shrugged. He didn't like it, but as she had made clear, Beth was the boss.

Beth reached over, gently grabbing Kyle's shoulder.

"Aly can do this," she whispered. "I need to know you can do this."

Kyle nodded.

Beth continued, louder now. "We don't win a speed duel, not today. Not this track. That other one's never been challenged in the stretch. Never had to gut out a win. You pull up alongside her in the stretch and we'll see what she's made of," she said. "I know what my horse can do."

The call for "riders up" came from the paddock judge. Beth gave Kyle a boost into the saddle as Lennie walked Aly forward into the parade ring. "Get the money," she called after him. Same line Jake had always used.

Dan and Beth stood shoulder to shoulder watching the horses being led around the walking ring. "Don't you start on me, either," Beth said.

Dan kept his mouth shut. He thought she was wrong, especially under today's conditions. He would have argued the strategy with Jake. Maybe this was Jake's plan anyway. Maybe he and Beth had talked about it. Dan didn't turn to look at her. He watched Aly and Lennie as they followed Zaqualina circling. This was more than strategy. It was simpler than that.

This was about trust.

"I would have given him the same instructions," Dan said, finally. He extended his chin and bobbed his head. "Good strategy."

"Bullshit," she muttered, just for his ears. A devilish smile creased her lips.

Twelve minutes to post.

Chapter 41

Three time zones away, Mickey Soldatov leaned against an ornate pillar while fixated on the television monitor across from him. The horses for the Oaks were being led onto the track. They would sing some silly song. It was a junior varsity attempt at being the Kentucky Derby.

The Santa Anita clubhouse buzzed with energy, as patrons lined up to get bets down. The serpentine bar to his left contained several dozen men with tall beers and short cocktails all struggling over their racing forms, trying to decipher a winning wager.

Mickey stepped into a line leading to a betting window. He had no intention of placing a bet. He had more important things to do. The line shuffled forward as gamblers at the head of the line called out their winning numbers. When Mickey reached the front he leaned forward on his elbows.

"Now's the time for my favor," Mickey said. Clayton Pinkney jerked back as though a rattlesnake had slithered into his window. Pinkney's head shot side to side as he scanned for a supervisor.

"Wha—what do you need?"

"I'm not buying a ticket," Mickey said in a hushed tone. "You are." A stunned face stared back at Mickey. "I want you to make a twenty-five thousand dollar wager."

"What?"

"In a few minutes I want you to make a bet. Twenty-five thou."

"Do you have the money with you?"

"I'm not making the bet. You are."

"I don't have twenty-five thousand dollars," Pinkney whispered, his hands trembling.

"You don't need it," Mickey said, smiling. "You have a printing press right here in front of you." He chuckled, tapping on the ticket machine. "You're like the federal reserve. You can create money out of thin air."

"I-I can't."

"You will," Mickey shot back. He'd dealt with guys like Clayton Pinkney all his life. They know right from wrong, but couldn't handle intimidation. He'd do it.

"I can't do it."

"Well, I guess that's what I'll have to tell Mitzi, just before I break that yapping mutt's neck."

"I'll get fired. I could go to jail," Clayton said in a hushed, but forceful tone.

"Then you'd better hope the horse you bet hits the board. I want you to bet twenty-five thousand to show in the Oaks at Churchill Downs." Mickey looked over his shoulder, then turned back. "No large tickets. Two hundred max per ticket."

"Tha—that's a lot of tickets."

"Just do it."

Clayton's head swayed slowly. "If I do this when will I get Mitzi back?"

"You do this right, Mitzi will be home waiting for you tonight. All safe and sound." It was a lie, but a necessary one.

Clayton drew a breath. "Then we're done? You and me, I mean."

"Yes, my friend, then we're done."

Clayton ran a hand over his unruly rooster tail on top of his head. "Which horse?"

"I'll give you a signal," Mickey said. "You just be ready. Or else no more woof-woof. Watch for my signal." Mickey turned to leave. "Talk to you after the race, partner."

Nine minutes to post.

Chapter 42

Pink.

It was everywhere.

Pink banners, pink hats, pink bow ties, pink shirts, pink dresses—the grandstand was awash in pink. Most track-side fans were in desperate need of a shave and shower. But this was Ladies' Day at Churchill, the Oaks. The air even smelled better.

"You forgot your pink shirt," Lennie said, eyeing the crowd from the fence just inside the track.

"I don't own a pink shirt." Then catching Lennie's drift, Dan said, "They're really going all out on this today, aren't they?"

"Been doing this for the past few years. Nice." Lennie nodded at nothing in particular. "Good cause. Time was, today was known as Louisville's Day at the races. The day before the Derby. Now so many fans and celebrities pile in the week leading up to Derby that it is everyone's day. Well, Ladies' Day at the track."

They watched the horses being led in the post parade. Once past the grandstand, then they'd warm up on the backside and head to the starting gate an eighth of a mile before the finish line.

"Damn, that's one fine animal," Dan said, as Zaqualina pranced past.

"It ain't a beauty contest," Lennie said. "It's crazy. But you see it all the time. Zaqualina may be the second coming, but at even money on this track at a distance none of these horses have ever run before? Lunacy."

They watched in silence, the announcer booming on the PA system.

"What do you think of Pinnacle Penny?" Dan asked. "That's the one Thoroughbred Nostradamus picked. What Milt said." Lennie gave a dismissive wave. Dan continued, "She look okay to you? She looks like—"

Lennie held his hand up stopping the conversation.

"Number five is Aly Dancer. Owned by Dan Morgan, trained by Bethany DeCarlo and ridden by Kyle Jonas."

"Christ sakes, man," Lennie said. "You're running in a Grade One race. At least take the time to listen to them introduce your horse. Smell the roses, dude. These don't come around every week you know."

Dan shook his head. "I know, but something's not right. I can just feel it."

Eight minutes to post.

~

Beth looked out at the expanse of racetrack below her. This was unfamiliar territory. As a groom she was accustomed to standing on the track where Lennie was now, waiting for her horse to return from the race. Of course she had watched races from the grandstand. Anyone who grew up on the circuit like her was more familiar with racetrack mezzanines than movie theaters or shopping malls.

This time was different.

This time she was Beth DeCarlo, trainer. She was preparing to watch her only charge engage in battle on the racetrack. She'd been on the track one way or another since she was six, but this was the first time any horse she had anything to do with was in a Grade One race.

She looked down at her shoes. Her wardrobe was even less prepared for this moment than she was. Mud caked her patent black pumps, which nearly slipped off several times in the sucking mud of the walk over. Her pants legs were similarly marked. Beth's arms were crossed and she rocked forward on the balls of her feet. Fingers were clenched against her elbows, not appearing pensive, but to keep from visibly shaking.

I hope I know what I'm doing.

Far below her Dan and Lennie were having a vigorous conversation near the entrance to the track. Ginny was there too, but he wasn't talking. Guy almost never did.

She glanced down the rows of box seats. She knew what to expect. Churchill Downs, as was customary with the Oaks and Derby, had provided box seats to the connections to each of the horses. Of course, Zaqualina's connections were next door.

Tad Stapleton stood confidently beside a stunning woman. Beth didn't know much about women's fashion, but she didn't need a Sherpa to know that the woman's dress wasn't on a hanger at Gap. She wore a broad-brimmed light blue hat that was pinned up on one side. An older man was with them, grey hair, combed perfectly. He had a boxer's nose and blocked chin. The man didn't seem very interested in the activity as his eyes shot around the track below him. He wasn't very talkative, either.

Then she heard the booming voice she dreaded. Chick Mangold.

"Hey, y'all. Beautiful day, isn't it?" He was speaking for the whole section of the grandstand. Beth swallowed, not sure she could speak if needed.

"Maiya, you look fantastic," he said, leaning in and giving her a double cheek kiss. "Okay, in a couple of minutes, Zaqualina will take care of business and we'll head down that stairway, jog over to the left and down to the track. The winner's circle is over there, just next to the tote board."

Arrogant jerk.

"And Maiya, don't you worry. They'll lay out a walkway across the track so you don't get those pretty Louis Vuittons all messy." He slapped Tad on the back, making a resounding pop. "Here we go, folks."

Beth looked away just as Chick made eye contact. "And good luck to you little lady," he said.

Little lady. Beth turned and gave him a nod of bored acknowledgement.

"First time in a Grade One." He chuckled. "They say you never forget your first time, darling."

Beth did her best to ignore him and looked for Aly Dancer warming up on the track. Chick went to his binoculars. *God, what I'd give to shut him up.* She glanced to the other side and exchanged polite nods with the crowd in the adjoining box. A touch on her arm startled her. She looked left. Maiya had her hand on Beth's forearm. "Good luck," she mouthed. Beth smiled and nodded.

Six minutes to post.

~

Aly Dancer galloped out powerfully. Kyle's legs were extended and he bent from the waist, bobbing with each stride. She seemed to be handling the surface well, but he would notice every few jumps that her back side slid sideways a touch as she dug for firm ground.

Kyle was at Churchill for one reason and this horse was it. Although the meet had just started the previous week, this was only his second mount. He needed a big share of the purse to right his foundering financial ship.

I don't know what Beth's thinking. We can go to the front, maybe we can't beat that other horse, but we can sure get a piece running our race. Making her come off the pace on this track of all times seems risky. We're going to eat an acre of mud running from behind. Why take the chance?

He adjusted his goggles—six pairs today. He would peel them off one by one, letting them hang around his neck coated with mud.

Be patient. Deep breaths.

This was far and away the biggest stage he'd been on. Nothing was close. All these riders are millionaires. All but him. He closed his eyes and rode with the rhythm.

Be patient.

A good showing today and he'd get more mounts. This was his chance to break into the upper echelon. Don't blow this one.

Aly Dancer was his one shot, his only reason for taking this route. He'd argued with Cyndi. She'd be home watching on TV. She wanted him home, but more importantly riding on the mid-Atlantic circuit where he'd have five or six mounts per day and a steadier cash flow and be home every night. He wouldn't be risking on one horse, all or nothing.

He promised her it would work out.

He'd promised her that many times before.

Aly's ears pricked forward. She glanced from side to side jerking on the pony that was ridden by the outrider alongside.

He glanced up the track at Zaqualina. That was one big filly. Who knows? Maybe she won't like this track. Big horses sink deeper in the mud, could tire her out. But from his review of the Daily Racing Form she hadn't found a surface she couldn't handle, nor had she found anyone that could finish within six lengths of her. Letting her loose on the front end was a big-time gamble.

Beth doesn't know what she's doing.

If Aly breaks sharply, I have to go to the front. It's her best shot. It's her only shot. If I take her to the front we'll certainly hit the board. Might even win. A strong finish will show Beth. I know what I'm doing. She'll take me seriously-—she'll have to. We have to go to the front. Beth is just plain wrong.

Four minutes to post.

Chapter 43

Mickey patiently watched the clock tick down toward post time. Bettors hustled past him to get in line at a teller's window. He tapped his program against his thigh. Decisions had been made. The plan was set. Now it was just timing.

He pulled his cell phone, drafted a text message and sent it to two numbers. One number belonged to Franco Wolletti. With a plaster cast on his right leg, and respect for recent history, Franco could be trusted. Vasily needed a favor. That was all that was needed to seal the deal.

The other number went to a cell phone in Phoenix. His brother, Maxim, was the recipient. Max had been released from Victorville Federal Penitentiary a month prior. With Mickey's help and a false identity, Max had been able to secure his first employment in ten years— as a mutuel clerk at Turf Paradise Racetrack. Timing was everything.

The text message was simple. One word. "Now."

Mickey pulled his program from the inside pocket of his blazer. He checked the number he'd written in large print to make sure he held it right side up. He walked toward Clayton's window. Half a dozen men were in line to make wagers, but Mickey was able to catch Clayton's eye. He held up the program for the little man to see. Clayton mouthed back the number. Mickey nodded and said, "To show."

Clayton's head snapped down the aisle behind the mutuel windows. He held out a palm to the next bettor in line and mumbled something about the machine being on the fritz. Then he placed a placard in the window indicating it was closed. The gamblers grumbled, but spread out looking for other windows where they could get a bet down.

Mickey watched as Clayton started printing tickets. Ten seconds later Mickey was out the side door, bounding down the stairs toward his car in the parking lot. With all attention on the upcoming race, no one would notice that he was leaving. By the time the race went off, he'd be wheeling his way through the streets of Pasadena.

Two minutes to post.

~

Clayton Pinkney slumped behind the closed sign on the front of his ticket window. He was crouched like a puppy caught peeing on the rug. Clayton looked down the aisle toward his supervisor, Beckstrom. He was as far away as he could be at the moment.

Sweat was pooling in his lower back. *I'm going to jail for this, I just know it.*

He continued punching tickets and looked back. Beckstrom was on the phone. Could they know already? Of course they did. They monitored everything. They'd know the tickets came from his machine. They'd know in the final count when they calculated overages. This would be the doozy of all doozies. Twenty-five grand and no money in the till. It was fraud. How would he explain it? What was there to explain? He was breaking the law, plain and simple. Case closed.

Jessie, his neighboring teller, shot him a worried glance. "Supposed to run out the tape," Clayton said, with little confidence. She wasn't buying it. They'd never run out the tape by printing live tickets. He wiped his forehead. Soggy.

Shit, I'm going to jail. Never see Mitzi. What am I doing? I can't go to jail. I can't run, they'll find me. I'll just pay it back. That's what I'll do. Pay it back. It will be okay. I don't have twenty-five thousand dollars. I'll get it somehow. Sell the place. They won't put an old man in jail. Not if he pays back the money.

Where's Mickey? He scanned the room. *Where is he? He wants these tickets doesn't he? The machine kept pumping them out. I've got time. I'll do smaller tickets. They won't notice it. Shoot, what am I thinking? Of course they'll notice.*

They see everything.

He looked over his shoulder; Beckstrom was still on the phone.

Shit, he's looking at me. Isn't he? Or is he just looking this way. Nope. He's looking at me. I'm screwed. They know.

One minute to post.

Chapter 44

Lennie was like a dog on point. He eyed the tote board like a scientist studying a strand of DNA. He could absorb it all in his mind. Where was the steam? Where were the soft spots? Early on regular bettors watched the multiple pages and columns on the tote board. With a few minutes to post, they only watched one number. The odds on the horse they'd bet. Lennie was different. He watched all the numbers. They told him a story. He was the only person reading the tea leaves and one of few people who knew what it could possibly mean.

Dan looked up at Beth standing alone in the owners' box. He needed to get up there.

"Look," Dan said, beginning to shuffle his feet. "I've got to—"

"I got it!" Lennie shouted. He jumped and reached for Dan, eyes still on the tote board. "I've got it. They're loading the show pool." Lennie shook his head. "Independent sets," he muttered. "Why didn't I think of that?"

"What? So what?"

"Look at the nine, Pinnacle Penny. Look at the show pool. Way too much—"

Ginny stepped forward leaning in to hear Lennie.

"That's Thoroughbred Nostradamus' pick," Dan said. "People probably thinking she may get a piece, but don't want to risk a win bet."

"No way. Look at the amount," Lennie said. "It's pouring in late. They're loading the show pool. Sure they're using the idiot tout to get extra funds to flow there, but this is over the top. Thirty thousand in the last minute. Shit, now fifty thousand. Jesus, never thought I'd see this."

"I don't get it. So what?"

"Shit. Should have thought of this earlier," Lennie muttered, then turned. "About thirty years ago a bunch of college guys at Pimlico pulled this off."

"Pulled off what?"

"They load the show pool on a horse that is absolutely going to run out of the money. It boosts the payoff for the horses that hit the board."

"And?"

"They increase the size of the pool to boost the show payoff."

Dan's forehead wrinkled and eyes squinted. "Yeah, but to get the payoff you have to bet and that evens the odds back out right? The money won on the bet can't outrun the money invested."

"Normally, yes. But these guys loaded the show pool on track at Pimlico, then their buddies on spring break in Vegas bet the favorite to show through the casino. Independent sets. Get it?" Dan's stunned look answered the question. "Instead of paying $2.20 to show," Lennie said. "The horse paid like nine bucks. You get an odds-on favorite to pay nine bucks to run third. It was magnificent."

"Who are they betting?"

"Who do you think? Zaqualina. Think she won't hit the board today?"

"Unlikely. But it can't work, the money bet to show on Zaqualina will reduce the payout. All the money on Pinnacle Penny will be lost. You can't change the odds and make it work."

"That's the beauty of it. Back then, the Vegas casinos didn't commingle bets. They just took bets and paid track odds. Bets in Vegas didn't touch the pool. The betting pools were independent sets."

"But now all tracks commingle bets, so does Vegas. You can't make a bet in North America that isn't commingled."

"They're not making the bets in North America," Ginny said.

Dan's head shot to the right. He'd forgotten Ginny was standing with them.

"Oh my God, they're betting offshore," Dan said. Lennie nodded. "How many books are there offshore?"

"Thousands. And none of them commingle bets," Lennie said. "Same scam. Load the show pool, bet the favorite to show offshore. Zaqualina is going to pay something outrageous to show."

Lennie's lecture with Milt from two weeks before hit him like a sledgehammer. "They're moving the odds," Dan stammered.

Lennie took his eyes away from the tote board and focused on Dan. "They're moving the odds, big time. How much would you bet on Zaqualina if you knew she'd pay three bucks to win and six bucks to show?"

"Shit, probably everything I got. But what's this got to do with Aly Dancer?"

"Don't know. Unless they were going to buy her and make sure she ran off the board. She's second favorite, if they load up on her, people won't notice. If she runs fourth or worse, the payoff gets big—fast."

Dan pulled out Lennie's phone and thumbed Bradford Bennett's number.

Ginny took off in a dead run.

Thirty seconds to post.

Chapter 45

"Stop the race!" Dan screamed into Lennie's cell phone. He looked at the upper reaches of the grandstand as if he could somehow make eye contact with the person he called.

"What? Who is this?" Bradford Bennett the Third said.

"It's Dan Morgan. You have to stop the race."

"What are you talking about? I can't stop it."

Dan quickly explained what Lennie had discovered.

As he was talking the PA system brought the crowd to its feet. "Ladies and gentlemen, it is now Post Time."

Nothing could be heard for several seconds as the cheering crowd gave their approval. He placed his bandaged hand over his other ear, but it didn't help. The Russian voice repeated over and over in his head.

You can't stop it.

"Look at the show pool for Pinnacle Penny," Dan yelled.

Not sure whether Bennett heard him, he started again.

"I heard you. We're looking at it."

"This is the scam Jake discovered. This is why they killed him."

Dan looked up where Beth was standing. One box over contained the Russian, Vasily. He stood calmly, even bored, as he gazed down toward the starting gate.

"Let me see if I understand this. Assuming you are right, and that's a big leap, you want me to stop the race to protect some online bookies that make bets on our races, but don't commingle with our pools. Is that about right? I have an obligation to protect *this* racetrack, not their illicit business."

He was right, but Dan dug in. "You have an obligation to the sport, to the industry. If the favorite pays a bunch more to show than to win, there will be questions and they won't be fun questions for the industry to answer. For you to answer. This sport has fought the perception of corruption and cheating since the first horse race took place. Don't give them your platform. Don't let them use your Kentucky Oaks."

"I'm not sure I can stop the race."

"What do you mean?"

"Once the horses step onto the track, they are under the jurisdiction of the starter until the gates open."

"Call him. He's got a radio. Tell him what's going on. He can stop it."

Bennett's voice disappeared and it sounded like he was talking with others with his hand partially over the receiver. Dan started up the stairs toward Beth. He looked over at the starting gate. They were starting to load the first horses. Damn it.

"Dan?"

"Yeah?"

"No go."

"You've got to!"

"Look with all due respect, Mr. Morgan, this isn't a Wednesday afternoon claiming race at Laurel Park. This is the Kentucky Oaks. We have a nationwide television audience—"

"All the more reason to stop it!" Dan interrupted.

"We have a live TV audience. They have a window in their broadcast schedule for this race. We can't sort this out in that time frame. There'd be too many people to ask. It can't be done. We can't delay that broadcast window. You know how hard it is to get this sport on national television? We can't screw with that. And, I might point out, this all assumes that everything you believe is correct. We even don't know that. If not, we all look like idiots."

"Scratch the nine! Scratch Pinnacle Penny! That's all you have to do. That fixes the pools. It fixes everything."

"We can't do that."

Dan tried to interrupt, but Bennett kept on. "We don't know why that money was bet. But it was bet legally as far as we know. And another thing. How would you feel if another owner was on the phone with me telling me to scratch your horse in a Grade One race right at post time? We'd get sued, you know that."

"Jake died trying to uncover this. He was man enough to risk everything to stop it!" Dan shouted. "Show the same courage he had."

"The race goes off as scheduled."

The phone went dead in Dan's hand.

You can't stop it.

Chapter 46

Loading horses in a starting gate was a rather routine matter. Well, to the extent that handling highly strung, muscle-bound athletes in a confined space could ever be routine.

The gate hand would take the horse from the outrider, walk the horse into the designated stall, step up onto a three inch ledge inside the stall, unclip the strap from the bridle, keep the horse's head straight, and hope for the best until the gates were sprung.

Most animals were well schooled at the process, thus making the gate hand's occupation like that of an anesthesiologist. Hours and hours of boredom interspersed by moments of sheer terror.

Frightened racehorses were known to flip over in the gate, toss a jockey, rip off a hoof, bust out teeth, or otherwise find harm's way while battling an iron and steel captor. The gate hand was just flesh and tender bones locked inside the iron gate. Getting the animal out of the gate in one piece was the desired outcome.

Kyle looked up and watched Zaqualina walk into the gate like a seasoned pro.

That's when the trouble started.

The gate hand had led Aly Dancer to the mouth of the gate. She stopped dead in her tracks. Tugging on the strap was futile. Aly Dancer was propped with hind legs dug in like a reluctant terrier. Two men linked arms and began pushing from behind, but Aly Dancer would have none of it. She kicked with one hind leg, but caught only air. These guys had learned how to stay away from danger.

"Come on Aly. It's okay," Kyle said, giving her a comforting pat on the neck.

"She's not on our problem child list, what gives?" the assistant starter asked, referring to the information provided to the gate crew about temperamental horses with a history of acting up at the starting gate.

"I don't know," said Kyle, futilely urging her forward.

Aly Dancer wasn't going into the gate. Her mind was made up.

~

Beth saw it before the crowd.

"Damn it," she said.

Dan looked over. After having hung up with Bennett he'd raced up the steps to join Beth. Her eyes were glued on the starting gate. He knew it wasn't good.

"She's acting up," Beth muttered. "Aly, don't do this. You're not a head case." They watched the struggle between men and animal. Beth shuffled her feet and appeared as agitated as Aly Dancer. "Something's wrong." She moved out of the box onto the stairway. Dan grabbed her arm.

"What can you do? They'll get her settled."

"Something's wrong. I have to get down there." She tugged her arm loose and ran down the steps toward the track. In seconds she disappeared among the standing throng.

~

"She ever done this before?" the assistant starter asked, trying to keep Aly Dancer straight in line for the gate.

"Never."

A fourth gate hand came over with a long twitch in his hand. Phillipe Calderon turned back from his seat aboard Zaqualina and watched the commotion behind him.

"Don't use the twitch," Kyle yelled. It was a method to prompt the horse to step forward. A few smacks with a slender firm stick, like a frozen bull whip, usually did the trick. It wasn't painful, more of an irritant to make the horse move. "Get that twitch out of here. Circle her, circle her."

The gate hand pulled Aly away from the starting gate and walked back up the track. Kyle was stroking her and talking soothingly. After they circled her several times, they led her to the gate. She propped again. Four other horses were standing in the distance waiting for their chance to load. Aly's antics were delaying the start.

Aly Dancer snorted and threw her head. She tugged back on the gate hand's grip like a Labrador pulling a chew toy.

"Get her in the gate." This came from the starter. "Use the twitch if you have to. I don't want to scratch her, but I will," he said, sternly.

The gate hand gave a shrug to the starter as if to say what do you want me to do?

"Circle her again," Kyle shouted.

The gate hand swung her around again, this time trotting. He turned her toward the gate and rushed her toward it. She went halfway into the stall and stopped. The two men returned, locking arms around her butt, and with their free hands they grabbed the starting gate and muscled her forward. After several seconds of standoff, Aly reluctantly stepped into the gate. The doors slammed shut behind her.

The clip was released from the bridle and the gate hand worked to keep Aly's head straight.

"After all that, she better run good, dude."

"She'll be all right," Kyle said.

Calderon looked over dismissively, like a king perched on a throne. Kyle looked to his right as the other horses calmly moved into the gate. Aly's legs were still propped and she leaned on the doors behind her.

"Come on, Aly. Get on your toes," Kyle whispered. He scratched her neck. "Come on, girl."

~

The man had sunglasses on.

That's what everyone would remember, those who saw him that is. Otherwise he blended perfectly in his official purple windbreaker and gold ball cap. As fans shifted their eyes from the tote board to the starting gate, other suspicious activity went unnoticed.

He smoothly drifted from the grandstand, leaped the fence and put a hand on the photographer who knelt just beyond the starting gate.

Touching people denoted confidence; that one belonged. Such was the code of the grifter and con man.

Sunglass man walked casually around the end of the starting gate. A ball of humanity surrounded the five horse who wasn't having fun at the moment. Four horses in the distance remained tethered to lead ponies. They waited. Everyone waited.

Once the five went into the gate, the assembly line started up again. Outrider to gate hand, gate hand to gate, doors slammed behind them. Bing, bam, boom.

Sunglass man strode up to the nine, Pinnacle Penny. Another gate hand in a purple windbreaker and gold ball cap approached from his right. He was young with a pimpled and pock marked face. Shards of blond hair stuck out and mud had been swiped across his face.

Sunglass man tapped him on the shoulder. There it was again, the touch. "I got this. Looks like they need help over there." He might as well have said, "Look, it's Haley's comet." But with thoroughbreds in the gate, there was always activity. Hard to be wrong with that comment.

"Whatever," the blond said, turning and going back toward the gate.

"Got the winner here?" sunglass man said as he pulled the horse toward the gate.

"You bet," said RD Gomez, the horse's jockey.

You bet, sunglass man laughed to himself. That's funny. You bet.

"One out," sunglass man shouted. This was repeated by several others. Jockeys hunched forward, adjusted their grips, leaned up and forward. The starting gate rocked and creaked its resistance.

Pinnacle Penny walked into the stall like a pro, like

it was a Tuesday morning workout back on the training farm. Sunglass man stepped up onto the ledge on the left side of the horse. RD Gomez was on his toes in the stirrup, bent forward. Being the last horse in, he had to be ready for a quick break.

Sunglass man was supposed to release the leather strap from the bridle. He didn't do that. Then he was to hold the horse's head straight for the break. He didn't do that.

RD Gomez looked at him through six pairs of goggles and puckered his face. Sunglass man was wrapping the leather strap around the iron stanchion on the inside of the stall—around and around and around. He'd effectively tied Pinnacle Penny to the starting gate.

Gomez shouted, "No, no." Several other gate hands and jockeys were crying in unison. A plea that the gate not open until they were ready.

Sunglass man didn't yell, "No, no."

He didn't make a sound at all.

Chapter 47

"Two out!" came the shout from behind Kyle. The gate rattled as horses shifted in their stalls, anxious for the break. Aly Dancer was shying from the front of the gate. Kyle had calmed her somewhat, but she was still reluctant. The gate hand wrestled with her bridle trying to keep her head straight.

"Let her be," Kyle shouted.

The man threw his hands in the air, backing away mere inches. "Fine. Have it your way, pal."

"Just leave her alone. Got her all riled up," Kyle said. He slapped open palms on her withers gently. *I'm here with you, baby. Everything will be okay.* Aly's head was cocked sideways to the left. "It's okay, girl. Time to go to work. That's all." She shifted her weight forward, her back feet sloshing in the mud.

"One out."

Kyle drew the reins in and twisted his fingers in Aly Dancer's mane. He rocked forward, knees in. With a tug she straightened her head and her ears pricked forward.

We have to break on top. Forget Beth. It's the only shot. She'll know I'm right when we win.

"Whoa, whoa," someone shouted to his left. The

starting gate shifted and creaked, its massive unforgiving forged metal resisted to the leaning and bumping of its inhabitants. "No, no, no." This time from the right. Aly Dancer shuffled her forelegs, ears forward. "No, no." Then as Kyle had become accustomed to there was a break of silence. Just a millisecond, but one that seemed to last an eternity.

The silence spoke volumes.

The split-second silence said, "This is it."

~

Pinnacle Penny's jockey, RD Gomez, had shouted the last set of "no's" to the gate crew. The man in the stall glared at him through the darkened glasses. With six pairs of goggles on, Gomez couldn't make out the finer features of the man, but the determination behind the stare said everything.

The gates flew open as bells rang.

Pinnacle Penny surged forward, then slammed sideways into the stall. Her body turned and jammed in the starting stall. Gomez flew upright, his head slamming into the green metal stanchion on the right side of the stall. The horse tried to jerk to the right, but she again slammed into the left side of the stall. Gomez fell back, but held on.

He could hear the field sprinting away from the gate. Disoriented by the head shot, Gomez twisted to stay on the horse. It was like a bull ride at a small town rodeo. Man and animal stuck in a confined space.

The animal lunged, but could not get away from the

gate. All that could be heard was the repeat of the gong when his head hit the gate.

A lifetime later, they were free. One foot was in the stirrup, the other flailed to the side. Within two strides he had his feet back under him, but the field was far, far ahead.

~

Aly Dancer slipped leaving the gate and immediately swerved left. Kyle expected to slam into Zaqualina when his mount lunged, but Zaqualina was gone. They drifted into the empty space she had left behind when she rocketed out of the gate.

~

And they're off. Zaqualina breaks sharply. Abelito on the inside. Lynn's Treasure from the outside. One back to Symbianna, Desert Image, Sunrise Sonnet on the outside. Aly Dancer another two back alongside Nanquette. Pinnacle Penny with a terrible start trails the field by fifteen lengths!

~

Kyle gathered Aly Dancer and straightened course. Quickly she was into stride. The first cold blast of mud and water hit Kyle like frozen buckshot. Aly's head was up swinging side to side as she was taking mouthfuls of dirt and spray.

Kyle shifted right to avoid the onslaught, but a horse next to him bumped them and kept them in the murky spray. He pulled down one pair of blinded goggles, only to have his vision blasted by the next wave of mud.

Jesus, at this rate, six goggles won't make it around the track. Good thing Beth wanted us to lay back. We don't have a fucking choice.

He tightened his grip and let the leaders move away. Kyle hated to lose touch with the front runners, but if he couldn't see what was ahead of them, they were already beaten.

~

Clayton Pinkney held a fist full of tickets. They burned his fingers. He swallowed hard trying to keep the vomit in his stomach. His crime was clutched in his ink-stained hands. Dizzy, he leaned against the wall. Beside him was a low bookshelf. Far down the alley of ticket windows Beckstrom was still on the phone, his back to Pinkney.

Jessie turned, a worried look on her face. Clayton put his hand over his stomach to signal he wasn't feeling well. He hoped she didn't notice the sweat beginning to roll from his hairline into his face.

In the distance a monitor displayed the race. He looked down to confirm the number, but it was etched in his brain. He would never forget the number. Number nine. At the bottom of the screen he spotted the string of numbers showing position in the race. Nine was last. Last, he thought. Figures. The horse wasn't even in the picture she was so far behind.

He covered his mouth as acid tried to escape from his throat. The back of his head hit the wall and his muscles failed him. He slid down the wall, knees collapsed, feet flat until he was bunched below the shelf to his right. Nearly invisible from Beckstrom's view. Only his quaking knees and worn Hush Puppies could be seen. He covered his tearing eyes.

"Oh, God. Arlinda, what have I done?"

~

The gate hands dropped to the ground and exited behind the gate. That is, all but one. The sun-glassed gate hand walked calmly out the front of the starting gate, separating himself from the rest of the crew. The tractor revved up and blew smoke into the air as it began dragging the starting gate off of the track.

"Hey, what the hell happened?" The voice came from behind the gate. It was surely directed to the man in the sunglasses on the front side, but a response was not forthcoming. "Hey, I'm talking to you!"

Sunglass man jogged to the outer rail and, like a gymnast on a pommel horse, vaulted over the rail and over the chain link fence into the grandstand. He didn't look back.

The crowd was shouting and all eyes were focused on the athletes on the track. This allowed the man to run unimpeded into the grandstand and strip off his windbreaker, glasses and hat. These were quickly deposited into the nearest garbage can.

Then the man became invisible, a wall of sound separating him from the race and a mass of bodies into which he merged like smoke. He casually rolled a fifty-cent piece over his knuckles as he vanished in the crowd.

~

Into the first turn, Zaqualina leads by three parts of a length. Abelito just inside. Symbianna and Lynn's Treasure one back. A break of two to Desert Image and Sunrise Sonnet, followed by Aly Dancer and Nanquette. Pinnacle Penny is outrun at this point. Opening quarter in twenty-three and two.

~

Kyle was able to get Aly Dancer into a steady stride and far enough back that the mud splashed on Aly Dancer's chest as it fell to the earth. He looked right and recognized the silks next to him. Nanquette. She was pinned to their side like Velcro. With a little bump, Kyle let Aly Dancer slip to the right for clearer running room. Together they were four lanes off the rail, but the going felt solid. It was the best part of the track, Kyle thought.

He looked ahead and saw a brown spray like several combined rooster tails shooting skyward. Another pair of goggles came down. He could count the horses, but barely identify them by color through the brown haze. He knew Zaqualina was up there somewhere.

Of that, he was certain.

~

Dan had reached the apron of the track when the race went off. Beth was nowhere to be seen. Groups of fans, separated into green metal-framed boxes, stood cheering, arms waving. The field roared past where he stood, but he could only catch glimpses of silks screaming past from the narrow spaces between the humanity.

Within the din, he heard Aly Dancer's name from the PA system, but he didn't have any context around it. Just her name floating in the air. *Where is she?* He scanned the area, turning completely around. No Beth. To his left a walkway led to the inside of the grandstand. He turned and rushed that direction away from the racetrack.

~

Zaqualina continues to lead by one. Symbianna has moved into second, Abelito on the rail. Break of two to Lynn's Treasure and Sunrise Sonnet. Two lengths back to Desert Image. Aly Dancer and Nanquette beginning to rally on the outside. Half mile in forty-seven and one.

~

Inside the grandstand, Dan spotted her. Beth was standing alone, head cocked up staring at a TV monitor. He ran over to her. She didn't pull her eyes away from the monitor. Despite the clamor he could hear her murmuring. "It's okay, girl. Everything's okay."

"How's she doing?" Dan said, interrupting her self-talk.

Beth glanced over quickly, then back to the monitor. "Nearly fell coming out of the gate, got hammered with mud spray for a quarter mile, went four wide on the first turn, but other than that, everything's perfect." As if to brighten the mood, Beth added. "They're going too fast up front."

Dan knew not to follow up. He could barely identify his own silks on the high definition monitor. The horse and rider were covered in brown muck. Somehow enough of the number "five" on the saddle cloth had survived.

She's never been behind like this. She's never seen this kind of competition, these conditions, this pressure.

I should have never started her in the race. Beth was hesitant, but I finessed her into it. Made her feel guilty if we didn't run. Stupid.

My ego put Aly in this place.

My stupid ego.

Selfish.

Chapter 48

Four furlongs to go and Zaqualina is clear by three. Symbianna's next. Lynn's Treasure just outside of her. Two back to Desert Image. Sunrise Sonnet inside her and Aly Dancer on the outside.

~

Dan's heart sank as he saw Zaqualina pull away from the field. She was as good as they said after all. "There she goes," he said quietly, not looking at Beth. He didn't need to tell her which horse he was watching.

Beth crossed her arms and stood defiantly. "She moved too soon."

Dan stood breathlessly. Beth was rocking back and forth slightly. She nodded her head forward as if counting. One Mississippi, two Mississippi. Then she tensed. "Now, Kyle!" she screamed. "Let her go!"

~

Kyle had Aly Dancer in a firm part of the racetrack, four wide from the rail. She had settled and was now running with purpose. He clucked to Aly Dancer and loosened the reins slightly. She took the hint, bowing her neck and lengthening her stride. They had a lot of ground to make up. Through his fourth pair of goggles he saw Phillipe Calderon's perfectly clean silks on the perfectly clean Zaqualina. They were extending their lead.

God, I hate that guy.

~

Out of the turn and into the stretch Zaqualina has four lengths on the field. Lynn's Treasure and Symbianna battling for second. Desert Image is…and on the extreme outside Aly Dancer is moving powerfully. Zaqualina leads. Lynn's Treasure on the inside, Symbianna…Now Aly Dancer moves past them. A quarter of a mile to go.

~

Kyle had no choice but to go wide. Two horses were losing pace down near the rail and their pursuers had staked positions outside them. It was one big mud ball and none of them were gaining ground on the leader.

Aly was moving now; trying to take her inside would stall her momentum. He shook the reins and she snorted her approval. Her ears were pinned back. She was ready for a fight. Giving that much ground to a loose front runner was crazy, but it was the only clear path he had.

"Come on," he shouted, grinding his knuckles along her neck. "Get 'em, girl."

Aly Dancer's momentum caused her to drift farther right, but she circled the mud ball. For the first time, they had a clear view ahead. Zaqualina was far ahead, well to their left. Kyle tugged down a pair of goggles. Nothing but open racetrack ahead of them.

As they straightened out of the turn a wall of sound hit them like a crashing wave. Kyle had heard about it among jockey tales, but this was his first encounter with it. His heart surged.

He pulled the whip and twirled it in a three hundred and sixty degree arc like a baton. He adjusted his weight. Aly Dancer changed leads perfectly like it was a morning exercise, but this was no exercise. She was all out. Kyle could feel her surging beneath him. They still had a long way to go.

~

"There it is," Beth yelled. "Come on, Aly. Go get her."

Dan was speechless. A ball the size of a grapefruit was in his throat. He couldn't swallow. He wasn't sure if his heart was even beating.

Beth uncrossed her arms and pounded a fist forward screaming at the TV monitor. "Take her down, Aly. Take her down." The grandstand sounded like a jet airplane on takeoff. Cheers, jeers and shouts all came together in a symphony of passion.

~

Down the stretch they come. Zaqualina leads. Aly Dancer challenging down the center of the racetrack. Two back to Nanquette and Desert Image.

~

Dan body-englished sideways as if he could shorten the distance between the two horses. Too far behind, too much ground to make up. He leaned further. "She's not going to make it," he whispered to himself. Beth was the only person who could hear him above the din.

"Like hell she won't," she shouted. "Come on, baby. Come on, Aly. You can do this!"

~

Kyle snapped her twice on the right side. Aly dug in. They were gaining, but they weren't going to make it in time. He switched hands and hit her on the left side. He knew she was giving all she had. They'd shifted through every gear. All that was left was heart.

He looked over at Zaqualina. Calderon was whipping furiously. Zaqualina was so far to Kyle's left that he couldn't gauge the distance. Two lengths? Maybe less?

He put his head down and pumped with the reins. His belly was flat against Aly and he scrubbed and pushed her neck with each stride. Her mud soaked mane slapped him as her head flew back on each stride. Fingers splayed, he pushed on her neck, pressing so hard his fingers could snap off at the knuckle.

Every ounce of energy was devoted to moving forward, no wasted effort.

Just ride it out. She's flat out.

His arms ached, his thighs burned. Mud ground against his teeth. His nose was caked over. He didn't dare look left.

Push, push.
Don't look left.
Farther, farther.
Don't look left.
To be so close. God, so, so close.

We won't make it. The ache in his gut was like a fifty kiloton bomb. The sensation wasn't fear. Fear was merely an emotion, like anger or happiness. Emotions went away. It wasn't physical. Though he could easily vomit his empty stomach out, what ached wasn't physical. What ached was his DNA screaming out in every direction, his very soul.

The ache in his gut meant he'd worked his whole life to be in this spot. To be right here, to be this close. He'd worked through pain, muscle tears, broken bones, insults, self-doubt and insecurity—just to be in this one spot. In this position he either broke through or would forever be an obscure answer to a trivia question.

What team lost to the Green Bay Packers in the first Super Bowl? The correct answer was, "Who gives a shit? The Packers were world champions."

The other team was made up of guys who almost won. Almost won, as in lost.

Your DNA knew. It always knew. You could never outrun your DNA. Your DNA would mark you as the guy who almost made it. Kyle didn't want to be that guy. The guy who almost made it.

In that moment there were two paths. The first led to desperation. That was always the wrong way. Desperation permits failure and error. The other path was called urgency.

Urgency was focused, precise, deliberate. It was relentless. Urgency was a drug. Urgency allowed a man to single-handedly lift an automobile off an injured child. Urgency allowed a soldier to carry a battle-scarred comrade two miles to safety, only to learn after the march that his ankle was shattered in the fire-fight.

Urgency was a drug.

You could not create it. You could not conjure it. You certainly could not buy it. No one else could hand it to you. Yes, urgency was a drug.

Only one thing was true.

When you were in that moment, when you were on the precipice, if you were worthy, there was a chance, a glimmer. You didn't find urgency.

Urgency found you.

"Come on, girl." He strained with every fiber. He pushed with everything he had. "Come on!"

Keep her straight. Ride her out. Don't look left. Just ride. Just ride like your life depends on it.

Because it does.

~

A sixteenth of a mile to go Zaqualina leads by two. Aly Dancer charging on the extreme outside. The mile in one thirty nine flat. It'll be these two to the wire. Zaqualina holding gamely. Aly Dancer absolutely flying down the middle of the track. At the wire, it's....

Chapter 49

The cheering reached a throbbing peak, then crashed. It was one of the oddities of nature. A horse race was an event that could produce fevered shouts one moment and, a split second later, silence or muttering sounds. For those in the grandstand it was too close to call. Those few on the finish line or with the benefit of a TV monitor knew. The hush meant thousands were wondering who won. For those in the right place, the answer was obvious.

Dan and Beth merely stood there. Beth had tears running down her face.

Several seconds passed in stunned silence, then Dan turned and whispered, "Oh my God. We did it."

Beth fell against him. "She did it," she whispered, between tears.

He hugged her tightly, wanting to squeeze her right through his body to the other side. Dan put his good hand over her blonde hair and pressed her to him. "You did it."

She shook her head, rubbing against his shoulder. A full on cry was now in progress. "Jake did it."

The embrace was an eternity. It held so much more than a horse race, a relationship, a deceased friend. It was an exhale after being submerged for four minutes. It was a release. Beth's sobs subsided. She pulled away and wiped her eyes.

Dan cocked his head toward the track. "I think we're supposed to be in a photograph or something, I don't know." Beth laughed and brushed back her hair. "At least that's what they tell me."

A mass of jubilant bettors raced toward them as they entered the narrow corridor leading to the track apron. Shouts, fist pumps, and eager voices swamped them as they swam against the current. None of them knew who Dan and Beth were. None of them cared.

They fought their way into the daylight and the post-race frenzy. Lennie, out on the track, was jumping and high-fiving any hand that came near him. There were many. The other grooms shared his exuberance. If they couldn't beat the big horse, they wanted someone else to and Lennie was the centerpiece.

Dan yelled as they entered the track. Lennie turned and rushed to them, hugging Beth and Dan like they'd just returned from overseas combat.

The PA system clicked on and the buzz kill for all winners blasted over the address system. "The inquiry sign has been posted on the tote board. Ladies and gentlemen, please hold all tickets."

"No fucking way!" Lennie screamed. Dan wasn't sure if he'd ever heard his friend utter a profanity, but the message was the same in Dan's mind.

"We weren't within forty feet of that horse," Beth said. "Can't be us."

"Can't be." Lennie was quick to agree.

None of the numbers were flashing on the tote board, which would indicate the horses involved in the inquiry.

That was of mild comfort. To the joy of Team Aly Dancer, the number five was on top of the board.

"It was the nine," Lennie shouted. "She didn't break with the field. That's the only thing the inquiry could be about. It sure as heck isn't about Aly. She flat won that race. She flat won it outright, no question."

The horses were beginning to return to the unsaddling area. They would have to wait for Aly Dancer. Dan saw Chick Mangold in a furious conversation with his groom. His arms waved, accompanied by sharp words that were thankfully drowned out by the louder and closer voices of celebration. Mangold looked up the track and made eye contact with Dan. Then he quickly shifted his gaze to the distance, waiting for Zaqualina to return. Dan smiled. The one glimpse was all he needed.

The PA announcer cracked the microphone again. "Ladies and gentlemen, the inquiry involves number nine, Pinnacle Penny. The order of finish will not be affected. Hold all mutuel tickets."

"Told ya," Lennie said, with gusto. "We're a winner! She's a winner!"

Dan watched Mangold lift his cowboy hat and run his hand over his perfectly groomed head. His eyes dropped and he walked toward them. Beth and Lennie were engaged in a fervent discussion of their own, the only discernible language was joy. Lennie gestured like he was riding Aly Dancer and waved his arm sideways indicating 'get to the rail.' Then he laughed and hugged Beth again.

A hand touched Beth's shoulder. It was Mangold. She turned with tears of joy on her cheeks. "Congratulations, Miss DeCarlo," he said, hat in hand and with no emotion.

Beth nodded and tucked her blonde hair behind one ear.

Mangold shook his head. "Hell of a race," he said under his breath. Then turned and walked back toward his groom. Other trainers slapped Beth on the back and offered handshakes. The battle was done, to the victor the spoils.

"That had to have killed him," Dan said.

She nodded again, fighting to keep from laughing out loud. "I was just wondering if I'd have done the same."

As was the custom at Churchill, the winning horse waited until all others had returned to the unsaddling area before prancing back from the far side of the track. In the distance, Dan could see Kyle fist-pumping in the air alongside an outrider and a journalist on horseback foisting a microphone in Kyle's direction.

The inquiry sign on the tote board flashed off. The PA system crackled to life again. "Ladies and gentlemen, due to difficulties with the starting gate and by order of the track stewards, number nine, Pinnacle Penny, has been declared a non-starter. All wagers made on number nine, Pinnacle Penny, will be redeemed. Again, number nine, Pinnacle Penny has been declared a nonstarter by the track stewards. All wagers on Pinnacle Penny can be refunded at all ticket counters."

A roar went up from the grandstand. Thoroughbred Nostradamus' followers will get their money back, Dan thought. Bennett did the right thing. Someone did, he thought.

Nonstarter. Dan smiled and looked up to the sky. Thank you Billy Barton. He promised to rub the statue next time he was at Laurel Park. Hell, maybe he'd take a picture. Billy Barton, he thought. Why you?

As was also the custom at Churchill Downs, the crowd stood and applauded as Aly Dancer made her triumphant return to the grandstand. Those in attendance were not merely bettors, they were fans of the sport and whether they cashed a bet or not, they stood and applauded. Dan found himself caught up in the frenzy as Kyle and Aly Dancer reached Lennie.

Kyle let out a whoop in full throat, fists in the air. The crowd responded in kind. Lennie high-fived him. Kyle's attempt at the high-five was such a roundhouse that he nearly flew off Aly Dancer's back. Once settled, he offered one to Beth as well. In her off hand she squeezed a sponge over Aly Dancer's head and cleared the mud from the filly's face. Aly threw her head up and down.

Kyle was talking a mile a minute and gesturing left and right as he recounted the race.

"That's Lennie's job," Dan said from behind Beth as she cleaned the area around Aly's eyes and nose.

Holding the bridle, she turned, smiling. "Once a groom, always a groom."

Lennie handed Kyle a water bottle. With his helmet resting on his thighs, he doused his head from the water bottle, scrubbed the muck from his face, then returned his mud sprayed helmet. Another whoop was unfurled.

Dan had lived for this one moment. Like all critical times in life—weddings, graduations, acceptance speeches—time accelerated and it was over.

Poof.

Participants struggled to slow it down, make it last. Make the moment last forever.

It never does.

The activities were a blur; the winners' circle, the

garland of stargazer lilies, the trophy presentation, the pictures, the microphones, the cameras, the handshakes from track officials and the Governor.

It all ended in a finger snap.

The one thing that lingered was the vision of Beth's calm graciousness. She gave all credit to Jake.

"Jake Gilmore was Aly Dancer's trainer, not me," she'd said. "I just led her over. All credit goes to him—and to Kyle-—and to the owner for giving me a chance. Someday I hope to accept the thanks, but not today."

Dan's smile nearly stretched over his ears. His heart was going to spontaneously burst—inevitable like a water balloon in mid-flight. He didn't care. This was that "God, take me now" moment. It didn't get any better than this.

Beth's words made his throat catch and eyes water.

Nobody noticed. Nobody, except her.

Chapter 50

They were alone again—the three of them, along with Aly Dancer making their way to the backside. Lennie continued exhorting the crowd and thrusting his fist in the air.

Aly Dancer's coat glistened in the sunlight. She threw her head up and down as if to say, "You want a piece of me?" She knew what she had done. Stack all those books on limited equine intelligence and animal instinct and set them on fire.

She knew she had done something special.

She knew she was special.

Saddle, riding cloth and weights had been removed. She carried the mantle of the champion, the garland of stargazer lilies. Tomorrow, the winner would get roses, but on Oaks day it was Lily for the Filly.

Splashing sounds pursued them. The noise originated at the Churchill Villages, a mini-grandstand and set of suites along the first turn of the racetrack. Seats were at such a premium at Churchill for the Derby and occasional Breeders' Cup that the grandstand was extended around the first turn. This was the Villages.

The sloshing grew closer; neither Dan nor Beth

noticed it, still caught up in the heady mist of being a Grade One winner. Lennie was giving a fervent lecture to Aly Dancer. She didn't seem to mind. She swaggered like a curvy celebrity on a red carpet.

The sloshing came nearer. A hand reached out to Beth's shoulder. She gasped and spun around.

"Skip Wilson, Daily Racing Form."

With hand over her heart, Beth said, "I know who you are."

"Congratulations. Big win."

"Thank you." Beth was getting better at these interviews. The rough edges from her early media exposure had been ground down. She was still far from being a pro, Dan knew, but big improvement.

Wilson moved quickly and stepped between Beth and Dan. He displayed his hand-held recording device as if to say, "You okay with this?" Hearing no objection, he clicked it on.

"Beth, did you want to be back so far early or did the poor break dictate your position?"

Beth considered the question for several steps. "I told Kyle to find a good part of the track and run his race. She's a very versatile filly. She doesn't need to lead and she proved that today."

"Were you concerned about going head to head with Zaqualina early?" He pointed the recorder toward Beth, though not in a threatening way.

Beth looked down at her shoes. They made sucking sounds as she extracted them for the next step. "I wasn't concerned with any particular horse in the field. Except mine. I wanted her to get a good position and run her race. If she did that everything would work out. And it did."

"I saw Chick Mangold come over to you after the race. What did he say?" The man seemed intent to draw blood somehow.

"He said it was a hell of a race. And he's right about that. He congratulated me…us. He's a gentleman. It wasn't easy for him to do that. Would have been very easy just to go on and not say a word, but he didn't. Have to credit him for that."

"Mangold said you were able to get on a firmer part of the track and that made all the difference."

Dan could see the ire start to rise in Beth. "Well, he's right. I think Kyle did find a firmer part of the track. I'll give you that. But Zaqualina had things all her own way. We didn't. She ran a mile and an eighth. Aly Dancer ran, I don't know, nearly a mile and a quarter…and still beat her. So yeah, we had the better of the track. She ran a shorter distance. We still beat her."

"Calderon said that because Aly Dancer was so wide, Zaqualina couldn't see her until it was too late. That if she had seen your horse, she would have dug in and held on. What do you think?"

Dan knew this was spiraling out of control. He reached over and touched Wilson's arm. Beth caught his eye; their minds met. It was like being tagged out in an all-star wrestling match.

"What Calderon meant to say," Dan said—the 'meant' came out a bit more sarcastic than he'd hoped—"was that Aly Dancer flew by him so fast, they didn't even see her."

"With respect, Mr. Morgan, I don't think that's what Phillipe was trying to say."

Dan spotted a smirk on Beth's face, and he continued. "I don't think I've ever seen anyone say it was unfair to go by another horse so quickly that they couldn't respond. Sounds like chicken shit to me. When did we start this thing where you have to slow down and let the leader 'dig in' and hold on? Loser talk if you ask me."

If there were going to be quotes sent around the barns tomorrow, better that they be Dan's and not Beth's. She needed to be diplomatic. Dan was a stranger to the backside. He didn't need to mark his words. He wanted Beth to know that he could play that part. To say all the pissed off, angry things she couldn't say—publicly. It was another yin and yang of their relationship.

Wilson's head snapped back as though insulted. Dan picked up on it. "Zaqualina didn't have so much as a daisy in her path to the finish line. And I mean the whole race. They had every option open to them. Aly Dancer got jostled at the start. Fell behind. Something she's never experienced, mind you. Ate mud and dirt for three quarters of the race." His voice was rising like a symphony ready to pop an ending. "And we still won. We still beat her. So they can make all the freaking excuses they want. We beat her straight up. We beat her fair and square. She had the better trip and we still beat her." As if it wasn't enough, he tossed in another, "We still beat her."

Wilson's face spread into a smile. He either liked Dan's remarks or liked that he was getting some great quotes for his story. Controversy sells, blood sells, he was getting a Red Cross donation right here.

Dan needed to calm the waters. He'd said his piece, taken the focus off Beth. He needed to end it by making peace with the racing brotherhood. "Listen, I don't mean to sound arrogant. I just feel like my horse ran a hell of a race and deserves to be the focus. Not the horse we beat."

Wilson nodded and after a few strides he clicked off the recorder. "That's fair." He appeared content to walk along to the backside. "It was a hell of a race, quite an upset," Wilson said off handedly.

Beth stopped dead in her tracks. Dan and Skip Wilson turned back after two strides.

"What did you say?" Beth demanded.

"I, uhm, I said hell of a race."

"No." She twirled her wrist. "After that."

"Oh, uhm, quite an upset." Noticing heat boiling up in Beth, he shrugged. His thumb passively hit the record button as he walked. "What? Just making an observation."

"Goddamn it," she shouted. "It wasn't an upset. I don't know how many times I have to tell you this." Her hands went up like summoning the gods. "But my horse has never been beat. Never. You got that? Take out your little pencil and memo pad. Write that down. This horse has never been beat. Write that down. Write it on your forehead. Never, never, never. Got it?" Then she muttered under her breath, "Jeepers."

Dan burst out laughing, as did Wilson eventually, though timidly and somewhat defensively. Beth couldn't help but smile as she tucked her hair behind one ear.

"Yes, ma'am—" he began, then seemed to catch himself. "Yes, Miss DeCarlo, I think I got it."

Miss DeCarlo? Dan thought.

Don't like the sound of that. Not at all.

Second time I've heard that today.

Might have to change that.

Chapter 51

The darkness filled with laughter. A light from the trainer's office and a distant street lamp provided the only illumination. They sat in the grass just off the shedrow walking ring. Two Dom Perignon bottles lay as dead soldiers off the side of the blanket.

Dan had Beth nestled in his arms. Lennie, Ginny and Kyle were sprawled on the ground. Between them a half disassembled case of beer grew progressively smaller. The garland and blanket were folded over the railing outside of Aly's stall.

Kyle called for another beer, then motioned toward Lennie. "So tell me again how this scam is supposed to go down."

Lennie chuckled. "Seems to me there must be a law against me talking to a jockey about a race scam."

"Come on. How's it supposed to work?"

Lennie leaned over onto one elbow. "Independent sets are—"

"Lennie. Stop," yelled Dan. "English, please."

After clearing his throat, Lennie started up. "Okay. Let me try this. In a normal situation, if you bet two dollars on a favorite like Zaqualina to show, what would you get back?"

"Two ten," Kyle said.

"Right. Five cents on the dollar. Now, if you wanted to bet a million dollars to show, your money is in the betting pool. It takes the odds down, so you want to bet your million someplace outside the pool."

"Okay," Kyle said. "So they bet with an overseas sports book, UK book."

"Essentially anyone outside the pool who will take a bet on the race," Lennie said. "So your money isn't driving down the odds. It's off the books. Independent sets. What happens is they flood the pool on a horse that they know is likely to run off the board. That increases the odds of your show bet. And they really flooded it here."

"But they had to bet a bunch on the horse to run out of the money, don't they?" Kyle asked.

"Sure," Dan said. "And that Thoroughbred Nostradamus hoax aided that. Guy should end up behind bars. He had to be in on it."

Lennie continued the lesson. "But let's say you put one hundred thousand into the show pool on the out-of-the-money horse. Based upon the size of the Oaks pool, quick math says Zaqualina would have paid at least six bucks to show. All the show payoffs would have been huge. So rather than your million bucks yielding fifty thousand, it yields two million. Big difference."

"Worth killing over," Dan said.

"So you can see," Lennie said. "The hundred thousand you put down to load the pool was returned many times over. The hundred thousand was just dead money."

"But, if you don't hit the board?" Kyle said.

"Then you're totally screwed," Lennie finished for him. "They didn't count on that happening, but a bad step, a broken leg, a slipped saddle. There's no sure thing."

It grew silent as they pondered the possibilities. Aly Dancer poked her head out of the stall and snorted.

"Why the Oaks?" Kyle asked.

"Because they controlled the favorite," Dan said.

"We don't know that," said Lennie. He exchanged a look with Dan. "But if I had to bet, I'd agree with you on that. They picked the Oaks for several reasons. First it is one of the only Grade One races run on a Friday. You know, outside of the Breeders' Cup. The betting pool is smaller than most Grade Ones."

"And," Dan said. "It's on national TV, so the stews can't delay the race because of the broadcast window. Even if they knew something was up."

Lennie pointed at Dan. "Bingo. And overseas books know it's a big event, so the action on the race makes sense. Not like they're betting on a Wednesday claiming race at Penn National. It's the perfect race. The perfect storm for pulling this off." The words trailed off into the darkness. They drank quietly.

In the distance, shadows of stable hands crossed the roadway. Minutes before, many had stopped to give their congratulations. Now they were just shapes headed for slumber.

Dan grabbed Beth's shoulder and shook her playfully. "Hey, you should be bouncing around like Christmas morning." She smiled and leaned away embarrassed. "Let's see," Dan said. "As a trainer you have one starter and one winner...in a Grade One race at Churchill Downs for crying out loud. That's a pretty fair win percentage. Don't you think?"

"And your ROI per starter is pretty impressive," Lennie noted.

"Ever the stat man, aren't you Lennie?" Dan said. "Can't give it up."

"You know how many trainers never run in a Grade One race in their lifetimes, much less win one?" Ginny said, cracking open a fresh beer. "I think your phone's going to be ringing the next few days with new owners."

Beth blushed and shook her head.

"Miss DeCarlo," Kyle said, mocking with prayerful hands. "I'll give you first call to ride anything in your barn."

"Oh, that reminds me," Beth said. "I get to curse and call you a pinhead now, don't I? See I'm still getting used to this whole trainer thing."

They laughed and pulled on their drinks. Beth suddenly turned somber.

"Your win, Beth," Dan said.

"That's what the books will say. But plenty of folks will think that Jake's training just hadn't worn off yet." A small smile eased across her face and she looked away.

"Fair enough," Dan said. "Next time it's all on you."

"I'll take that bet," she said.

"It's a beautiful world," Dan said, looking up into the night sky. "Aly got her first Grade One win. So did you," Dan said, pointing at Kyle. "So did I." Dan cocked his head in mock humility. "Lennie made money today, course he always does." He stretched his arms out, yawning.

They sat silently for several moments, their smiles lingering.

"Here's to Aly Dancer," Beth said.

Drinks were hoisted in her direction.

"Wait," Dan said quietly. "I've got one." They looked at him as he paused. Dan raised his beer. "Here's to Jake Gilmore." They nodded. "He was a good man."

"Helluva good man" Ginny said.

They toasted the air and took a drink.

"Guy gave me a chance," Kyle said. "Not many people like that."

"Me too," Beth said softly.

For this group it wasn't the night before the Derby; it was the night before a friend's funeral.

Dan stirred and sat upright. "I made a phone call after the race." All eyes went to him. "Rachel Compton."

"Who's that?" Lennie asked.

"Jake's sister. Wanted her to check with the family." He paused and flicked straw off his trousers. "If it was all right with them, I wanted Jake's casket to be covered with the garland." He thumbed over his shoulder at the stargazer lilies. "Want him to be buried with them. The man earned the right."

Beth teared up and nodded her head. She set down her beer and hugged him tightly around the neck.

As the owner I'm entitled to keep them, Dan thought. But that would be just plain selfish.

And that's just not who I am.

Not anymore.

~

Two miles across town Tad Stapleton was enduring a verbal tirade.

Part Russian, part English, mostly profane, Vasily was taking turns screaming at Tad and Sergei Cheskov in person and Mickey on a cell phone. His face was red and veins pulsated along one temple.

Tad wondered if the guests in the suite next door were picking up every word. Vasily apparently didn't care.

"I wanted that fucking horse bought. You fucked that up," Vasily said pointing at Sergei. "I had this whole thing set up perfectly. You and Anton fucked it up."

"You still made money V," Tad said. The instant he spoke he knew it was a mistake. Sergei glared over at Tad as if to say "why?"

It was a cat-like move. One second Vasily was standing in the middle of the suite, the next he'd slammed Tad against the wall. Vasily gripped Tad's throat in one hand, the cell phone was in the other.

Tad had always feared Vasily. Feared his dead eyes and flash of anger. This was it. He'd gone too far. Tad's arms raised to half-mast in surrender. Vasily's vise-like hand closed both air and blood flow. The dead eyes were locked on Tad, frighteningly unemotional.

Tad dared not strike at the man. Bad would spin into deadly. He looked into Vasily's eyes. Tad's chest was burning, lurching for air. His mind numbed, throbbing. This was it. This was the end.

With a flick of the wrist Vasily tossed him to the ground like a cigarette butt. Tad crumpled and stayed down. Eyes watering and gasping for breath, he knew not to get up, even if he could.

"I made fucking five percent, you putz. Should have made a hundred percent, hell even more if you guys did your jobs right. That means you cost me at least a ninety-five percent return. You fucked it all up. You cut my profit, you morons. I don't consider that making money."

Vasily turned to the cell phone. "Mickey pull in all the accounts, close them all out. Put half in the Canadian account and half in Cayman." He drew two deep breaths, but couldn't stop himself. "Motherfuckers."

Mickey must have said something because Vasily stopped and listened. "Okay, do it."

He slapped the phone shut, dropped it on the marble floor and stomped on it until it was unrecognizable. As he walked away, he pointed at Tad. "Clean that up." Tad didn't have to be asked twice. Before he walked into the bedroom suite, Vasily turned to Sergei.

"Offer him a million five."

"Million five won't get her," Sergei said timidly. "Not after winning the Oaks."

Vasily stared through Sergei, then turned to Tad. Time stood still. Vasily slowly pointed toward Sergei. "You want to end up like Anton?"

The question didn't require an answer. Sergei shook his head anyway.

"Offer the million five," Vasily said. "If he doesn't take it…kill him."

Author's Note

I love reading fiction. I love it almost as much as I enjoy writing it. One persistent thought I have when reading though, is "Could that *really* happen?"

I can suspend reality for a well spun science fiction tale if the story has some thread of reality. In a murder mystery I'll wonder whether a person can really die that way. Can a bullet really do that? Are the clues contrived?

You get my point.

So as a reader you may have a question and I'll ask it for you.

Could the scam described in *Dead Money* really happen?

It already has—many times.

Some were documented and investigated, others existed below the radar.

As long as there are non-commingled betting opportunities, there will always be the chance for manipulation of pari-mutuel pools.

One of the more renowned scandals occurred in January of 1932. Aqua Caliente was a racetrack in its infancy. Located in Tijuana Mexico, just a stone's throw from the US border, it became a haven for Southern California gamblers.

Agua Caliente was famous for another reason.

It was one of the first racetracks in the world with automatically calculated pari-mutuel betting. Prior to this feature, gamblers made fixed odds bets with bookmakers at the track. Pari-mutuel betting grouped all the bets together and recalculated the odds every minute. No matter what the odds were at the time a bet was made, the payoff was determined by the pari-mutuel odds at post time.

Aside from being a boon to betting efficiency at the racetrack, there was a side benefit the track officials didn't count on. Bookmakers could now take bets on Agua Caliente races. Prior to pari-mutuel betting, the bookmaker had to create his own betting line for odds on a given race. Pari-mutuel betting opened the door to bookmakers to simply take bets and pay track odds.

If a patron wanted to bet fifty dollars on the seven horse in the fourth race at Agua Caliente, it was a bet. The bookmaker and gambler could look up the results the next day in the newspaper and pay off the bet, or not depending upon the outcome.

Baron Long, businessman and part owner of Agua Caliente racetrack was furious at the northern bookmakers. In Long's mind, they were taking revenue from the track. Rather than travel to the racetrack, gamblers could stay home and place bets on Agua Caliente races with their local bookmaker. Baron Long was going to make an example of them.

He travelled north and located several of the biggest bookmakers of the time. Being away from the track, Baron Long wanted to know if he could place some action with them. Being dutiful and compassionate entrepreneurs, the bookmakers agreed. Long bet several thousand dollars among several bookmakers. The bets were all to win on a horse named Linden Tree.

To their credit, the bookies had done their homework and had little to worry about. Linden Tree was a huge favorite and had morning line odds of 1-3. This meant that if those odds held at post time, a three dollar bet to win would yield one. One thousand dollars bet to win would garner $1333 if Linden Tree actually won the race. Not a big risk for the bookmakers, so they readily took Baron Long's action.

Two minutes to post time of Linden Tree's race, someone on track at Agua Caliente made several huge bets—thousands of dollars to win, on every entry—except Linden Tree. The on track odds for Linden Tree shot up. The race went off. Linden Tree won handily.

Linden Tree, a horse that was supposed to pay $2.60 for a two dollar win bet, paid twenty dollars to win. A bookmaker that took $1000 of Baron Long's action had planned to pay out $1333 if the horse won. Now they owed $10,000 for every thousand dollar bet.

Baron Long had made his point.

In some circles a bet with a non-commingled bookmaker became known as a Linden Tree bet.

Another name for the scam was a "Dog Out Bet." It is based upon the same principles, but targets the place and show pools rather than the win pool.

On July 16, 1981 a middle aged man in a gabardine suit walked up to the betting window at Pimlico racetrack three minutes to post for the third race. He wagered $5000 to show on a horse named Mister's Mistress. Then he made a similar bets on long shots in the sixth and seventh races.

The man in the gabardine suit presumably had a bad day. But the scam wasn't in Maryland, it was in Las Vegas. Like the situation with Baron Long and the bookmakers,

Las Vegas did not commingle bets with US racetracks until the 1990's. This made Las Vegas books susceptible to a Linden Tree style bet. Friends of the gabardine suited man had a very good day in Las Vegas, cashing bets on favorites that paid more to show than they did to win.

In the third race, favorite My Edelweiss paid 3.40 to win, 2.40 to place and 4.40 to show.

The seventh race was where they made their biggest strike. Noble Side won paying 3.60 to win, 3.40 to place and 9.40 to show.

The man in Maryland manipulated the show pools, his friends in Las Vegas bet and cashed at track odds. Their bets were outside the commingled pool and therefore did not lower the odds on their chosen horse.

Although casinos executives are loath to talk about losses and betting scams, Hank Heffron, manager of the sports book at Barbary Coast Casino said, "They got us. They made a bunch of bets and probably hit every book in town." When asked if the casino honored the wagers, Heffron said, "Yeah, we cashed them. But it won't happen again."

Really?

As long as there are non-commingled betting services that pay track odds, there will be the risk of a Linden Tree or Dog Out scam.

As any good reader of fiction, you still might be suspicious. You may think technology has changed, that speed of information forecloses scams like this. Las Vegas bets are now part of the commingled pools. Digital fingerprints make illicit bets harder to pull off.

You would be right.

But if you're convinced that a Linden Tree or Dog

Out bet won't work in today's environment, check out the fifth race at Thistledown Racetrack on May 21, 2012.

Also by Steve O'Brien

Redemption Day

They shall be for you a refuge from the avenger of blood. He shall flee to one of these cities and shall stand at the entrance of the gate of the city and explain his case to the elders of that city. Then they shall take him into the city and give him a place, and he shall remain with them. (The Holy Bible, English Standard Version, Joshua 20:3-4)

Prologue

Killing by an empowered government was deemed justice. Be it a convicted death row inmate or an unfortunate battlefield enemy, death was righteous. David Allen Wolfe agreed with the premise. Where he disagreed was with which government was authorized.

That made all the difference.

Wolfe grabbed the long neck and killed the remainder of his beer. A loud burp erupted, and he signaled the waitress for another round. He leaned forward on his elbows and scratched his three-day-old stubble. Two men sat across from him. At six foot four and two hundred forty pounds of twitching muscle, Wolfe towered over them even while seated.

"You got wheels, Brother Kevin?" Wolfe asked.

Kevin Landers nodded. "I got a guy."

"I don't give a shit if you got a guy. Do you have the vehicles?"

"Yeah, Jesus, yeah, I got the vehicles," Landers said at first looking at Wolfe, then staring down at his beer bottle.

"This is getting serious. We gotta have clean communications. I don't need no bullshit. I ask you something, you tell me. Got it?"

"Yes, sir," Landers said sheepishly.

The waitress, a chunky blonde trying desperately to look like she was still in her twenties, placed three more beers on the table. As she reached forward to gather the empties, Wolfe slipped his hand up her backside. She jumped forward and jerked away, giving him a stern look. Wolfe laughed heartily and blew her a kiss.

"The fuck you laughing at?" Wolfe said to Gibson, the smallest of the three with round wire rim glasses framing his eyes like fishbowls. Gibson stuck the beer bottle into his mouth to wipe the grin.

Though early afternoon, the tavern was dank and shadowed, a hole with a small bar, where two geezers occupied all but one seat. One vacant booth separated the trio from the front door that hung precariously on worn hinges. Chicken wire covered the sparse windows, and mildew was the fragrance of the day.

The waitress was the only thing about the place that drew any interest from Wolfe. She was his type. Female.

"Talk to Merton?" Wolfe said to Gibson.

He swallowed hard, "Yes, sir, spoke to him this morning. We've got a secure line set up—"

"Secure line, my ass," Wolfe said leaning against the table with a menacing stare.

"We're set," Gibson said, avoiding eye contact. "We can upload from the compound, and it's designed to route through several sites. Not traceable."

"Everything's traceable."

"Well—it would take a hell of a long time to figure it out. By the time anyone does, we're gone."

These guys were good, Wolfe knew, but leaders imposed their will at all times. He knew that was what kept leaders in charge, but in his field what kept them alive.

"Mert okay with it?"

"Mert's good. He's the last man in the chain, so they'd have to walk it back from him."

"He won't give them shit. Mert won't talk. He's solid."

Gibson nodded.

Now back to Landers. "We're gonna have a run-through tonight. Get the vehicles there. We're gonna practice til it's perfect. I got Jackson's boys meeting up later tonight. Those guys seen time in Baghdad and Irbil. They got skills. They won't be at the compound. But even if they come around, nobody goes to the shack, 'cept us. Got that? Nobody."

Wolfe took a long pull on his beer. He let out a sharp whistle and motioned to the waitress for the check. "When this goes down, we'll have those lawless bastards, FBI, justice, sheriffs crawling up our asses. Nobody goes to the shack without my okay and nobody talks about the shack."

"What shack?" Landers chuckled.

"Damn straight."

~

Sarah rang the register, waited, and ripped the receipt from the machine. After slapping it into the plastic check holder, she walked it over to the table where the men sat. She made sure to keep her distance from Mr. Grab-ass. Without so much as a thank you, she moved across the room back toward the bar.

She had to put up with idiots like this. Over time

Sarah had learned how to diffuse a bad situation. That meant dealing with morons like this guy for minimum wage plus tips.

Tips, yeah, that was a joke.

I don't need this to escalate, she thought, particularly since it's just me and Zeke running the place today.

Zeke was a good friend, but hadn't been in a fight since the early days of Vietnam. No, if things went south, Sarah was going to be on her own. The only other inhabitant of the bar was old Luke Skinner. At somewhere north of eighty years old, the best he could do was fall off the bar stool and cause someone to stumble over him.

She'd thought about moving out of the county, up to Winchester, get her a real paying job. But the rents they charged up in Winchester always backed her off. At least here in podunk, Yellow Spring, her mobile home was paid for, and all she had were community fees for a place to live. The one thing she got in the divorce that was worth a damn. Well, other than her daughter.

Heck, what was she thinking? Kelly was still in school, would be for a bunch of years. No moving to Winchester. It wasn't going to happen anytime soon. Jobs were hard to come by in Yellow Spring, so it was in her best interest to just keep this job until something else came along.

The men sauntered past her toward the front door. She ignored them, though making sure to keep them in her peripheral vision. From the corner of her eye, she saw Grab-ass staring at her. Then he stopped, about four feet away. She froze.

"See ya, sweet cheeks," he said.

She looked down, wiping imaginary water droplets off the bar.

"I said see ya, sweet cheeks," Grab-ass said, this time in a booming voice.

She looked over and stared directly into his eyes, mustering all her courage. For a second, they were locked. Though attractive enough and unlike the losers she had to date in this area, his eyes were grey and electric. It was like the eyes didn't connect with the rest of the body, like they were controlled by some other being.

After three seconds that seemed like three years, he started moving again. Eyes were still on her, but at least he was moving toward the exit. When he finally turned his head to leave the building, she exhaled fully.

The men piled into a rust-colored GMC pickup, Grab-ass, of course, driving. What a creep. He was still staring toward her from behind the steering wheel. He put the truck in reverse and backed away in a wide arc. The truck was shifted and burned rubber, spitting gravel as it careened onto the highway and out of sight.

Never seen them before; hope they never come back. Sarah ambled to the booth the men had occupied, slipped the check wallet into the front of her jeans, and plucked up the bottles. She wiped the table down holding the three empties aloft.

Zeke and Luke were engaged in a deep conversation about when old man Tucker closed up the hardware store, before or after the drive-in shut down. They always rambled on about some nonsense. The bottles chinged and thudded as they went into the oversized plastic rubbermaid.

No tip, she was convinced. She slipped out the wallet, opened it, and stared. Then she turned it slightly sideways and stared more. Zeke and Luke turned their attention toward her. She lifted the multi-colored document out of the wallet and examined both sides of it, holding it in the air like a flattened earthworm.

"What in hell's name is this?"

Chapter 1

April 15

 A white-haired man in red striped suspenders appeared in the doorway. With hands on the door frame, he leaned in. The message was simple. "You're fired." Then he was gone.

 Nick looked up from his desk at the empty doorway and exhaled loudly. The footsteps clicked two doors down the hallway. "You're fired." The clicking of heels became more distant and a final, "You're fired" was delivered. All became silence.

 A bespectacled imp of a man walked through Nick's doorway with a clipboard and tossed a document on his desk. "This is your severance agreement, Mr. James. You have 21 days to sign and, if you agree, your severance will be paid on the eighth day following receipt."

 "Get out, Briney, you blood sucking ferret."

 Briney continued undeterred. "I must remind you of the obligations of the covenant not to compete which you signed with the company. Your network account is being—"

 "I know the drill."

"Terminated. Please leave all papers and materials with your desk. We will review everything and mail your personal belongings—"

"Okay, okay, enough with the good Nazi routine."

"To your residential address on file. Your security badge for the building has been deactivated, so once you leave, you won't be permitted access."

"Get out of here."

"It's been a pleasure having you work with us at Center Tech and I wish you the best of luck in the future."

Having read Nick his rights, the man spun around and scurried two doors down the hall. "This is your severance agreement—"

Nick leaned back in his chair and surveyed the paperwork on his desk.

Should I call someone? Who would I call? Kate? No, can't call her.

He picked up the document the ferret had left behind and scanned it. Twenty-two thousand five hundred dollar—three years of work and this was the final insult.

His report on domestic terrorist groups lay unfinished on his desk. He stared at it briefly, then disengaged. He tapped his computer, and his e-mail had been erased, his network connection had been shut off. Damn efficient. They've had a lot of practice.

A head appeared around the corner of his door frame. "You okay?"

"Yeah. I guess."

Dave Winters walked in and plopped down in the client chair next to the desk. He was twenty pounds overweight with a receding hairline accentuated by no evidence of a comb or brush having passed by recently.

His black pants and white shirt looked like he'd slept in them, and the knot of his tie never quite made it to the top of the collar, which was okay since the top button was missing anyway. "Sorry, man. I didn't know."

Nick nodded. Dave was from the adjoining office. The one who had been skipped over in the massacre. "Pays to be on the fed payroll."

Dave nodded this time.

Winters was actually employed by the Department of Homeland Security, a lifer. Nick was a contractor or had been until three minutes ago. The agency had "feathered" contractors from Center Tech and lifers in adjoining offices down this corridor of the massive limestone building on Pennsylvania Avenue.

Feathering, Nick thought. Nice expression. What it meant was the lifers were surrounded by people who actually did the work and had performance expectations. Lifers were the ornaments on the Christmas tree. Contractors were the tree that held up the ornaments. The tree always died and a new tree would be brought in to hold up the shiny, glittery baubles.

Firing a lifer was next to impossible, Nick knew. Unless they bludgeoned their supervisor with an axe and the full College of Cardinals happened to be eyewitnesses, they were invincible.

Even if they force fed the boss into a wood chipper, the union challenges and Byzantine process to terminate them would run through the offender's expected retirement date, which was damn early anyway and loaded with lifetime benefits.

Productivity didn't matter, he thought; intelligence didn't matter, competence didn't matter. They were cloaked with the impenetrable shield of "the civil servant." Lifer's could play Texas Hold 'em all day on their computers or run pornographic websites from their taxpayer financed server. The worst that could happen was "reassignment."

Winters had been Dave's advocate and friend. He was more of a mentor than a co-worker. He knew the politics and where the battle lines had been drawn on each of Homeland's initiatives. Winter's sage and candid advice had kept Nick out of more than a few scraps over the years.

Winters had taken Nick under his wing. He became the sounding board for Nick's research. The subtle shake of his head could alter Nick's strategy and a favorable word could elevate an otherwise ignored research report. Winters knew the game. He'd played it more than two decades, first at State, now at Homeland.

He was the only person Nick could truly confide in, the only person Nick had ever told the true story about his father. Of all his co-workers, Winters was the one Nick would miss most as he emotionally packed his belongings.

"Briney's a piece of work, isn't he?" Winters coughed at him as Nick shook his head.

Another head appeared in the door frame. This one with long brunette hair and tears. Nick waved her in.

"It's not right," she said, snuffling.

"Doesn't matter what's right. It is what it is," Nick said. "It was the DOMTER contract. When that got defunded, it was just a matter of time before Center Tech reacted. Kind of surprised it took this long. Hey, at least we got fired by Galbert himself. He didn't send some pin striped, Ivy League lieutenant to do it."

She slid along the door jamb and entered the office leaning against the wall with her arms folded. She was five feet tall, if she stood on tiptoes, with a white blouse and blue knee length skirt. A jangle of bracelets adorned one arm that rattled and clinked as gravity dictated.

"What am I going to tell Rick? He's going to be so pissed off. He just bought that damn boat last week." She tried to laugh, but couldn't quite make it and covered her mouth.

"You'll be okay, Kathy," Winters said. "You've got SCI with a bunch of tags. That kind of security clearance is worth plenty, at least in this town. Somebody will pick you up. You, too, Nick."

Nick laughed and shook his head. "Did my full lifestyle poly two months ago. Bastards. Not sure it was worth going through all that crap if I was going to be laid off. Good planning on their part."

"What about the non-compete?" Kathy said.

Winters turned toward her. "Those things aren't worth shit in this industry. Just sound nice to shareholders and investors. They aren't going to enforce it; you watch."

"Easy for you to say," she said.

Winters tossed his hands in the air and turned back to Nick for validation.

"Probably right."

The sound of heels clicking on the granite came echoing down the hallway. Kathy snuffled again and rubbed her eyes. They waited.

Peter Logan stepped into the doorway. Based upon the prior footsteps and location of his office, he was the third of the Center Tech terminations in their wing. He was tall and lean with his blond hair brushed back perfectly. Peter stood there wearing his pink dress shirt and navy sport coat with hands on his hips. No trace of anger or disappointment framed his face. He quickly scanned the people in the office. "Anybody want to get a drink? I would have sent an e-mail, but—" He shrugged.

Nick looked at his watch. "One-thirty? What the hell. We'll beat the happy hour crowd."

About the Author

Steve O'Brien is the author of *Elijah's Coin, Bullet Work* and *Redemption Day. Elijah's Coin* has been added to the reading curriculum in multiple secondary schools throughout the US and has been incorporated in a university ethics course. The e-book version of *Redemption Day* was an Amazon.com Bestseller. Steve is a graduate of the University of Nebraska and George Washington University Law School. He lives in Washington, DC.